A TIME OF TESTING

✒️ *A Time*
of Testing

BY JON R. LITTLEJOHN

CONCORDIA PUBLISHING HOUSE

Saint Louis

PZ
4
L7812
Tʋ

Concordia Publishing House, St. Louis, Missouri
Concordia Publishing House Ltd., London E. C. 1
Copyright © 1965 by Concordia Publishing House
Library of Congress Catalog Card No. 65-28173
Manufactured in the United States of America

Contents

23677

A TIME OF TESTING

The
Walls
of Jericho

Karl Mueller soaked up the sights and sounds of April like a thoroughbred colt too long in the barn. His feet pressed deep into the turf. The primulas and daffodils grew so dense in the grass he feared he would trample one and threaded his way back to the gravel.

The scene was quite enough in a rustic English way — a pair of schoolboys flying their kites, some ducks and swans dozing on the pond, a horse-faced nanny playing gently with her charge, a tourist couple unlimbering a camera before the cathedral.

As his shoes grated on the path, Karl spied the only soul who looked as if he really belonged in Bishop's Monksham. By dress and manner he might well have been a sexton or gravedigger, the sort that gathers obsequiously wherever the tower of a cathedral rises from the landscape.

This one would stand out anywhere. He wore a rough jacket of Harris Tweed in fustian brown, with a cap to match. Elbows and sleeves boasted patches of leather, protecting him against the decades, like the honored battle insignia of his regiment at Ypres.

He wore another mark even more striking, a scarred chunk of lumber where his left calf should have been. The wooden limb was somewhat darker where it touched the ground, as if it had soaked up the rains and dews of the priory gardens for decades.

For a man with a wooden leg he did not seem at all hampered, any more than by his age. He carried what was certainly the most unusual tool Karl had ever seen. It was a length of wrought iron as tall as he, with a rough handle that appeared to have been turned by a blacksmith.

He hopped spryly across the slope that rose from the millpond to the cathedral, like a robin cocking his head for worms, and twisted his rod beaklike into the soil. It seemed so odd Karl smiled. Surely the sexton wasn't aerating the soil or making holes for drainage or anything so simple as that. He appeared much too solemn. Karl would have to ask next time the conversation waned over a light ale at the Cross and Mitre.

There was really no one else Karl could address. He tried to erase his amusement. "I wonder, please, if you could direct me to the Abbey Gatehouse?"

The sexton pushed his probe another foot into the ground. "That'd be his lordship's residence. Have you an appointment?"

"Yes, he's expecting me. To tea. In five minutes. So you see I don't have a great deal of time." The accent was clearly American.

The sexton was not one to hinder the path of progress, but on the other hand he could see no earthly reason why the bishop would have the least interest in taking tea with an American. "That be the house there, t'other side of the wall. You've got to take the path and come in from the highroad."

"Thank you. You've been most helpful." Karl could not take his eyes off the odd tool and the odd little man who wielded it. He must really find out what it was all about.

Had he not walked across the meadows, there would have been no mistaking the Abbey Gatehouse. Just off the highroad rose the sort of ornamental tower the Benedictines once loved to build as entrances to their monasteries, perhaps to remind them of the pillar of fire and cloud of smoke that always went before.

The path to the bishop's palace was a blaze of color —

tulips, hyacinths, daffodils, forsythia, almond, cherry, even some late-blooming snowdrops. The facade was clearly Georgian, with twin white pillars and a heavy brass knocker, clearly a later addition. The original walls must have been hundreds of years older, when flint and mortar were as popular as bricks and stone.

The knocker was what one might expect of a bishop. Even for the massive oaken door it was a bit big to be in proportion — a 10-inch casting of the angel Gabriel. The bell of his trumpet was what struck the brass plate, announcing not the end of the world, in this case, but the arrival of visitors.

The massive timbers swung back to show a kindly, grandmotherly face, and at a lower level the wet, black nose of a high-voiced little Corgi. "You must be the American vicar."

"Yes, ma'am."

"Do come in. We've been expecting you, haven't we, Alfred? That's the dog. He has such an inferiority complex we've taken to calling him Alfred the Great. To build up his ego."

The house was clearly older than Karl had guessed. The open timbers in the hall had seen the smoke and fog of centuries, maybe as old as Queen Elizabeth.

"I'm Sarah Ellingston-Harte. The bishop's mother. Josie's grandmother. I suspect she's the one you've come to see, isn't she?"

Karl was somewhat taken aback. Sweet as she was, the old lady needn't be quite so frank. She showed him to the drawing room.

"I knew one of her friends in Chicago. Naturally, when I had the call to Bishop's Monksham, I promised to give her a hello. That's when she invited me to tea."

"Yes. That was my idea. I overheard your conversation on the phone. I'll call her. And the bishop'll be ready for tea too. Don't be too formal with him, will you? It makes him stuffy."

Karl was more and more intrigued. No wonder Josie had referred to her as the Queen Mother. "Queen bee" was more like it.

With the sun bright and the breath of spring heavy over the land, he was somewhat surprised to see a fire on the grate. Not a warm one but just of smallish boughs the wind might have blown down. To give the long, low room a touch of cheer.

Over the mantle like a family coat of arms hung a pair of oars. This, he knew, was a trophy far rarer than the head of an elephant or tiger. Where the oars crossed was a plaque with the great seal of the University of Cambridge, below it a smaller one of Christ's College. So the old boy had been an athlete, and what was more, the kind of an athlete to mount his trophies in the drawing room.

"Hello." Karl had not heard her enter the room. "I'm Josie. I'm so glad you could come."

"It was kind of you to ask. I'm Karl, naturally. How much did Judy tell you? That I'm one of her oddball friends, the kind the States was happy to lose?"

"No, hardly. Just that you were a preacher and a little conservative. Dark clothes, you know, and no sports car, and only one drink."

Josie had the same twinkle as her grandmother, with slate-blue eyes that looked slightly out of place against the chestnut shock of hair, and an upturned nose that reminded one of a mischievous elf. She would be fun to know.

"I wasn't angling for an invitation, you know. But I did think you might want to catch up on the news of Judy. She's to be married this summer, you've heard?"

"Yes, she told me all about him. When she wrote of you. Said she always thought you were an Englishman at heart."

"With a name like Karl Mueller? That's about as English as Hengest and Horsa."

"Or the Battenbergs. Mountbattens, I mean. Don't run yourself into the ground just because it sounds German. That's where we got our royal family."

"Over here I really ought to Anglicize it to Carl Miller."

"You do have a point. We *are* rather insular. But look at all the famous here who are foreigners — conductors and painters, sculptors and designers, publishers and lawyers, even clergymen."

"Clergy?"

"Professors anyway. Daddy says they're not really English, even if they're third generation; but if *they* aren't, who is? Just check the faculty at Cambridge or Oxford or Edinburgh. Germans and Dutch and Scandinavians galore. *You* couldn't say this in a bishop's house and still be polite, but *I* can. We couldn't provide our own, so foreigners drifted in to fill the vacuum."

"Now don't be so modest with your Anglicans. Many of the books I read at the seminary came from the Church of England. Almost as many as from Germany or Scandinavia."

In the doorway the bishop scraped his pipe with a penknife. "My baby daughter talking theology?" he laughed. "What does a social worker know about theology?"

Josie made the introductions.

"How do you do, Karl? Welcome to Bishop's Monksham."

"Thank you, Your Grace. How do you do, sir?"

"Not at tea, Karl. None of this 'Your Grace.' It's all well and good in a letter or when the Queen comes to pass out maundy money or I'm sitting on a platform with the Lord Mayor. But not in the house. Not at tea. You see, I don't even wear gaiters."

"I noticed, sir. Is it just at home?"

"No, not really. They're not very comfortable, mind, and far more expensive than ordinary trousers. At Lambeth meetings, of course, one has no choice. Or at confirmations. But here in my own diocese I can sometimes be a better bishop without them."

Karl paused at the bank of windows, gazing out across the sweep of the lawns. In the afternoon sun the towers of the cathedral cast long shadows across the valley. The boys with the kite still played on, and the aged sexton with the wooden leg still probed the earth with his iron bar.

"Tell me, what's the sexton doing? He is the sexton, isn't he?"

Josie laughed. "Old Tom Swopes. Lost his leg at — where was it, father — Ypres? The first World War. Been in Monksham far longer then we, and his father and grandfather before him. Sextons run in the family. It's a matter of pride. When he came to, in France, after the operation, he wasn't worried about the lost leg. Just asked the doctor if he'd still be able to get around enough to be a sexton."

"Oh?"

"His sort's a shilling a time in the villages, but you don't often find them in the towns. His father was famous on the bells. You'll still find the name on the brass plate in the bell chamber. Oh, but you asked what he was doing. Looking for graves."

"Graves?" Karl looked quizzical.

"Yes," the bishop took up the conversation, "graves. A good parish register should not only say *who's* buried and *when* they were buried but *where* they were buried. That's what bothers Tom. Ours doesn't. Not before 1600 anyway. He has some queer notion the lawns were all part of the churchyard once and that children shouldn't play over the dead. Sometimes he does hit something solid, but without digging up the landscape it's difficult to say whether it's a coffin of a chunk of flint."

"Are the graves really so scattered?"

"Somebody's graves, I imagine. The Celts or the Romans

or the Saxons or the Elizabethans. As many people as died here over the centuries, they'd have to be buried somewhere. But even if the meadows were full of graves, it wouldn't make any difference. There's nothing wrong with the boys flying their kites there or a nanny giving a baby some sunshine. That's the only way some people ever get near the church, and I'd hate to lose even that contact."

The garden outside was a lush growth of green. The roses showed their first buds, and would soon be bright with color. The laurel and the boxwood and the birches sported the bright foliage of April as if they had put on their best for Easter.

"My father would love this climate. A lot of Americans don't, you know. But it's, well, *moderate*. A little rain, a little sun, almost every day. Not too cold and not too hot."

"Just right for roses, eh?"

"I should say! He loves the fancy ones — the grandifloras and the teas and the floribundas. At home, of course, we mulch right up to the crown, or the frost will get them. That's nearly impossible with a tree rose."

A soft creaking from the hall and the padding of slippers announced the arrival of the tea cart. Sarah Ellingston-Harte followed it through the door. "The maid has Saturdays off, so I've made the scones myself."

"You're in luck," said Josie. "Granny makes better ones anyway."

In the elaborate ritual of tea, Karl Mueller was no newcomer. He'd been in England only two weeks and in Bishop's Monksham only five days, but from the first he knew that tea would be a problem.

As a parson he'd discovered he could never turn down a second cup, possibly even a third, without fear of offending his hosts. And to put it frankly, three pastoral calls in a single evening — well — three calls times three cups was simply too much tea.

But today there would be only one invitation. A proper English tea in the home of a lord bishop. And not merely a lord bishop but a leading bishop, not quite of the rank of Canterbury or York but one whose prestige and seat boasted just as proud a history.

The bishop of Bishop's Monksham did the honors. A careful peep into the pot, where the swelling leaves of the Darjeeling perfumed the air. A careful hand replacing the cozy. One cup to each saucer, with the clear tinkle of ancient and well-preserved Spode. A probing finger outside the silver urns of milk and water to see they were properly hot.

"Very nice, Mother. Very nice. We'll have to give Grace more days off."

"Don't flatter me, son. I'm well aware of your little tricks. Since you were two years old." The touch of honey in her voice also carried a hint of mischief.

"The scones. I used to think they were best only when the snow lay on the ground, but they make me just as hungry in daffodil time."

"There! That one's sincere. I'll accept it. Why didn't you just say you were hungry?"

The bishop snickered. "You've just arrived in England, Karl?"

"Yes, sir. Two weeks ago. I was here once before. Just after I finished the university. For two years with the army engineers. They were building a runway at Stony Hinge in Hants. But of course that was before my seminary days."

"Josie tells me you're a Lutheran."

"Right. They're not many of us in England, of course, and I suppose we're often thought of here as a sect."

"Oh, no! We may be a bit stuffy or a bit ignorant, but at least we know our history. We'd be in bad shape if Luther hadn't had all those scraps with Henry VIII. Did a good deal for the Church of England, even if he didn't realize it. And of course we practice fellowship with the Church of Sweden. They have apostolic succession too, you know."

Karl was not eager to push his views in the midst of tea. It was not just the prestige of his church or the feeling of propriety. It was his status as a guest. Proper guests, in England of all places, didn't start controversies over their hosts' tea.

But His Grace the Bishop was not to be diverted any more than he was to be diverted from wielding the implements of the tea maker. "There's a kind of theology even in brewing a pot of tea. And pouring it. Ask any debutante to do the job" — he glanced toward his daughter — "and she'll invariably pour the milk in first and then add the tea. But of course that's not U."

"Upper class," Josie laughed. "Don't really pay any attention, Karl. That's just the latest fetish at Lambeth. They say the Queen has a theory about pouring the tea first. Prewarms the cup. And now there's not a bishop in the realm who doesn't ape the Queen."

"All wanting to be archbishop," Granny added.

Karl had not really had a good chance to examine the room. He had been too intent on the oars and the views over the gardens and the conversation. In the far corner, away from the fireplace, loomed an ancient piano, flanked partly against the figured tapestry at the windows.

What caught his eye longest were the pictures — ancient sketches and maps that might have dated from the birth of engraving, Roman ruins, town plans, a sheet of vellum from some aged tome of a monastery, figured with a red-and-black script from the missal for tierce.

"Granny says you're doing some spadework for a Lutheran mission in the New Town."

"Yes. It's still experimental of course. We don't know exactly what to expect."

"I can imagine."

It was Sarah's cheerful interjection that kept the chat on the rails. "Competition for the Methodists and the Congregationalists, Alred. He wouldn't think of besieging *your* little bailiwick."

"It is a bit delicate, I admit," said Karl. "I've been through it all with our man in London, Doctor Dennis. The last thing in the world we want is to steal sheep. An Anglican's an Anglican, a Methodist a Methodist, and that's that. If a man hasn't been to church in a decade or isn't baptized, then of course we're playing the game straight if we try to land him for Christ. He's just as much a heathen as a fetish-worshiping Hottentot."

"Right you are. But don't you think it might be easier to try and convert the Hottentot? After all, he's never heard the Gospel, but a man off the street in a country like ours — he's scarcely been able to avoid it. Bible readings at school, churches on every corner, preachers galore on the radio and television. If the Englishman's not a Christian, it's not because he hasn't had a chance."

"To tell the truth, Dr. Ellingston-Harte, you're right. I'd probably be happier among the Hottentots. As a missionary, I mean. Somehow a job in the middle of Africa, something like that of Dr. Schweitzer, seems far closer to the true calling of the disciple than anything here in Britain or America. But the men at the seminary thought I'd be just right for England — my time here with the army, I guess. And there *is* a challenge here. I can't deny it. To see if a new approach won't wake up a few of the sleeping Christians. A seedbed operation, if you will. Still and all, I haven't really given up the thought of Africa. Maybe it's just that I don't know what I really do want."

"Good for you. It hits us all, that search for a cause. I had to do an episcopal tour of Basutoland a few years back. I nearly resigned my see and stayed. Stirred the blood, seeing all those new Christians thirsting after God. With not enough men to teach them. If I were a few years younger —

Sarah interrupted. "Now don't say that, Alred. If you're really too old and crotchety, I could go along to look after you."

The bishop laughed and continued. "We've been expecting you, of course. As a matter of fact, the incumbents at St. Saviours and St. Michael's have expressed some concern. Most of the local folk attend the cathedral. That's the fashionable thing. So that leaves the other two with smallish flocks. Only St. Swithums doesn't seem to be worried. The vicar there says the Romans and the Methodists haven't upset the apple cart, so why should the Lutherans? No one goes to St. Swithums anyway. And of course you have to remember he's not quite typical of the Church of England."

"We're not so concerned with the townsfolk. It's the cockneys from London who've come out to the New Town. They're the ones without any roots. Those are the toddlers that need baptizing and the Teddy boys who need confirming."

"You're quite right. We *are* a bit behind the times when it comes to evangelism. We don't have the American touch. Yet you must remember we're old, with old traditions."

"That's why I feel a little out of place, indulging your hospitality. To our minds England is — well — a bit post-Christian. The customs and culture are not pagan by any means. The kids in school still get their Bible history and memorize their catechism, but there's not much of a living faith."

"That's an acceptable way to put it. In fact it's just what our younger bishops are saying. But give us time. We'll come round yet."

"By rights we Lutherans should probably be working in Denmark or Norway or perhaps even France. They need a twentieth-century faith as much as England. But of course there's the question of language and culture. With a smallish amount of money, England is a better spot to experiment. And certainly in a New Town we won't tread on quite so many toes as elsewhere."

"If you were an Anglican, I'd have to agree with you. But — well, since our churches have so much in common, it seems a little like one brother competing with another."

Karl was not altogether pleased with the conversation. He hated to spoil the tea. Yet the challenge of minds could not be avoided merely by denying it existed.

"I've been somewhat hesitant myself, to tell the truth. I wouldn't have taken the job if I hadn't spent those two years with the army. I'm convinced something is needed. English faith is stagnant. Not only the C. of E. The Romans and the Methodists. That's why the Lutherans are here. We can't do it alone, but we can at least help."

"That's quite an order, you know. Old St. Augustine invaded Kent with forty monks. When there was scarcely any population at all. And even he didn't finish the job. In his lifetime, I mean. Are there many Lutherans here?"

"Clergy?"

"Yes. And people."

"No, not really. Perhaps a dozen who conduct their services in English. Australians, Canadians, Americans. There's quite a colony of Lutheran servicemen, you know, and diplomats and engineers and business folk. And several score of pastors for the northern Europeans. The Danes and Finns and Swedes and Norwegians and Germans. And then of course there're the refugees from the war. Forty thousand, we reckon."

"Still Lutheran?"

"Many, yes. They brought their own clergy. Latvian, Estonian, Polish, Hungarian. Settled mostly in the big cities. London, Birmingham, Cardiff, Leeds, Glasgow. Of course a good many have turned Anglican."

Karl studied the bishop's face. The lines there were gentle, not angry, even if they were a bit perturbed. Behind the glasses and the blue-grey eyes one could almost sense the wisdom and experience that had made Alred Ellingston-Harte a bishop. Real tortoiseshell in the frames, Karl noted. Not the shiny plastic of a cheap imitation.

"It's not that we resent competition, we English. We wouldn't think of crowding you to the wall. In fact, with the Lutheran refugees here, you've every valid reason to be here. And yet down deep we may be a little like the Roman Church. Jealous of what we have but not too eager to work at keeping it. Still, I think you'll be far more welcome here than say at Naples or Palermo."

"Too much so, maybe. At least with the Teddy boy set. Just because they like hamburgers and popcorn and jazz, just because the pastor is an American, they get interested. Not in the church. Not as a matter of faith. Just for the American atmosphere."

"There now. I feel better. So long as you know what to expect, so long as your feet are on the ground. Sometimes I'm a little taken aback by what passes for faith, especially in America. Crusades and conversions and faith healings and all that."

Alfred the Great sniffed gently at the tea, as if he had been completely forgotten. "Here, Alfred," said Josie. She tested the temperature of her cup, added a spoonful of sugar, poured it into the saucer, and set it on the tiles before the fireplace. "That's for you."

"This is all too theological, Alred. Can't you men talk anything but shop?" complained Granny. "You'd think this was Lambeth."

Josie had scarcely been able to get a word in edgewise. She was more like a child of seven who sensed she should be heard but not seen than a mature twenty-two. "Tell us something about your trip, Karl. Did you fly? Did you stay long in New York?"

Karl sat back and relaxed, glad that the conversation was no longer touchy. He did not regret broaching it. Sooner or later it had to come. And if he were to be starting a Lutheran mission in the midst of a cathedral town, one might as well beard the bishop in his own den. Reach an understanding. Clear the decks in person, so that rumors did not grow out of all proportion.

He was justly proud of the afternoon's performance. Of course his feelings toward the C. of E. were still mixed. She was a proud old dame, sometimes too proud. But at least God understood her, and Karl too, in time. And he hadn't been as bitter as he might have been. About all those royal chaplains who were Lutheran, for example.

That was usually all it took to rile a dyed-in-the-wool C. of E. man. Tell him the Supreme Head of the Anglican Church wasn't always an Anglican but a Lutheran. Now, maybe, but not historically. What of the House of Hanover, from George I right down through Victoria and Edward VII? Brought their chaplains with them for the royal court. From the Church of Hanover. Germans. Lutherans, every last one of them.

Karl had been decent and honest about it all. He hadn't ruffled feathers just to make a fluff. He hadn't said he wanted to live in England just to admire the swans or visit the castles or write picturesque letters to his friends in America. He was still a man of God, and that was why he was here.

After all, maybe he did have a great deal in common with the man who sat across the table, the man who signed himself "Alred ✠ of Bishop's Monksham."

The
Sound
of the Cuckoo

It was a delightful way to face a new day — the sound of a cuckoo, off in the shrubbery. Every minute or two the rough *cuckuck* echoed across the garden, bringing back happy dreams of Karl's boyhood and his mother's clock.

Lying there half asleep, he had never really thought of the cuckoo before, not as a real bird. Cuckoos existed only in the realm of dragons and elves and fairy godmothers. In the world of the *Brüder Grimm* and of make-believe.

In the pub last night, before closing time, the talk had turned to cuckoos. They were thick this year, said the regulars at the Cross and Mitre, and already mating. Old Purbeck, the retired commercial traveler, said he had counted eight on the village common. In a week or two the eggs would be laid, and the magic mating cry would fade to a cheerful trill.

Karl pushed back the blanket. Poking its face through the cluster of beeches and limes in the garden, the sun climbed smoothly up the horizon. The light streamed against the spread.

From his bed he examined the room. For a week now it had been home — the Cross and Mitre, an old-fashioned country inn. Once it had been an outlying house of the Benedictine priory, a sprawling stone building of six or eight large rooms. The new part of the structure was half-timbered Tudor and twice the size of the old, catering to a half-dozen residents and an occasional transient.

Karl was quite content at the Cross and Mitre. The food was completely palatable, especially the Dover sole and the

Aylesbury duckling. Even for a preacher the public bar was no disadvantage, for it was quiet and out of the way. It attracted little custom except for the regulars — old-timers mainly, who lived there on the Little Wealdstonebury Common and dropped in for a half-and-half or a pint of bitter.

From the corner window one could see all the way to the abbey fishpond, where the mists of dawn still fluttered ghostlike over the waters. The little Aublin meandered crazily across the meadow. Farther upstream, almost lost in the midst and buried behind the towers of the cathedral, one could make out the Roman ruins.

The forum and the amphitheater and the arena, the fossa and the dyke and the hypocausts. Under the care of the Minister of Works the ruins brought hordes of tourists piling into Bishop's Monksham to spend their shillings just as the Roman legionaries had once spent their denarii.

Karl liked his room. On the fireplace wall, where a shelf of wainscoting ran head high across the width of the room, stood a dozen pewter tankards. Over the mantel was a steel etching. It was so artful, in fact, had he not known better, he might have credited it to Blake or Dürer.

It was a tableau showing Richard the Lionhearted and a magnificent retinue of knights, eager to besiege the lands of the Turk. There stood the king in all the splendor of inlaid armor that had cost some Nürnberg armorer a decade of his best labors. There sat the knights astride their chargers, and in the background the bowmen with their shafts, the pikemen, the swordsmen, the squires, the blacksmiths, the lackeys, the couriers, the sutlers.

Somehow the picture reminded Karl of his job. He certainly didn't want to think of himself as a Richard the Lionhearted, and yet in a way, despite all the lack of pomp and circumstance, his work was just as colorful. And maybe just as futile. At any rate the picture established a rapport, a common purpose, and at the same time served as a sly comment on trying to accomplish the impossible.

Laden with the scent of blooming hawthorn, the air flowed gently through the open dormer. Karl drank deep, his nostrils flaring like a thoroughbred that has just finished the course at Ascot.

He couldn't help remembering everything he had heard about the English spring. Of course this was not his first. Yet a country inn in a cathedral town was not exactly the same as a quonset BOQ with an army battalion. The banks of white clouds woollier than wool. The brilliant blue of the skies, more brilliant than the Aegean.

"What is so rare as a day in June?" he quoted. "Then if ever come perfect days." But it was not yet June, and his scholarly mind told him he'd better save his poetry for the proper season.

How did the other one go? He was still not fully awake, sitting at the edge of the mattress. "Oh, to be in England, Now that April's there!" Who was it that wrote it anyway? Keats? Shelley? Byron? Wordsworth? About the glories of April Karl quite agreed. But he, to be in England, had given up his native Michigan. And the poet, whichever one it was, seemed to prefer his adopted Italy to his native England.

Standing in the bottoms of his pajamas, Karl rose to face the day. From the leaded windows he peered out at the garden, a bit too formal for his taste, with its measured paths and symmetrical plots.

This was Saturday. *The* Saturday. He picked up from the desk a starchy sheet of vellum and the envelope that had brought it. Not vellum really, he told himself. Laid paper, heavy and antique. He read it again, as he had a score of times, and grinned.

"Madam Sarah Ellingston-Harte and her granddaughter Josephine request the pleasure of your company at the St.

Swithums Sale of Work and Bazaar Saturday afternoon April 15 at two." Scribbled in the bottom corner, in the same hand but hardly the same spirit, was a lighthearted postscript: "We'll call for you in Old Christopher at the Cross and Mitre. OK?"

For a woman in her 70s Sarah Ellingston-Harte was certainly spry, both in mind and body. It was as if the two families she had reared, first her own and then that of her son, had kept her as fresh as a fountain of youth.

Promptly at two Old Christopher came chugging up the drive. Even if she had lived through the blitz and the buzz bombs and was beginning to show her age, the ancient Austin still boasted a royal pedigree. Her black paint was of recent vintage, and the coat of wax gave her a sheen equal to any modern upstart.

In the boxlike sedan Sarah and Josephine sat as erect and formal as the Queen and The Queen Mother in the royal carriage. Relaxing there on the stone lion at the entry to the inn, with the hitching-post ring in his fingers, Karl was surprised to see Sarah at the wheel.

The clock at St. Saviours had not yet gone two, but that proved nothing. St. Saviours' clock was a notorious timekeeper. And a bad clock, coupled with a verger who thought more highly of his dark ale at the Three Feathers than of minding the timepiece, led more than one schoolboy to be late for classes.

In a prim black dress Sarah Ellingston-Harte shoved the brakes hard against the floorboard and kicked up gravel on the walk. "Hi, Yank," she said. "Ready? You ever been to a sale of work and bazaar?"

Josie was in as good spirits as her grandmother. "Father says we're to keep a sharp eye on Granny." She turned and swung open the back door. "Not let her buy up a whole roomful of embroidery and needlepoint. Or slip out to the garden with one of those old-age pensioners and propose marriage."

"Me? I'd rather marry off my granddaughter first. Like I did her brother and sister. Then I'd be a free woman again."

Somehow the girl looked older than the Saturday before, the day of the bishop's tea. She wore a soft tweed suit in a becoming brown, and a pixie tam. Probably, thought Karl, this is what she wears at work. So the poor cockneys whose homes she visits didn't take her for a stripling straight out of the university. Which was more like the truth.

At a jaunty angle on their lapels both girl and grandmother sported mammoth daffodils. The flowers at any rate gave a certain festive air to the day, though the clothes, Karl thought, were a bit conservative even for a church bazaar. Sarah let out the clutch with a jerk that chattered the gravel and set the daffodils nodding gently.

"You've never met Old Christopher before, have you?" Josie asked. "This was the first car father ever owned. Named for St. Christopher, the patron saint of travelers. There's a new one now, a little Morris. Dad usually uses that. That's New Christopher. But Old C. here is still the favorite whenever there's an occasion of state."

The lordly steeple of St. Swithums already hove into sight, a 2-minute ride from the Little Wealdstonebury crossing. Even by foot it would have been hardly an 8-minute walk from the parish church of St. Saviours, where most of St. Swithums parishioners went to say their prayers and hear their sermons.

They came upon the churchyard abruptly, just round a sharp bend at the foot of Sevenoaks Hill. Perhaps that explained how quaint and lovely the church looked, for all her age and history. Karl had looked her up in Baedeker. She did not rate much space in the tiny chapter on Monkshamshire, but even a few lines put her head and shoulders above most of the parish churches.

Like a good many others, she dated back to the Benedictines, when Archbishop Lanfranc was so busy in the Home
Counties. "Eleventh-century Romanesque apse," Baedeker had
commented, "later refurbished in somewhat Puritan taste with
Purbeck marble. . . . Twelfth-century font, leper's squint,
double hammer-beam roof with gilt angels, excellent six-
teenth-century brasses. Lady Eliza Horton, sometimes lady in
waiting to Henry VIII, buried in churchyard."

"It's really a shame about St. Swithums," Josie had begun. "Such a lovely little church. But nobody ever attends.
It's just a hop, skip, and jump from St. Saviours, which of
course packs them in by the hundred. Sunday at evensong
anyway."

"At least they've still their sale of work and bazaar,"
Sarah added. "That's the only time in the year but Easter
when anybody belongs to St. Swithums. Your father says the
church commissioners have even considered it for the list of
redundant churches."

"How I'd like to have her stone by stone in Connecticut!
But that would take a Rockefeller. From the outside she
looks exactly like every seminarian's dream of what a church
should be. Not ornate, maybe, but churchly."

"That's the trouble with you Americans," said Granny.
"Trying to uproot Old World culture and transplant it to a
new frontier. If I had a choice, I would trade you St. Swithums
for one of those splendid aluminum-and-glass things you're
so good at. With the pulpit in the middle, and the pews all
round."

It was Josie who continued. "Tell me, Karl. This business
about Africa and the missionaries. What you were talking
about Saturday. Given a choice between a lovely, old church
like St. Swithums and a job with Hottentot evangelists —
which one would you take?"

"You put me on the spot, Josie. I — I'm not sure. I hope
I don't ever have to make the choice. A pleasant, old village

church, with the bells calling the countryfolk to worship —
that's what the painters loved to paint and the writers loved
to write about. Still and all, there'll be painters and writers in
Africa too one day — once they learn to read and write. Now,
what Africans need is modern St. Thomases — to read them
the Gospel and then to explain it."

Old Christopher drew past the lich-gate and the line of
cars, seeking a parking place. The graceful tower of St.
Swithums reached 50 feet skyward, skillfully fluted in the
light and airy style known as Perpendicular, with a touch,
perhaps, of Decorated.

From each buttress a gargoyle poked its head, with a
mouth gaping wide to carry the rains from the leaden roof.
They were the only sort of dragons St. George would ever
find in the length and breadth of England. Along the base of
the south wall, where the winter sun had penetrated, fans of
ivy boasted their survival. Higher up on the wall there was
only the tracery of once-dormant vines, now with a sprightly
new foliage.

Granny parked the car with a certain slambang approach.
She was not really reckless or incompetent, Karl reassured
himself, but simply forceful. This was how she lived and
apparently also how she drove.

Karl helped first Sarah and then Josie from Old Christopher. "You really ought to know something about St.
Swithums, Karl," said Sarah. "Old Geoff Thorkill is rector here,
and he and the Ellingston-Hartes are not on the best of
terms. Alred, I mean, not the rest of us. So every year we get
a formal invitation to the bazaar, and every year Alred dis-
covers something that needs doing that day. Like pruning the
holly."

"Oh?"

"It's really rather funny. Geoff is a peculiar sort but really
quite a scholar. Long ago he gave up daily matins. Says he
can read the offices just as well at the vicarage. Nobody

else ever came anyway. And only a handful on Sundays. It's a long story, really, and you probably wouldn't be interested."

"Oh, but I would. It's a fine chance to learn something of English churches and people."

"Well, ever since he's been bishop, Alred has been fighting to get the advowson of St. Swithums. He can't even name the vicar. And if you can't put a good man into the spot, at least a reliable one, and the parish is just down the road from the bishop's palace, what will people think? That's Alred's attitude. How can you run a diocese if you can't even run a parish?"

"What's an advowson?"

"That's the right to name a parish priest. It used to go with the land. The squire could name his own. Often one of his sons or his friends' sons. Nowadays most of the advowsons have been transferred to the bishops. But a few of the landowners are stubborn. Like Todd Fortnum here at Green Gables Hall. He's not even an Anglican. A spiritualist. A Scotsman. One of the leading spiritualists in all Britain. When he bought the hall, he also bought the rights of the church. To name the vicar, I mean. And he's stubborn. It's he who's so keen on Geoff Thorkill."

"How's that?"

"Well, Geoff's quite a scholar, as I said. He's written a book and dozens of articles on ancient music. Plainsong and the Sarum missal and early counterpoint and Palestrina's modes and the baroque organ. Even if he's not a spiritualist, he's an eccentric old bachelor and a scholar, and that's what the squire likes about him."

"Isn't there anything the bishop can do?"

"Not legally. Geoff isn't a heretic or anything."

"Tell him the flap about the organ, Granny."

"Oh, that! Yes, that's the best. Well, way back when I was a girl, some organist at the Royal Academy persuaded the bigwigs at Lambeth Palace to put all organs in the west end. Mostly, they're wherever was convenient. West end, south porch, north transept, often at the side, in a kind of chantry."

"Yes?"

"Ever since, *where* the organ stands has been a kind of touchstone. Of how effective a bishop is. How many churches he can persuade to move their organs to the west end. Here in Monkshamshire of course, with our ancient churches and with scarcely any destroyed during the war, Alred simply hasn't done very well. Not on that score."

"Don't you think the country folk are a bit more bull-headed than city ones?"

"That's it too, p'r'aps. But Geoff Thorkill didn't help matters any. There's a wonderful old organ here. With manual trackers. Rumor has it, it dates back to a pupil of Johann Sebastian Bach. At any rate the parish register says it was installed in 1769. Older than your country, in fact."

They walked up the flagstone path, past the pair of yews flanking the south porch, past the limestone slabs that served both as coffin lids and tombstones. On the slope behind the church the breeze swayed a candy-striped awning where tables of handwork and cakes attracted a crowd of people and a buzz of chatter.

"You tell him the rest, Josie. And show him the church. That'll be more exciting anyway. I'll go look up Sadie Haskins and have a gossip." She left them at the south porch, where the oaken beams, gray with age and weather, supported a slate entryway.

"I guess Dad was quite anxious to make a good impression. It was the first year he was bishop. The organ had always stood there in the music gallery, off the transept. See, about even with Granny. Mr. Thorkill would sit there by the day, tinkling away at the keyboard, gazing out over the meadow to the towers of the cathedral."

"Sounds like a good setting for a murder mystery."

"Yes. By Dorothy Sayers."

"Right. Just the proper mix of quaintness and religion."

"One day the organ quit. Ciphers all over the place. And there was no choice but to dismantle it and start from scratch. Everyone knew of course that it was too fine to discard. The tone was excellent. None of that vibrato and viola d'amore that belong in a theater."

"Go on."

"In a recent case the Chancellor had ruled that no new organ could be installed except in the west end, preferably the west gallery, without a special faculty. There were churches of course where you could decently make an exception. But Mr. Thorkill didn't even bother to ask. He just called in the organ builders. A skilled French firm in Lyons with a good deal of experience in baroque organs. An English firm would have raised questions perhaps, knowing how the bishop felt. But the Frenchmen dismantled it where she stood and rebuilt her in the same spot."

"And your father didn't like it?"

"He was furious. He used to be stuffy when he first became bishop. Now experience has moderated him. He wasn't really so angry about the location. In fact, with the music gallery there, the transept is as good as anywhere. But what made him furious was that Mr. Thorkill didn't even ask."

"I see. The local vicar knows best. And when the vicar has the support of the squire, well, he's almost as impregnable as a bishop, right?"

"That's about the size of it. They've never really been on good terms since. Fortunately of course, in a dormant parish like St. Swithums, it doesn't really matter. But it still rankles father."

"It's a bit amusing in a way."

"It is, really; Mother used to gaff him about it mercilessly when she was alive. But it's been good for him, and I think he can laugh about it now."

After the brightness of the April sun, their eyes were half blinded in the darkness inside. The organ spoke gently from somewhere above, so soft it could have been a muted violin. Scarlatti. A Scarlatti rondo. Hardly church music, Karl noted, at least not in the purest tradition.

"That must be Mr. Thorkill now," the girl suggested. "But surely he wouldn't desert his own bazaar?"

Karl took in all the glories of the church. There by the entryway, as a symbol of entrance to the kingdom of God, was Baedeker's 12th-century font. An exquisite chunk of limestone showing signs of age but attractive nonetheless.

Like others its vintage, it boasted a bowl large enough to immerse an infant, not one of these modern ones hardly big enough to dunk a cricket. Around the stone was a frieze of the twelve apostles, their faces lost to the ravages of time but still good art even in silhouette.

Built into the wall was an ancient piscina, where the water of baptism or the wine from the altar could be poured out on a bed of sand beneath. Overhead the roof displayed magnificent timbers of oak, with coveys of angels on the trusses and bosses that still showed faint traces of paint and gilt. Not completely waterproof perhaps, but inspiring in spite of the drips.

The altar and pulpit Karl liked best of all. He was fond of stone altars despite the cold touch, for there was something lasting and eternal about stone that even the costliest of wood did not offer. The lines looked clean and sharp as if they were only a century old, though the design was clearly Perpendicular. A copy, probably, of a famous altar somewhere else. He must remember to ask.

Josephine was already at the pulpit, just at the edge of the chancel steps, peering up toward the gallery.

"Oh, it's you, Josephine. I'm glad you could come." From the organ bench a little wizened monklike face leaned over the rail, squinting through steel-rimmed spectacles.

"Mr. Thorkill. Aren't you ashamed, running off from your sale of work and bazaar?"

"Ashamed? My music needs me. Besides, I do go show my face every half hour. That's really all that's necessary, don't you think?"

"Mr. Thorkill, I want you to meet a friend. Karl Mueller, who is starting the new Lutheran mission at the Community Hall. Maybe you've heard about it."

"No, but then I don't get around much. How do you do, Mr. Mueller? Excuse me for not coming down. A Lutheran, you say?"

"How do you do, Mr. Thorkill. Yes, sir, that's correct."

"Glad to hear it. Did you come to hear the organ?"

"No, not primarily. To see the church and to visit the bazaar."

"I thought maybe you were like my other Lutheran friends. From the Continent. Great lovers of music, the Lutherans. Germans, Swedes, Danes, all of them. Too bad we don't have it in the C. of E. If I'd known you were Lutheran, I'd have switched to Johann Sebastian. Or Sweelinck. Come to think of it, I'll do it right now. You show him about, would you, Josie? You know St. Swithums as well as I. And mind, don't forget the leper's squint and the bell tower."

Josie did not forget the leper's squint or the bell tower. Bells were common enough, and Karl knew enough about changes to appreciate the wall full of bronzes the ringers had accumulated, marking their perfect peals. But a leper's squint he had never seen before.

Josie explained it as professionally as a guide, yet with a personal note. "In the Middle Ages leprosy was common. You couldn't deprive a leper of his worship just because he was diseased. Many of the churches knocked a hole in the wall at eye level and inserted a pane of glass, so the leper could stand outside and observe."

The organ in the loft had switched to a toccata and fugue.

Karl paused now to rub at a brass in the floor, marking the grave of a knight. "Do we say good-bye to the vicar?"

"I think not, really. He'll be happier just with his music. Besides, we'll probably see him again outside."

From the dank air of the church, smelling of damp and incense and candles and linen, the air outside was a welcome change, smelling of wet earth and blossoming orchards.

On the plot behind the church the chatter of the bazaar hinted of a swarm of people and happy conversations. "Tell me, Josie, why all these yew trees in every churchyard? Are they really a sign of immortality?"

"Where'd you hear that, Karl?"

"I'm not sure, to tell the truth. Maybe in one of the guidebooks, or perhaps when I was here with the army."

"It's just an old wives' tale. A yew doesn't live forever, even if it does hold its leaves through the winter. There's a better reason than that."

"Oh?"

"A practical one. One that would appeal to a countryman. Or at least a country parson. You don't find yews much in the towns, you know."

"This really is Dorothy Sayers."

"No, there's no mystery about it. Just common sense. A churchyard always has the best lawn in the village, and the only way to keep out a hungry cow is to scare its master. A yew is poisonous, and half a dozen mouthfuls would be the end of the cow. So to keep out the cows and make their owners keep them fenced, the churchwardens plant yew."

"Who says the English aren't practical?"

At the bazaar the crowd was still growing. For so small a parish it appeared a booming success. Karl was surprised how many English crafts were represented there — tatting, weaving, needlepoint, wickerwork, baskets, tooled leather, water colors, silverwork, woodcarving, almost anything you could name. Table after table groaned under a load of handiwork.

He was even more surprised by the range of folk who were there — all the way from his lordship the mayor right down to a sheep crofter who lived in the abandoned lockhouse on the Monkshamshire Canal. There were simple farm folk from the countryside, girls who coated candy from the chocolate factory, butchers and fruiterers, leatherworkers from the shoe plant, linemen from the County Electricity Board, sisters from the Monks and Essex Hospital.

There was even a collection of vicars. Josie made a point of introducing Karl to each of them. One was Edward Hopeton, the vicar of St. Saviours. Another was Lancelot Evans, the vicar of St. Michael's and All Angels.

Meeting them one after another, Karl could have guessed their theological position from their garb. To be truthful, he'd already heard, and what they looked like merely was full confirmation.

Hopeton was a youngish man, an Evangelical, in a soft grey flannel that some might have thought a bit too gay for a clerical collar. Evans, on the other hand, was as black in his garb as a Roman, right down to the felt in his hat. You could almost smell the Anglo-Catholic, as if he had not left the incense and holy water back at St. Michael's at all.

Geoff Thorkill was there too, for a few minutes at a time. To see him in the light of day, apart from the shadows of the organ loft, made him seem almost human. His spectacles, with their steel rims, did not seem perfectly round. The corners looked squared off in the fashion of Wolfgang Amadeus Mozart. But maybe it was simply Karl's imagination.

They found Sarah back among her cronies and quite happy to be rescued from the gossip. But she was far from ready to go home. Between the rounds of tea, Karl was quite certain she intended to introduce him to everyone in the whole crowd. It was not that he was unsociable. It was not that he resented the introductions.

Somehow Josie sensed it too. He was always introduced as more than plain Karl Mueller. That might have been flying under the proper flag.

Instead Sarah consistently added that he was the new Lutheran vicar. He could quite as easily have passed for a friend of Josephine's. Any girl could bring a friend home from London for the weekend and not attract the slightest attention. Even the bishop's daughter, in fact.

But when one was introduced as a Lutheran at an Anglican bazaar and under the wing of His Grace the Bishop's mother and daughter, he felt he was taking an unfair advantage. It was a mixing of Beelzebub and Jehovah which the prophets would have railed at.

On the surface Karl's afternoon could not have been more pleasant. There was just that one annoyance. Why didn't the Ellingston-Hartes put up a fight instead of smoothing his way? Didn't they know that some of the folks he met might be the very souls whom he would try to win, whose doorbells he would ring?

Was he a camel who had been cheerfully invited to put his nose in the tent with no fear that the whole camel might soon be inside? What were they trying to do — pretend they were all one happy family, Anglicans and Lutherans?

When he knelt down to his prayers that night, safe in the upper reaches of the Cross and Mitre, he admitted he ought to thank the good Lord for a happy and instructive day. But he was not quite sure what direction the good Lord wanted him to take. Was it a fie on the bishop's house in spite of his kindness?

Should he strike out on his own against the weaknesses of Anglicanism? Or should he feel his way more slowly until he knew what he was doing, until he knew the direction of the wind? Should he cut off his ties with the bishop's family?

If he could. That Granny, she was an activist of the first water. The kind one can't cut himself off from. And Josephine? Well, if first reactions meant anything, he might make a Lutheran of her yet. By way of marriage.

The
Game
of Darts

The study would have done honor to a manor house or even to a college at Oxford, with a huge fireplace at one end, of narrow Elizabethan brick, and every wall lined with the tomes of a scholar. It was not large, as studies in England go, neither was it small. Round the long table in the center one could quite comfortably seat a dozen, with plenty of room for elbows and knees.

Ensconced at the head of the table, Dr. Paul Dennis leaned back against his chair and fumbled with his pipe. He was fond of his briars, with an appreciation most men have only for horses or dogs. He liked the South African ones best, with their large bowls and the patina that never seemed to dull, even if the owner were careless.

Under the open beams of the ceiling sat a dozen young men of the cloth, a few in clerical collars, a few in country tweeds, a few in Ivy Leagues, and one straight from a bandbox on Savile Row. Dr. Dennis was by far the eldest, and even he, with a youthful head of hair and a quick perception of all that passed, could hardly have been much more than 45.

As was the custom at the Tyndale Conference, the host led the morning devotions. In this case it was Dr. Dennis. The 16th edition of the Nestle Koine lay open before him, and his happy little exposition was on the second letter of Peter. His younger colleagues, to judge by the shifting of feet, were far less interested in the Greek than he, though their editions were largely the 20th or the 22d, and their seminary Greek in theory should have been less rusty.

This month the Tyndale Conference had convened at the Lutheran Church of St. James, on a freehold not two blocks from the South Kensington tube. It was a pleasant part of London, with stately old apartments and gardens. St. James fitted into the pattern, the dean of Lutheran churches in England, with a history that dated back to George I.

In its day it had hosted many a Lutheran from Germany, and along about its 200th birthday it reluctantly decided its second language should be English. Too many of the younger folk were slipping away to the Anglicans, if not by confirmation, when they went to boarding school, then by the slower route of marriage.

More than any other vicar in its history, Paul Dennis had championed the new look and the English language. His accent betrayed him at once as an Australian, and for those who were in the know, an Australian from the vicinity of Adelaide. In some ways he was more English than the English.

His war record as a chaplain would have put to shame many a brigadier. He was with the 23d Light Armored at Arnhem, with a citation for valor. With shells bursting on every side, from his unarmed jeep, blazoned with a cross, he jumped from shell hole to shell hole, seeking out the injured and the dying.

The end of the war brought him to London, on a Rest and Recreation, before heading home to the dreary outback of Australia. He was not particularly fond of his homeland, now that he had seen Europe at first hand, and he did not relish the kind of ministry to scattered handfuls he had once known.

His name was as English as they come, the gift of a *father who had died when Paul was a boy*. His mother, an immigrant from Germany, was a solid Lutheran. His whole outlook on life, as an Anglophile, was his father's, and his faith his mother's.

The title of doctor was still fairly green, the honorary gift of his seminary in Adelaide, which was justly proud to have one of its graduates making such a name for himself at the center of the Commonwealth. He still asked his colleagues not to call him doctor, just plain Paul, though an acute observer could note that a tactful mention of the title gave him an unmeasurable glow of pleasure.

His wife was old-line British from a not very well-to-do baronetcy in Devon, and though she was hardly a Lutheran in the sense she had forsworn her Anglicanism, she at least worshiped regularly with him and was quite happy that the children be trained from Luther's Catechism.

As a newcomer to the conference and the sole bachelor in the crowd, Karl followed the Greek text only with considerable compulsion. Most of those who sat there at the table with him he already knew by first name — Doug Harting, Ted Gruber, Milt Howeisen, Hans Mutli, Gene Bratlich, Tony Grandtwanger.

He had to smile at the names. They sounded not at all English. Teutonic, every one of them. Like the delegates to the cantonal council of Uri or Unterwalden. By passports they were fairly well split. American, Australian, and Canadian. This, Karl had come to realize, was all part of the plan.

The architect of this plan was none other than Paul Dennis. If one were to build a strong Lutheran Church of England, he reasoned, the wisest course would be to have English padres. And lacking these, at least someone from the Empire. Australian perhaps, or Canadian, though Canadians might be falsely taken for Americans.

It was not that Americans were less capable or suitable. In fact, since the salaries and funds came mostly from America, a good number of Americans was essential. It was the Americans who held the purse strings, even if it was the Australians who could hand out the doctorates and fight for the true faith in the land of the fathers.

Karl felt at least a tinge guilty. He really ought not to be woolgathering, in the midst of Dr. Dennis' train of thought on 2d Peter. But somehow he could simply not settle in.

It was often little things that diverted him. This cigar smoke, for example. How could a preacher afford cigars, on £600 a year? At one and six a go, with most of it to Her Majesty in tax, it was like taking food out of the kids' mouths. Preachers simply couldn't afford cigars. Or were they getting them in illicit packages from home, tax free, or from their parishioners at the embassies?

The books that lined the study were the pride and joy of St. James and of Dr. Dennis. He often spoke of them as "The Lutheran Library," in a reverent accent — tomes, pamphlets, incunabula, in English, French, and German, that had been gathered by generations of Lutheran vicars. Anything that touched on Lutheranism, anything that affected the Reformation.

They were so complete, in fact, that Karl had his doubts about the bibliophiles who had assembled them. If they had spent half the time visiting their flock that they had spent roaming the bookstalls, St. James might have been far healthier over the centuries. But for a greenhorn with only a month of service in the Lutheran Church of England, this was rank heresy, and he thought he'd better stifle the wild notion.

Karl speculated once or twice about the visitors up near Dr. Dennis. A missionary en route from Mozambique and a Lutheran padre from the outskirts of Paris. They had their spiritual missions too, distinct but nonetheless intriguing. He wondered if the challenge of the Gospel for them was greater than in England.

For three weeks now he had been pounding the pavements at Bishop's Monksham, especially among the workers of the New Town. It was not that he disliked walking the streets and passing out handbills and pushing doorbells. It was not that he resented the doors slammed in his face or the curt refusals to talk, even when he had ignored the signs on the gate: NO VENDORS, NO HAWKERS.

He considered himself mature and knowledgeable. A trifle too intelligent, perhaps, for a good evangelist, but a padre who loved his Maker nonetheless. But one had to approach people somehow, even if they were annoyed.

He got a certain lift from the Tyndale Conference, from meeting those his own age who were doing the same work. Not all of them had the talent or drive of a Paul Dennis. And with their poverty-stricken parishes, none of them had a building in the class of St. James. Most were in the New Towns or the slums, just as he, trying to reach the unreachable, trying to gather the young folks and the children.

A few of course had already graduated to a plant of their own, with meeting rooms and church and parsonage, not always with money of their own but from America and Canada. Even so, they first had to have a going church, and only then would the bigwigs back home kick in for a permanent building.

Often as he lay awake at the Cross and Mitre, his head filled with dreams and his stomach with tea, he wondered just what appeal Lutheranism had to offer. The Lutheran Gospel was no more powerful than that of the Anglicans, though perhaps it was under tighter controls. You couldn't be a Lutheran Communist, for example, without being unfrocked, nor even one who denied the Virgin Birth. But then you didn't often find one of those in an Anglican pulpit, either. At least not for long.

Was the difference one of method rather than doctrine? Was it New World activism versus Old World patience? Was it the Gospel preached in a form which made sense to the 20th-century factory worker? Stewardship, the envelope system, the sprightly church papers, the four-color Sunday school leaflets, the filmstrips, the movies?

Karl felt more and more remiss. He must pay attention. He must listen. He must not go off woolgathering.

He was not very successful. Fortunately he was at the far end of the table. He noted Doug Harting, across from him, daydreaming too. Perhaps of how the baby had kept him awake teething, or whether he and his wife should take their holidays in Cornwall or the Shetlands. Karl smiled a little. Paul Dennis wasn't really bad as an exegete. In fact, Karl couldn't have done as well himself.

It was an enjoyable and fruitful way to spend the day, the Tyndale Conference. Karl looked forward to many more. He had heard much of the Tyndale days, more from the wives, to tell the truth, than from the clergy. By local custom the group met monthly at one of the churches. Since St. James was so central, and perhaps also because of the guiding hand of Paul Dennis, six meetings a year were at St. James. The others shifted about, sometimes as far away as the little mission in Hereford or Southampton.

There was a certain rivalry over lunch. The womenfolk, those who were not too saddled by babies to travel, often organized a kaffeeklatsch at the parsonage while the men lunched at the local pub. This freed the women of cooking chores and made for a pleasant change from the usual routine.

The preachers, for all their pose as men of the world, often gave the game away. They couldn't quite find the right street for the pub, or they din't know the whereabouts of the men's room.

Karl was the only new man this year, though there had been three the year before. He was somewhat envied, both as a newcomer with news of the great Lutheran world outside and for his status as a bachelor. Yet he was a little pleased to have the French padre there and the African missionary, to scatter the attention.

The conference wore on, questions of practice, of money, of doctrine, of relations with other churches, of budget, of printing, of publicity, of casuistry. By four the meeting broke up, early enough for those who lived within reasonable distance to get home at reasonable hours. Only the padre from Hereford stayed on, to catch a morning train.

Though the pattern was still new to him, Karl Mueller thought it somewhat odd that Dr. Dennis had asked him to spend the night. Doug Harting would be there, from Hereford, in the sprawling Georgian town house. Karl could have been home in an hour.

After a pleasant supper with the Dennises the plot began to thicken. Paul got out the Consul and loaded his cohorts for a ride to Chelsea. They parked behind the Bull and Calf, a pub that used to be a favorite of Thomas Carlyle.

It was a free house of course, and that meant one could be choosy what he drank. He didn't have to take Watney's or Bass or Worthington's just because the brewery owned the pub and sold only their own. Of the three padres, only Doug Harting wore a clerical.

In Chelsea, of course, not even the bartender was likely to notice. Besides, a clerical collar added a certain tone to the place and, what was even more practical, kept just enough damper on the spirits to save the innkeeper's china. All in all, any guest in a dog collar was doubly welcome.

The more Karl came to know Paul Dennis, from the pink-shell glasses down to the brown brogans, the more he admired him. Paul was certainly no stick-in-the-mud. He knew London cold. This pub for instance. None of the younger brethren would have been half as much at home there, and most would not even have known it existed.

They started with pints of half-and-half, drawn a little too warm for Karl's taste, from the oaken keg. For the sake of atmosphere he liked the heavy pewter mugs, though the taste of metal reminded him of Boy Scouts and tin cups. At eight the evening was still young, at least for Chelsea. A few customers lounged on their elbows over near the telly, and a man and a woman talked seriously off by the window.

"Anybody back at the darts, Fred?" asked Dr. Dennis.

"No, sir. And most welcome ye are." The voice had a wee smack of the Irish in it.

The padres ambled lazily through the double arch, a little cautious of their mugs of ale. Tall as he was, Doug had to stoop an inch to clear the lintel and spilled a drop in the process.

There was not much light there in the room behind the bar, just an old hurricane lamp that had been wired for electricity. But darts in a pub is not so serious a game one really has to see.

It did not take more than a handful of darts to mark the champion. Paul hadn't been an athlete for nothing. Either in his chaplain days or when he had steeled his muscles at inside right on the soccer field, he had also learned something of darts. Not that an athlete really had an advantage, Karl mused, but there was probably at least an element of muscle control and rhythm.

Between pints of beer and barrels of talk, in the haze of cigarettes and the smell of draught, Karl finally learned the evening was not purely sociable. Things were getting so amiable, in fact, he couldn't really remember all the details. Perhaps it was just as well.

The talk drifted to Dave Preusser, a young graduate straight out of the seminary who had worked in Brighton New Town a couple of years back. "Dave had all kinds of gifts. No doubt about that." It was Dr. Dennis doing the talking. "But he just couldn't adjust to an English parish. The people and the work and the witness."

"How long's he been gone?"

"More than a year now," Doug answered as if he and the boss had prearranged a sharing of the conversation. "He was with us only nine months."

"Did you have to ask him to leave?"

"No, nothing like that. It wasn't morals or honesty or anything so serious."

"One of the biggest factors, I imagine, was the car. The minute we put through the LCE scheme for buying cars half on the church and half on the individual, Dave was a different man. In nine months he saw more of England and less of his work than all the rest of us together."

"What of his family?"

"Oh, he wasn't married. Just a bachelor. In fact, that was the other problem. Two or three nights a week he had to be in London. A play or a concert or a nightclub. He did have good taste, you must admit."

"No doubt about it. He knew only the best families. The New Town was a bit grim for him socially, and the car was just what he needed as an entrée to the upper crust. That and his sparkling chatter."

"Where is he now?"

"Home in Canada. A suburb of Toronto. Doing a good job too, we hear. The Synod President was through here last fall and spoke very highly of him. Hadn't even heard of his difficulties here."

In the flow of conversation Karl felt at times not so much the man who was throwing the darts as the man who was the dartboard. But he was a little glad they had all had their pints. Now he knew where he stood, with no punches pulled.

A bachelor, they were telling him, was suspect. Especially a bachelor who was rich enough to ask for a car. Or a bachelor who showed an interest in the fair sex. Or a bachelor who was too knowing or too cultured.

"What do you need to chalk out, Karl?"

"A double three."

"Loser pays for the next round. OK?"

Karl was not certain he could even see the double three.

He hefted a dart between thumb and finger and let fly. Doug booed and Paul gave him the raspberries. The dart stood mockingly in the double three. He wondered whether it was a symbol. Had he won, or had he lost?

Opening
Gambits

Except for the clerical collar, Karl Mueller might well have passed for a managing director. The soft flannel of his suit was just a shade off black, in a soft lamb's wool that would make any bespoke tailor proud. Compared with a normal English style of short waist and too long sleeves, the cut boasted a touch of American influence.

But no tailor would have guessed wrong on its origin — one of the better houses along Savile Row. Four fittings it had needed, and the way it set off his 6-foot frame was worth every penny of the $75 it had cost. He had never felt guilty about the price, despite the fact he was the only Lutheran padre in England who would even consider paying 25 guineas for a single suit.

Back home the price would have been altogether reasonable, and since he had specifically waited to buy new clothes, to take advantage of the English quality, he saw nothing wrong at all with maintaining the price and upgrading the quality. Let the other padres stick to their £8 varieties if they liked.

For him there were no little mouths to feed or hands to glove or feet to shoe. Besides, he had worked hard in his seminary years, getting his tan and muscles mowing the lawns on the estate of a beer king. With the GI Bill taking care of the board and tuition, he had managed to salt away $2,000. It was not a lordly sum, to be sure, but at least it was a pleasant backlog.

If he wanted a nice suit, he could afford it. If he wanted a glass of wine with his meal, he could afford it. And when he heard of the Lutheran car scheme, he had not hesitated at all to put up his half. The little Morris Minor made a great difference. It changed his whole point of view.

He no longer felt himself a minor peon dependent on the whims of a feudal bus or train. Rather he was a man with a car, a man of responsibility, a man in whom the Lutheran Church of England had invested not merely £70 of boat fare and £50 of monthly salary but £300 of car. In a way, by the standards of the Presbyterians or Anglicans or Methodists or Romans, a car put him in the class of a bishop.

Ever since he had wheels, he had become a new man. It was not so much a practical help, perhaps, as a psychological one. It gave a lift to his spirits. He no longer resented ringing doorbells till nine-thirty at night in the New Town. Down at the end of the road would be his little wagon, and there would be no half hour's wait in the rain if he missed the bus.

Though he may have been a pioneer at Bishop's Monksham, the mission techniques he used were hardly new at all. Across the Atlantic they were at least a generation old and for all that, with a few changes, dated to the days of the circuit riders. With differing success they had found a home in half a dozen New Towns scattered across the face of England and, best of all, in the suburbs of London.

Karl's method was simply a churchlike, businesslike way of preaching the Gospel. That it was American gave it at once both an advantage and a disadvantage. Pious folk of the conservative sort felt that their own methods and ways of worship were perfectly suited to the English, but the younger sort, taken up with angry young men and rock-and-roll and American clothes, were ready to take a fling at an American kind of congregation.

The New Town already boasted a little handful of Lutherans who had come up from London — a postman and his family, a baker, two old maids at the Monksham County Bank, a Polish gardener, and a Latvian display artist. Working at new jobs and living in new homes, these folk were nearly as much strangers as Karl, but at least they provided manual help in sticking up hoardings, passing out handbills, and ringing doorbells.

For three solid weeks he had run a series of movies at the Community Hall, every night promptly at seven. He had deliberately chosen an early hour to entice the youngsters, and with considerable success. The movies would have been nothing extraordinary in America, but to an English audience they were a novelty: religious kinescopes from TV, films on stewardship, mission flicks that boasted a touch of Hollywood glamor.

There was no attempt at church services in the usual sense, though of course there were always a few announcements about the worship that was to start some weeks later, and a few words of Christian welcome and prayer. Paul had a nice touch for these, not so much as an evangelist as an interested Christian friend, eager to be of help but quite careful lest he intrude on someone's privacy.

The tea that followed each movie was no small attraction. Give a pack of English youngsters all the sweet, brown tea they can drink, for free, and a stack of cakes to go with them, and they will not only come again, but they will bring along their friends. Eventually, according to Karl's hopes, their parents.

The first phase of the campaign was now over. A dozen or more movies had been shown, thousands of cups of tea had been drunk, and hundreds of doorbells had been pushed. This was the big night. Sunday. High tea was long past in the modest row houses of the New Town, and soon a little trickle of old-timers would be headed off to the Cathedral or St. Saviours for evensong.

As Karl looked about him at the Community Hall and took a last look at his sermon, he hoped at least a few of the evening churchgoers would stop off with the Lutherans. The hall itself certainly would not attract them. Built just after the war, with a kind of makeshift fiberboard that was scarcely even weatherproof, no matter how patched and asphalted the seams, it looked downright uninviting.

The framework showed girders and ribs of steel, a bit rusty now after a dozen winters. Once upon a time the fiberboard had been painted a strong cream, but through the dirt and rust it was now hard to tell there had ever been any color there at all.

The hall outdated even the Town Planning Board. It belonged to the days when Monksham New Town was still a gleam in the eye of a Socialist planner. At first it was intended to serve only the folk who lived on the Little Wealdstonebury Common. Now that the New Town had blossomed in the meadow, however, with thousands of newcomers fresh from London, no one knew quite what to do with the old hall.

Some thought it might make an acceptable overflow for the new civic center, as a day nursery and youth center. But for the most part it was simply a castoff. The commissioners were quite pleased at the interest the Lutherans showed and even more pleased with the £5 a week they offered for rent.

Through three weeks of films and an extra three weeks of doorbell pushing, Karl Mueller had been awaiting this night. The night the mission really began to function. Not just as a cinema or a tea shop but as a real church.

He and Dr. Dennis had enjoyed working it out. They'd designed a portable altar of plywood, easy to slide out of the way between services. They'd scoured the secondhand shops of Kensington to find suitable frontals and a damask reredos. The hangings showed signs of age of course, but in such magnificent cloth there was still the majesty of the church. And what more could one ask for five guineas?

The appointments for the altar were of French vintage, to judge by the marks on the sterling. From Bordeaux, and perhaps a century old. Two baroque candlesticks, not too ornate, and a Latin cross to match. They'd found them at a shop in Cambridge, perhaps where some landed squire had once brought them for a family chapel.

What had been hardest to dig up was an organ. In so small a hall of course the piano would have worked just as well. But Karl wanted an organ, a little reed organ like the one his grandmother once owned. It took a score of inquiries and a dozen false starts, but he finally found one.

The tone was not altogether perfect, but at least it would give a churchly touch. He bought it on sight for £8 from a furniture man in Bury St. Edmunds. The hauling and the cleaning cost another £8, but he still reckoned it a bargain. Like the altar, the organ could also be rolled out of the way.

At twenty to six Karl inspected the hall to make sure everything was in order. The baker's boys had come round early to arrange the chairs, and their mother was setting up things for tea in the adjoining kitchen. At the sight of the organ Karl smiled, wondering what Geoff Thorkill and his fine old baroque manual would think of these Lutherans and their reputed fame in music.

He was just a bit perplexed because so few folk had come. It was still a quarter to six, and he did not yet have reason for concern. Half a hundred New Towners had faithfully promised their presence, but where were they? Besides, of course, there was that chartered bus of Lutherans from London who had volunteered to see the first service at Monksham New Town off to a flying start.

In his clerical collar, with a touch of shadow beginning to show from his morning's shave, he stood in the entryway. The sun was still high in the sky, on a bright June day, and the clouds scudded swiftly before an easterly breeze. Three turnings down the road and catercornered across the common he could see the south porch of St. Saviours. There were few worshipers there, he noted, though the clamor of the bells from the steeple told him it was not too long before six.

He heard the phone ring in the hall. "It's for you, padre," the baker's wife told him. And it was. On the other end of the line he heard the woeful voice of Norah Westlake. She sounded as if she were in trouble.

"I just rang up to say I couldn't play," she was saying. "One of the boys has slammed the car door on my fingers and cut them pretty seriously. In fact, I'm at the hospital now. One of them will need some stitches."

"I'm awfully sorry to hear it, Norah. For your sake and not just ours. But don't worry. I'm sure we'll find someone to play. Not so well as you, perhaps, but enough for the hymns. Will you be able to come at all?"

"We'll try, certainly. But I can't be sure. The doctor is on the wards, and it depends how soon he can get here."

"Thank you for calling, Norah."

"Not at all, pastor. I'll ring off now. Cheerio."

"Good-bye. Hope the finger isn't serious. Thanks again."

Karl brushed a thumb behind his ear, as he often did when he was annoyed or startled. He tried to remember what one of his engineer buddies might have said, back with the army at Stony Hinge, when a dragline snapped. But that was hardly the way to get in the mood for a divine service.

The bus from London was drawing up outside the door now, and none too soon. What had been a gentle trickle of worshipers became a flowing stream. The New Towners would be pleased to see they were not alone, a curious handful. In fact the crowd that poured off the bus appeared to be people of substance and importance.

The clothes they wore and the way they carried themselves and their whole demeanor spoke not of workers in a factory but of the middle classes, of clerks and secretaries and bankers and tailors and engineers and salespeople and maybe even a stray doctor or lawyer.

There would be no trouble with the singing tonight, either the liturgy or the hymns. The singing could go *a capella* if need be. Karl hoped he would still find an organist or at least someone who could pick out a melody on the old piano that had been left there.

At ten to six he raised the question with Fred Ertling, whom he knew as a staunch elder from St. James in London. Most of the busload Fred knew well, and though he squeezed his brain for a potential musician, he was not very successful. If they could find one among the Lutherans, Karl knew, the liturgy would go easier. But ask as they would, they found no one.

At five to six the hall boasted as many as a hundred worshipers. In fact it was nearly full. Karl stepped to the front of the altar, not yet in his vestments, and stated calmly what had happened. Was there perhaps someone in the audience who could play? Even just with one hand?

It was not an auspicious start. In fact Karl felt he was even more the center of attention now than when he would later stand at the lectern. He got no response. This was not unusual perhaps, since so many of the adults were really from London and so many of the New Towners were children.

Three rows from the front, on the side aisle, an older woman with wrinkled skin and dirty-gray hair nudged the girl beside her. Karl had not noticed her before, a few years out of her teens probably, and on closer look rather stunning. She rose, though there was a certain look of reluctance and annoyance in her face.

"I'm really not much of a pianist, but perhaps I'll be better than nothing."

"I'm sure you will. We don't have a great deal of time. Perhaps if you could come to the vestry, we could look at the liturgy."

Fred Ertling was there too, and Karl was glad he was. Under the tweed coat the girl was — well, svelte might be the best description. As if she were a receptionist or a model or a dancer. The line of the eyebrows was a bit overdone and the lipstick too bright, but she was a girl who had natural beauty in spite of the overlay.

"Since there's so little time, perhaps it would be simplest for Mr. Ertling to sit with you at the bench. Is that suitable? He knows the liturgy well."

"Good. Then I needn't feel lost. Would you like me to play softly during the offering and the prayers?"

"No. I suppose most Lutherans don't, at any rate."

"Fine," she said with a hint of tease in her voice. "That sounds more like C. of E. than Methodist."

It was already three past six by the time Karl twisted his long torso into a cassock and surplice and stole. He did not like to be rushed like this, especially for the first service. It was not the proper mood. There was not even time for his usual prayer, the one he had memorized in Latin from the writings of Luther. Practically he felt it better to skip his own petitions than to keep the flock waiting.

In the light of the difficulties with the organist the service moved more smoothly than one could have hoped. She was not a gifted musician perhaps, but the notes were correct and the tempo sprightly. With a bit of practice she might have been far above average.

All during the service Karl had little reason to think about the music. Ever since April he had dreamed about his first service in his first mission there at Monksham, and with that sea of faces before him, framed by the rough I-beams of the hall, he felt the fires of Pentecost at work. It was as if he were a mere tool of the Holy Spirit, who was certainly making good use of Karl's talents and abilities.

In fact some of his hearers likened him to Billy Graham, who more than once had made a God-pleasing splash in the religious waters of Great Britain. There was the same evangelical fire, the same blond hair, the same youthful drive, the same devotion to a worthy cause. He was moved himself, seeing especially the faces of the younger ones, knowing that they were being fed with more than just tea and cakes.

In 45 minutes sharp the Lutheran evensong ended. There was a kind of jubilance in the air, of quiet friendliness and success. The happy chatter of those who moved to the adjoining room was good proof, and Karl was at his best, moving easily among the New Towners to make them his friends.

Man for man there was a Londoner for each New Towner, a solid Lutheran for every one who was searching for a faith. For psychological reasons this was extremely healthy, that the newcomers have plenty of company. Karl glowed. By all accounts there had never been so successful a first service in any of the missions. He could just picture the pleasant smile when Dr. Dennis heard the news, probably that very night when Fred Ertling got back to London.

There were the second cups of tea and the thirds, and then the Londoners boarded their bus for the hour's drive home. Karl waved them off, along with a dozen youngsters. Not far from the doorway he could see the little old lady in gray and the girl who had played the piano. It was almost as if the old lady wanted to seek him out, to share a bit of the night's glory.

"We're really most obliged," said Karl. "Without you and without the music I'm afraid the service might have been a bit dismal."

"It was a pleasure to be what help I could. Mum, you wanted to meet the vicar, didn't you? This is my mother, Mrs. Dunning."

"How do you do?"

"I did so want to come. My husband, you see, used to travel in Germany a good deal and admired the Lutherans so. Naturally, when I saw your hoardings, I insisted Carole bring me tonight. Maybe I'm being a bit sentimental about my husband. His grave's in the churchyard at St. Swithums."

"I'm pleased you came. Your daughter too. She makes a lovely organist. Will we see you again?"

"Carole lives in London. Just home for the weekend. And I don't get about much. Rheumatism. And old age."

"The crowd is rather gone and I won't be missed. Could I give you a lift home?"

"That's really most kind. Carole can't get the top up on hers, and I dread facing the night air. One has to drive so slow."

Karl was taken aback. It was not often that elderly grandmas and their attractive daughters went careening through the night in a convertible or that they owned a car at all. He was more shocked to see that it was a little, red MG, bright with chrome spokes and mudguards.

"Tell you what, vicar." Carole flicked her dark locks away from her forehead. "I'll go ahead and scout the route. And you can give Mum the warm comfort of closed windows."

She was a bit slow and awkward, old Mrs. Dunning, as Karl held the door of the Morris Minor. She settled into the seat with the cautious air of people who know their bones are ancient and fragile. Two cars ahead, Carole was revving the MG.

Karl turned over the engine and flipped on his lights. He really did not need them yet. It was merely a kind of sign he was ready to roll, and more considerate than hitting the horn. He switched them off again, and Carole took the lead.

They moved along the houses of the New Town, the glare of the setting sun flaring from the windows, and took a hard right to the Causeway Road. Three or four houses down, nicely shielded by a hedge of laurel and rhododendron, Carole pulled into the drive.

The house was hardly what one would expect for a widow and her daughter. This was rather the kind of cottage that was sought out by bank directors or solicitors as a home away from London. Thatch roofs and half-timbered walls always brought a premium, Karl knew, no matter what their age.

The garden was well cared for, that he could see in the last glimmers of daylight. Just what the flowers were was not so easy to make out. Either the old lady was quite a hand at gardening, or she hired good help.

"Why not come in a spell, vicar?"

"Why not call me Karl?" After that fire engine race your daughter led us down the road," he laughed, "there's nothing left to be formal about."

"OK," Carole answered. "Mum can put on the tea. Or better yet, we can slip across to the Fighting Cocks — damn! I forgot. It's Sunday."

"Carole. I do wish you wouldn't swear."

"Sorry, mum. I guess it's just the company we keep."

"The young man's had enough tea, Carole. I think there's still some Guinness in the pantry."

"Not for the moment, thanks. But I would enjoy seeing the cottage. In the twilight it's a little like the candy house in Hansel and Gretel. Is it just as magic inside?"

"Carole's spoiled me, really. Not many old-age pensioners in a cottage like this. But one day she wants it for her own, and I guess you might say I'm kind of a housekeeper. When she brings her friends up for the weekend."

"Mum, you know that's not so. It's your house. After all you've scraped for me, I'd be an ingrate not to keep you in style, now that we've a bit of money."

Karl didn't know exactly what she meant by a bit of money, but his savvy of England was enough to know that this kind of house and this kind of furniture didn't come from the salary of a barmaid or a secretary-typist.

The beams inside were smoky with age, and opposite the door, filling the whole corner, was an Elizabethan fireplace. The flooring was ancient parquetry, scrubbed white with the pumice and elbow grease of centuries. The bay window bulged outward with its panels of leaded glass, fresh with the quiet colors of begonias and geraniums and ageratum.

"Like it?" asked Carole. She could see the vicar's eyes moving swiftly about the room, like a little boy in a candy shop.

"It's — it's quite remarkable."

"Picturesque, really. Too, too! We searched for it a long while. The roof leaks, but one has to expect that from thatch. It was a coaching stop once, back in the days when Dickens roamed these parts. You can read about it in *Pickwick Papers*. Charming but not too practical when it comes to heating and plumbing. But we like it."

"It's — well, it's an American's dream of Merry Olde England. I didn't really think these places existed."

"They don't, many of them. The buildings, yes. We've had to search hard to accumulate the furniture. Not much of the genuine country stuff about anymore. Not where you can lay your hands on it at any rate."

As they were making the tour of the house, Karl had his first real chance to examine Carole. She moved with a certain grace he had first missed. And there was something about the eyes, a bit Oriental, he thought. His first notion that she was tough and cold and determined and manly was beginning to soften.

In the study the oaken walls were hung with every item from a ballet that even Faust might imagine — a mobile made of dancing shoes, African masques, silver-spangled tutus, a pair of swan wings, a flimsy headdress of golden lace. The walls were plastered with signed autographs, so thick one could hardly see the wall. Every star and starlet of the Continent was there — the Sadler's Wells, the Royal Danish, the Bolshoi, the Ballet Russe de Monte Carlo.

He was a bit embarrassed. "I guess I should have tumbled right away. Carole Dunning. Of the Sadler's Wells. It just didn't ring a bell. I've seen you dance too. Three years ago, in the *Nutcracker*. You should have said you were Carole. *The* Carole."

"She's rather good when she's at home, vicar. In London she can't walk down the street without a string of autograph hounds. Little girls mostly. But at home she's still just plain Carole."

"Don't be too sure it's just little girls. Once, when I was here with the army, we loaded up a bus and went down to London to see her. For a year the barracks had more pinups of Carole than of Marilyn Monroe. And I'd give you odds my old officers mess wouldn't know whether to be more surprised, if they were here tonight, to see me in a clerical collar or to see me with Carole Dunning."

With the tour of the house a thing of the past, dusk settled quickly over the garden and the fields beyond. Not too far up the slope one could make out the silhouette of the cathedral, and across the river the cluster of buildings and trees that marked the site of St. Maudlin's College. Mrs. Dunning excused herself and padded up the staircase.

"She's really not at all well." Carole waited a moment until she was certain her mother was out of earshot. "It's not just the rheumatism. Her heart too. That's why I try to spend my weekends home. Not whole weekends in the ballet business. I usually drive up Sunday morning and go back to London Monday."

"I still feel a little embarrassed. I'd never have asked you to play if I'd known."

"Don't be silly. Me playing was Mum's idea. Didn't you see how she nudged me?"

"Yes, but you really didn't have much choice."

"I'm glad no one recognized me. The makeup probably. It's a little darker than I wear on the stage. And a little more tweedy. Wouldn't do at all to have Carole Dunning mixed up with your mission, you know. Some reporter from the rags get a pic of that, and you'd be ruined for life."

"Oh, now, you're exaggerating."

"Not at all. You're too green at the sociabilities of ballet." She lowered her voice. "Mother's a horribly light sleeper. Why don't we go out on the veranda? It's not cold, and the flowers are worth smelling."

The red brick of the terrace glinted softly from the yellow lamp within, softly polished with a hard carnauba. A retaining wall rose a foot about the terrace and boasted a blanket of sweet peas and clematis. Overhead the stars began to poke holes through the sky.

"Like a drink? There's some gin in the car."

"I would, thank you. Sunday or no Sunday. It's a good nightcap for a happy day. Can I get it?"

"No, you'd never find it. It's in the boot under mountains of clothes. Mother doesn't really like me to drink, except beer, I mean. It cuts down the company of course, having only beer to serve. But then I've plenty of social life without bringing them up here."

She moved gracefully into the darkness. Karl heard the boot hinge and then the kitchen door. A light flicked on in the pantry. Three minutes later she handed him a gin and lime. If the whole tumbler was as strong as the first sip, he would have to drink cautiously. A parson picked up for driving under the influence had just about had it.

"Cheers!"

"Cheers! Now I'll be able to tell my grandchildren I once spent an evening with Carole Dunning."

She laughed. "Just so you don't tell them you spent the night! A vicar too."

He was not sure of her intentions. Her eyes were no longer steady, as if she were a drink ahead from the stop in the kitchen. It was pleasant there in the garden, and he saw no reason to cut it short.

"Tell me, Carole, how does it feel to be a ballerina? Being a prima donna, with tours all over the Continent?

Command performances before the King of Sweden and the Prince of Liechtenstein? Someday writing your memoirs and having your own little school of balletomanes?"

"I wish I knew. I do wish I knew. How do you say it over there — that's the sixty-four-dollar question."

"I suppose we all wonder now and then. Why I'm a padre, for example. Why I'm a Lutheran. Why I'm in England. Somehow, when I saw you at the piano tonight, you looked like a happy little country girl. A milkmaid or a cook or a typist. You're young enough, you know. But I knew it wasn't true. The makeup, the clothes, the manicure, the whole bearing. In fact I figured you for a model."

"That's a pretty compliment. With all these muscles too. A good ballerina doesn't have a body, you know. No breasts, no thighs, no throat. Not like an ordinary woman. Just hanks of muscle." There was a touch of bitterness in the voice. Carole finished her drink. "Freshen yours a bit?"

"No, thanks. I'm not used to it yet."

"Mind if I do?"

"Not at all. You're over twenty-one, aren't you?"

She grimaced back at him, showing the effects of the gin, as a woman who knew she was closer to 25 than to 20. She stood in the cottage door, another drink in her hand, staring up at the stars in the Great Wain.

"Thruppence for your thoughts."

"I'm not sure they're fit to tell a preacher. But then you look mature enough. It's just that — well, when I get back to little old Bishop's Monksham, sometimes I wish I'd never seen a tutu in my life. There's something clean here and pleasant, and I miss it."

"Nostalgia?"

"Partially, I suppose. Homesickness for the joys of a child. Innocence of heart. There's none of it left in the ballet business, take my word for it."

"How do you mean?"

"Well, you asked for it." She sipped heavily from her drink. "It takes more than dancing to reach the upper rungs, you know. Scores of girls can handle their feet and their hands and their bodies. To reach the top you've got to give a little more. Special favors here and there, to get the parts. And that's only the beginning. Even at the top it takes some haggling and enticing. There may be exceptions, but most of us are just like Cleopatra."

"Don't you think you're exaggerating?"

"What do you think I am? A schoolgirl? No, I've been at ballet too long. Eight years. Ever since I was sixteen. Maybe I'm too frank. That's the fault of the gin. But at least I'm not exaggerating."

Karl had downed only half his drink, and he could already feel it racing through his veins. He had seen Carole down two and guessed that the true number was probably three or four.

"We certainly don't want to waken your mother. And if your eyes are half as glazed as mine, you'd better get some sleep. Have a show tomorrow?"

"Yes, but that's a long time off. That's what we do have, vitality."

"I've got to be going. Can you make it to your room?"

"I could drink this much more and still make it to my room." He doubted it, but then he didn't know her. "I'm sorry if I embarrassed you. I'd really like to see you again. I'll give you my London card, and if you don't phone me one night when you're on the town, I'll telegraph you a personal invitation. Is that fair warning?"

Karl guessed she was probably more temperamental than drunk, though one had to know her better to be sure. "Fine. I'd love it. But first we must rinse out these glasses. Your mother's too dear a girl to have the smell of gin in the morning." He poured the rest of his drink into the ivy.

"No, that's a woman's work. It'll help me clear my head. Tell you what. Drop off the bottle in the MG on your way home. Stick it somewhere out of sight, OK? And you'd better be running along to your Cross and Mitre. A vicar is suspect after midnight, you know."

"Were you serious about London?"

"Certainly. I'll write you a note when I'm sober. Run along now. Got to take care of yourself."

"G'night. And thanks."

"Thanks for coming over. I feel a lot better."

Karl inched his way across the dark lawn. He turned the starter as gently as he could, as if that would keep down the whir of the engine. With a touch of alcohol still in his brain, and a good deal else, he was glad the Cross and Mitre was only a half mile away.

The
Hind and
the Hounds

Outside the wrought-iron gates of the Ellingston New Hospital, Karl Mueller glanced at his watch. The June sun reflected from the crystal, and he had to look again. A quarter to three. Fifteen minutes early. Ah, well. He would take a turn around the street.

The name of the Ellingston New Hospital was misleading. It had only a faint connection with His Grace Bishop Ellingston-Harte, and it was certainly not new. Nonetheless Josie took a good deal of kindly repartee about *her* hospital.

To tell the truth, the Ellingston in question was one of those freebooters of the time of Francis Drake who had made his money somewhat questionably on the high seas and perpetuated his name with grandiose gifts to charity. As a hospital for the poor, with vast endowments and income, the institution was as old and famous as London's best — St. Bartholomew's or St. Thomas' or St. George's.

No one could come up with a reasonable answer why it was called New. The best bet was that there had been another sickhouse there in Kentish Town, however small, and the founder wanted no mistake. On the part of local historians, of course, this was pure conjecture, for search as they would among the dusty bundles in Her Majesty's Record Office, they could not come up with an explanation.

In spite of a long record for charity, the Ellingston New was hardly a hospital one would choose if he had a choice. However adequate the staff, however competent the equipment, it bore too much the marks of its environment. Kentish

Town was hardly the fashionable end of London or for that matter acceptable even among the middle class.

In spite of the new blocks of flats and council houses, it still wore the air of a slum straight from the pages of Dickens. The castoffs of society seemed to make it their home, the unemployed from Jamaica, the stevedores from Nigeria, the porters from Smithfield Market, the dustmen who plied their brooms in the streets of greater London.

Even the plane trees had a look of disease and dirt, as if this were an island the welfare state had forgotten, with enough grime on the leaves one wondered they stayed alive. The hospital too had a forlorn look, even as it rambled four stories high across acres of slumland. One wing alone glistened bright and new, of the six one could see from the street, though the scarred graft with the older brickwork showed where a German buzz bomb had done its work.

Karl Mueller sauntered through the wrought-iron gates. It was still five to three, and he had allowed plenty of time. He remembered what Josie had once said of the gates — too beautiful to be melted down for gun barrels, even though the rest of the fence had found its way to the smelters.

He had never been to a Founder's Day tea, had never even heard of one. He was not quite sure what to expect. That he was here at all, in fact, was by accident.

For a month he had chosen Wednesdays for a preacher's Sunday, a day to take life easy and get away from it all. He could drive leisurely down to the big city, browse through the stacks of Dr. Williams Library, meander among the byways of Billingsgate, watch the sidewalk artists beside the National Gallery, take lunch at the Fisher's Arms, check the latest theology at Mowbray's, and perhaps cap his day with a play or concert.

Two days before he had phoned through to Josie at her flat in London. Would she be free on Wednesday night, he asked, and would she like to join him for dinner and the theater? He remembered distinctly how casual he had tried to sound, though he was not completely at ease.

He had not seen much of her in the past month. It was not because he was disinterested. There was no denying he thought her worth developing and, from where he stood now, even courting. On the one hand, however, he remembered what Dr. Dennis thought of young vicars who mixed church and courting, and on the other, he was a mite leery of his relationship with the bishop.

Either ground demanded caution. That, in fact, was precisely why he had contacted her in London. There, one among millions, she could come and go as she pleased, but at home she was the daughter of the bishop, with one eye cocked for the local gossips.

Josephine Ellingston-Harte was not free, she regretted, for Wednesday evening. There was a Founder's Day dinner at the hospital, the biggest affair of the year, from which even an assistant almoner would be missed.

But if Karl were to be in town anyway, why not come round for tea? A good many celebrities would be there, the Bishop of London, the Mayor of St. Marylebone, the Prebendary of King's Cross, and Karl might enjoy meeting them. Say about three in the afternoon.

Through the brick portals of the main entrance the hospital struck Karl like any other hospital, clean despite its age, and smelling of soap and disinfectant. In spite of the ancient plaster and wood, the waiting room shone with chrome furniture and plastic covers, a little out of place, perhaps, in so ancient a setting.

He pulled gently at his coat to make certain it draped properly. He smiled, thinking back to his bath that morning. In fact he had even changed suits, once the trousers were on, wondering just what he ought to wear when he showed up at the hospital. With church dignitaries about, would Josie want him in a clerical, as a Lutheran, or would it perhaps be safer to dress neutrally?

In the end he wore a plain collar and an Irish tweed, half green and half brown, which was fine enough in cut and cloth to pass daytime muster for almost any job one might think of — a reporter, maybe, or a doctor or an advertising man or even a man of the pulpit. This way Josie could introduce him as a vicar if she liked, but it wouldn't be putting any pressure on her.

She was there waiting, just as she'd promised. "Aha! Right on time. The tea's not for another half hour, you know. Maybe you'd like a look round."

She wore a dark-blue tailored suit that was nearly as straightforward and businesslike as a schoolmarm's or, for that matter, a schoolgirl's. But the chestnut hair and the upturned nose and the twinkling eyes belied anything drab. She was so full of life, Karl thought, she was not really English.

"Maybe you'd better brief me on the tea. Anything special you want me to be or say?"

"Just yourself, silly. I see you're not in your dog collar. Is that for me, or did you want a freer hand in your roamings through Billingsgate?"

"You wouldn't want me to get into a big argument with the Bishop of London, would you? We still could, of course, but there's no point egging him on."

"Don't be so considerate. There's likely to be a Roman or two here and probably a Methodist or Presbyterian. In dog collars, I mean. To make sure they're noticed and get a second cup of tea. But I like the thought behind it anyway. It gives me room to maneuver. There'll be a mob here, of course. Every councilman in the borough — every parson, lawyer, manufacturer, doctor. They've all been invited. Thank goodness they stay home, most of them."

"Is there much to it?"

"No, not really. The Mayor of Kentish Town is the big fish. Nominally he's chairman of the trust. The superintendent presents him with ten red roses as full payment of the year's rent. The tradition goes back — I don't know how far — somewhere in the sixteen hundreds."

"Is that it, Founder's Day?"

"Just about. After the tea there's the report of the superintendent, how many patients, how much money, how many rooms, onward and upward — that sort of thing. Probably wouldn't interest you. It doesn't me, I know. And then there's the stuffy little dinner. The staff officers and the board of control and a score of the dignitaries."

While she talked, she led him down the corridor. A crush of visitors blocked the way, chatting elegantly and milling about. Just beyond lay a huge room, apparently a dining room, cleared of tables and chairs. A century earlier it might have been a ward, where the pallets of the sick cluttered the floor.

"There." Josie's voice pointed to an elegant figure in a cutaway coat and striped trousers. "That's the Mayor of Kentish Town. With the gold chain of office. It's funny, really. He's an overgrown shoemaker at heart, and a Socialist at that. Hires five or six assistants in his little shop. But he was voted Mayor, and now he has to attend all the functions. Everybody knows he hates this medieval folderol."

"Why does he go through with it?"

"Tradition, I guess. If fifteen other generations submitted, why shouldn't he? Who's one little Socialist mayor to derail the train of tradition?"

"Look at those dresses. You'd think this was a showing by Dior."

"They are a bit overdressed, aren't they? For daytime anyway. Look at the duchess there. The Duchess of Malmorend. Bet she spent more on that gown than she pays her gardener in three months."

"Hello there, Miss Josephine." The voice came from somewhere behind them. "It's a pleasure to be here at your hospital." A plump, balding figure in a clerical collar and gaiters and a purple stock smiled pleasantly.

"Bishop Grayson," Josie greeted him. "It's all my pleasure. And Mrs. Grayson." She shook hands warmly. "I want you to meet an American. Lady Grayson, may I introduce Karl Mueller. Bishop Grayson, Karl Mueller. The bishop's see is St. Marylebone, which has as many ties with the hospital as Kentish Town itself."

"Every year seems to draw more and more to Founder's Day, doesn't it, dear?" commented Mrs. Grayson. "With all these traditions it seems there are more press people than anyone else." A flash bulb popping across the hall startled her. "I do hope it won't ruin the atmosphere."

"Now, dear," the bishop quieted her, "we mustn't belittle the fourth estate. Who else helps us stamp out the death-watch beetle and encourage the Historic Churches Preservation Society?"

"I do hope your friend isn't with one of those horrid news magazines, Josephine."

"Oh, no, Mrs. Grayson. You can be just as frank as you like."

In the shuffle the bishop and his lady went their own way. "They really aren't so peculiar, Karl. They just give that impression."

"I find them quite exciting. The salt of the earth. Independent, and not afraid to say what they think."

"To a point. But she *is* eccentric, you've got to admit, and it's a tribute to the bishop he got where he is in spite of the handicap."

On a little platform at the far end of the hall stood a stately cake. The white frosting gleamed bright with symbolic roses, bigger and redder than in life. There was no doubt the cake could serve a regiment, and as if to prove it, a golden saber gleamed slantwise from the top.

A handful of officials clustered round the table, joshing back and forth as a crowd of photograhers jockeyed for position. The mayor took a guarded pose behind the cake, as if he were really not happy about being in the public eye. The superintendent fiddled nervously with a shock of long-stemmed roses.

There were no words at all, just a formal bow between the two men, and the handing over of the flowers. Flash bulbs snapped, a ripple of excitement passed through the crowd, and then there were general cries of Huzzah and Congratulations and Hear, Hear.

Really, Karl thought, a ceremony like this should have a script writer. Ancient formulas and dialogs, Shakespearean gambits and parries. But perhaps it was best the way it was. A conspiracy of silence unbroken by the centuries, even if the actors had little to work with.

If they really wanted to impress the press, at least they could garb themselves in the dress of their ancestors and present scrawny little roses of the time of the Middle Ages instead of these pampered hybrids straight out of the pages of Mr. Cuthbert's Rose Catalogue.

With the roses out of the way, a handful of caterer's men scurried to distribute chunks of cake. Even in postwar Britain, convenience still ranked high. The liveried servants busied themselves chopping up servings with a kind of hasty precision that did not at the same time preclude an aura of dignity.

It was over and done, and for all the happy chatter of hundreds of guests, no one was the least disturbed. With cakes and sweets and tea so close at hand, why find fault? A happy stomach was its own excuse for being.

Karl and Josie edged gently toward the tables, stopping occasionally to greet a friend. Most of the crowd were in fact strangers, but for Josie there were acquaintances on the staff, many of them not much older than herself, and they took some of the edge off the feeling of strangeness.

Karl valued the tea as something to store away in the file of experience. Except for the time of day, it was not far different from a cocktail party. A vast throng of guests largely unknown to one another, little cliques of friends who appeared more interested in avoiding their own loneliness than in meeting others, the excited buzz of chatter that did not ring true, as if everyone were wearing his best face.

By the time Karl and Josie had gone through their cake and tea, others were beginning to edge toward the doors. Karl looked somewhat anxiously at his watch. Four-twenty. He felt a little sorry for Josie, with the formal dinner still to come, and wondered whether she might not have been happier to go to the theater.

The leave-taking was pleasant enough, even cordial. "I'm sorry it wasn't too exciting," said Josie. "They didn't make much of it with the new mayor. Were you bored to tears?"

"Never, Josie. And a fellow does have to take tea somewhere, doesn't he? But if I'd taken you out to the ABC, I wouldn't have had to share you with three hundred others."

"Flirt! Where'd that line come from — Gilbert and Sullivan, or the latest West End musical?"

"That's what America does. Corrupts the youth. Betcha any other daughter of Boadicea would take a compliment at face value and not run it through an analyzer."

Across the street a pair of urchins were pitching gravel at the street light. It tinkled softly against the globe without enough force to smash it.

"Will I see you soon?" Karl asked.

A flip of her shoulders sent the chestnut curls flying, and the upturned nose grinned. "That depends how soon you ask me."

With just the trace of a bow, like some 16th-century

knight, Karl took his leave and strode quickly across the highroad. It had been pleasant repartee, but then when people were too clever, one could not always take the words at face value.

His little Morris stood a full turning away, behind a massive Daimler, on the corner near a tobacconist's. A bird in the hand, he told himself, was worth two in the bush. And Josie was still in the bush. Tonight at least.

What to do next? Stop for a light ale? No, it was still closing time. Have an early dinner and go to Sadler's Wells? From his shirt pocket he took out a diary and sought the little schedule of entertainments from the *Times*. Plays, opera, ballet, concerts, lectures, exhibits.

Perhaps because he was lonely or chagrined, perhaps for a reason he could not explain, he thought of Carole Dunning. Would she be dancing tonight, and had she really meant what she said about phoning? The prospect was worth considering, and he fumbled through the diary for her number.

Outside the tobacconist's stood one of Her Majesty's flaming-red phone booths. Karl put four pennies in the slot and dialed the number, MAYfair 6243. The phone had rung only once when he heard her voice. He pushed Button A and heard the coins drop.

"Hello, Carole?"

"Yes."

"This is Karl Mueller. You know, the padre from Bishop's Monksham."

"Oh, yes. So you were brave enough to call, were you?"

"So far, at any rate. I've been knocking about town today, and the plans for the evening have fallen through. If you were dancing tonight, I thought I might come round and watch. Sadler's Wells or Covent Garden?"

"Neither, Karl. It's an off night. 'Smatter of fact, I was having dinner with Willie at the Chungking Coolie. Have I told you about him?"

"No, but then there's not much reason why you should."

"You're wrong there. He could do with a padre, and maybe you're the type."

"What do you take me for, a flaming Jeremiah or a shouting Savonarola?"

"Neither, but then you are dedicated, and it does show. M-m-m-m. Tell you what. We're having dinner at seven. In the little room on the second floor in back. Just tell the waiter you're with Willie and me."

"Won't I be crashing a party?"

"No, not at all. I've brought friends before. Willie often does. Business pals. You can't tell who'll show up. No, you needn't worry. It's not as if we were George Sand and Frederic Chopin. It's just that Willie and I are both lonely, and this way we don't have to eat alone."

"Who is this guy? You speak of him as if he were the Prime Minister."

"You don't read the right papers. The *News of the World* and the *Sunday Pic.* Willie Gavin's his real name. The papers usually call him Willie the Knife. He once did eighteen months in Wormwood Scrubbs for wielding a blade. The name has stuck, but now that he's grown up and sophisticated, he can afford to hire someone else to do the dirty work."

"Do I bring my cosh? He sounds intriguing. Not for you, maybe, but in general."

"It's on Frith Street. Two turnings from Shaftesbury. The west side. You can't miss it."

"You'd be surprised. But in this case the incentive is good. See you at seven."

"Good. You'll enjoy it, I know."

"At seven then. Good-by."

"Cheerio."

Karl turned the switch of the engine and heard her purr into life. She was a loyal little beast, his Morris. She took him wherever he wanted, without let or hindrance. Some day he must really keep a log of his journeys. Mile by mile, so he could tell just how much he used her for work and how much for pleasure.

For parking he knew a sheltered spot on Soho Square. He might as well settle the Morris for the evening and do his few blocks of tramping on foot. It beat fighting the five o'clock rush.

The Chungking Coolie was a block south. He walked past it. With two hours to kill, he could ramble among the pigeons on Trafalgar Square, keep an eye on the June tourists and the sidewalk artists, browse among the bookstalls off Charing Cross Road. It sounded so exciting, in fact, he was sorry he had only two hours.

The sky was still bright with daylight and busy with the sounds of scurrying secretaries. Like ants the throngs of shoppers and workers dove into the subways and disappeared into the earth in an unending stream.

The drifting clouds were a shade too somnolent, and even with the skies half clear Karl sensed rain. In the northwest, up in the neighborhood of Oxford or High Wycombe, there were murmuring sheets of lightning. But no matter. If it rained, Karl would hop a taxi back. The fare was cheaper than a cleaning bill.

He skirted along the fringes of Trafalgar Square, where you could see the vast streams of white-collar folk storming out of Whitehall. It was appalling, in a way, how people devoted their whole lives to a paycheck. No wonder the country folk of Monkshamshire thought so little of London, with its timeclocks and grime and pressure.

He found a warm chunk of limestone in an out-of-the-way corner, on the steps of the National Gallery, and looked down over the fountains. He had almost forgotten the Founder's Day tea and Josephine Ellingston-Harte. He had forgotten Carole Dunning too, and Willie the Knife. He had even forgotten the round of activities that kept him occupied at Bishop's Monksham — the committees and the telephone and the doorbells and the Bible classes and the confirmation lessons.

He sat there absorbed only in himself and in what passed before him, like an immobile thinker from the chisel of Rodin. The afternoon sun was still warm and, so close to St. John's Eve, still high off the horizon. Barring a storm, there were two or three more hours of daylight.

He enjoyed the sun and the passers-by, and he sat there most of an hour. An organ grinder cranked romantically at the curb. Car after car tried to honk him to the sidewalk, but as a proper Italian, and a musician at that, what was safety of life and limb in terms of a fine location? To beat the whir of the traffic and the annoyed complaining of the horns, he simply cranked the harder.

By six-thirty the hum of traffic waned, and the hustle of feet that scurried toward the suburbs was replaced by those who were coming in for an early dinner. Karl brushed off his tweeds and stretched himself. The stone was colder than he thought, and he was a trifle stiff. He ambled easily up Charing Cross Road, peering from window to window.

At five to seven he found himself under the sign of the Chungking Coolie. The neon lights burned bright even in the daylight, and with the Chinese atmosphere he thought himself not in Soho but in Whitechapel. The proprietor bowed low, swinging wide the door.

"Are you alone, sir?" The accent was not easy to understand.

"I'm with Mr. Gavin and Miss Dunning."

"Ah, yes. Welcome. Willie's friends are always welcome." With unusual warmth he led the way upstairs. In the main dining room on the ground floor the early theater crowd had jammed every seat, spilling over into the smaller rooms at the side.

Upstairs the proprietor seated Karl at a table alone, a

table that might seat six or eight. It was in a private room at the back of the second story, and by its trappings a place reserved for special guests. One waiter was there, but only one, and the proprietor engaged him in a flurry of Cantonese.

"What would you like, sir? Mr. Willie has his own. While you're waiting. Some whiskey or sake or Danish beer?"

"The Danish, I think, on a warm day like this. Is it cold?"

"Yes, sir. Right off the ice."

Karl glanced about him. There was a tinge of mustiness in the air. The walls gleamed with murals of painted silk, and the lights shone gently from the leaded chandeliers and Chinese lanterns. In wainscoting and in screens there was a small fortune, with carved ebony, jade, and ivory that gave the room more the look of a museum than a restaurant.

The beer was as cold as promised, a strange thing for England, even in a Chinese corner of England. "Does Mr. Willie eat here often?"

"Most every night, sir. Most every night. Four, five times a week. We greatly honored. He mostly run this part London."

Karl knew he would have to do further research on Willie the Knife. *The Reynolds News* and the *Daily Mirror* and the *News of the World*. This chap seemed to have as impregnable a fame as Robin Hood or Alfred the Great. Not a good prospect for a Lutheran parish possibly, but one who needed it nonetheless.

Karl's daydreaming was interrupted by the happy chatter from the doorway. Carole Dunning entered first, with the lithe tread of a dancer, and then a big hulk of a Romeo, taller even than Karl, with flashing teeth and curly, black hair.

"So this is your discovery from Bishop's Monksham!" He put out his hand boisterously and pumped Karl's. "You know

I don't ordinarily eat with parsons, but when they're Americans and friends of Carole's, well, that's a different story."

"Don't let him snow you, Karl. He's more bark than bite. Bet you've never picked on a padre in your life, Willie."

"Now there you've gone too far. I don't, usually, you're right. But in my younger days — well, there was this bishop at Ascot, see. A regular young pimp and the bachelor type, who always went up to the tenner window. Ordinarily I wouldn't consider picking a preacher's pocket, for more reasons than one, but he was the insolent sort, and pickings were slim — and well — there was an even hundred pounds in it. Course I felt guilty afterward — went round to St. Martin in the Fields and slipped a fiver in the blinking poor box."

"You didn't!"

"I did! Even claimed it off my tax as a contribution."

If one had not known her, Carole might have passed for the perfect effigy of a mobster's girl. The lipstick was heavy, the mascara dark, the black satin too tight across the hips and breasts.

"She must like you, preacher. She never dresses up for me. Sexy, isn't she? We're just lucky she's not in beachcomber's pants and pirate's shirt." The accent had a hint of Irish, from boyhood days, but with the dark, wavy hair and the Roman nose, Willie could easily have passed for Italian. The soft, gray shoes and the blue pinstripe with wide lapels proved him a man of good taste — a shade Continental maybe, but a man of taste all the same.

"You in a soul-savin' mood tonight? Or shall we just have a good time?"

Karl hesitated. "I can do both, Willie. Save souls and have fun at the same time."

"Sure, sure. I was just tryin' to get a rise. Don't take me so serious." He glanced at the bottle of Tuborg. "I see Frankie's taken good care of you. I'll have to remember him in my will. Ready for another, padre? And what'll *you* have, Carole? The usual?"

"No, some wine, I think. It's too warm for gin. The rain makes it muggy."

"All right, Frankie. Champagne to start with. We can always switch later. The Heidsieck, eh?"

The waiter polished three glasses, then disappeared for a minute or two. He came back with a bucket of ice and a magnum of champagne. "Is that what you wanted, sir? Or the '53?"

"This is fine, Frankie. I wouldn't know the difference anyway."

As Willie poured the drinks, the waiter appeared with the menus. In a vellum binding so handsome and costly Karl knew they were for this room alone, the menus were mostly Chinese characters and numbers, with here and there a comment in English and French.

"What would you like to start with, Carole?"

"Something to celebrate, I think. The padre's introduction to Soho and the Chungking Coolie. Bird's-nest soup, or shark fin with awabi and cuttlefish."

"Good. That's your forte, anyway, soups. Tell you what, Frankie. Just a small bowl of the shark fin for me. And two of each for the others. Then they can eat whichever they like best."

"Just the small ones, Frankie. So we don't spoil our appetite."

Chinese food was not Karl's specialty. He liked it all right, but no one who grew up in the Midwest, far from the sidewalks of Frisco and New York, could really claim to be a gourmet in Chinese. Tonight would be a real test.

His eyes wandered restlessly among the murals, but in his heart he was trying to weigh the characters who sat across from him. A straying young dancer from Sadler's Wells, and a bruising Irishman who was some kind of kingpin in the London underworld.

"What would you like to follow, Carole?"

"Not too heavy. It's warm tonight, and besides, if I gain another pound, I'll need a new set of tutus."

"Tell you what. I'll order the padre the specialties of the house. You can eat as little as you like. Myself, I'm on the hungry side. All right with you, Karl?"

It was the first time Karl had heard him use his proper name rather than padre or parson or preacher, and it seemed a sign of acceptance.

"I've had a late tea, but then there's been a good deal of walking since then. I'll help clean up Carole's leftovers if she's not hungry."

"That's the spirit." He motioned with his finger. "All right, Frankie. Let's have a braised duckling, with almond and tangerine stuffing. And something light to go with it. Lobster balls. Sweet and sour pork, that's always good. Shrimp chow mein. And fried rice and crispy noodles to fill in the chinks. The Chinks, get it?" Frankie obviously did not, but Carole's smile brought a smile in return.

"Fried vegetables?"

"Yes, I guess. We can't eat just meat. While we're waiting, bring in the Liebfraumilch, would you? And the special stuff from Spain. You know."

In the cuff of his sleeve Willie wore a linen handkerchief in the Oxford fashion of the '30s. He certainly knew how to dress, there was no doubt about that. Only the tie might be out of place — a red paisley against a blue-gray shirt and the dark-blue suiting.

In wool the tie might have had the proper tone, but in silk it stood out a shade too bright. The colors a barrows boy might wear. In contrast, Karl's clothes were those for a country weekend, the soft Irish tweed as green as it was brown, the tie grayish with flecks of green.

With the last of the champagne toasted and drunk, Willie turned to fresh glasses and the bottle of Liebfraumilch. A splash in the glass, a sniff, a roll of the tongue, and he pronounced it good. He filled each glass in turn, with a deft turn of the wrist.

Karl noticed the watch on his wrist, and the distinctive crown that marked it as a Vacheron-Constantin. Solid gold, he'd bet — the kind that cost £200 if you bought it at Cartier's, plus another hundred to Her Majesty's Customs.

"Cigarette, padre? They're my own special brand." He flipped the lid of the cardboard box. "Manufactured in Alexandria, by a firm of French brothers." And as Karl had expected, with no customs stamp in sight. "You've got more in common with Carole than I thought, padre. She says I'm a boor to smoke during the meal. Ruins the taste of the food. But that's why I like her. To keep me on the straight and narrow. Like my mother should have done."

Carole's smile was pleasant, though with just a smirk of superiority. Karl wondered how they had ever got together, this kingpin of the underworld and starlet of ballet. Attracted solely by loneliness?

In the doorway the proprietor was hosting another party into the room. It was a family group, a man, a woman, a girl just starting in her teens, and someone who could have been an uncle or guardian.

"Hello, Mr. Gideon," Willie greeted.

"Hello, Willie. Still eating up the Chungking's profits, I see."

Willie laughed. "Have to wangle the business somehow, Mr. Gideon."

Carole nudged him with her elbow. "Do you really have to shout across the room, Willie?" It was kindly in tone, but a rebuke nonetheless. A little, Karl was reminded, like a nanny and a naughty child. He could not keep from grinning.

"That's the head of Enterprise Pictures. Has his offices

just down the street. He's a good customer. I really had to say something."

"I'm sorry. I guess you did. But you could have been a shade quieter. And perhaps not carried on the conversation unless he wanted to introduce the rest of his party."

Willie drank gently of the Liebfraumilch. It was warm from being too long in the glass, and he poured more from the still cold bottle. Meanwhile Frankie approached with mincing steps and a steaming tray of food.

He tested each plate with his fingers, to make sure it was not burning to the touch, and then polished it thoroughly with his towel. With a flourish of dexterity no one but an Oriental could duplicate, he skimmed the glass cover from the duck and placed it lovingly on the table. Already the golden breath and the steaming aroma drifted across the room.

Next came the pork and the lobster balls and the shrimp and the fried rice and the vegetables, this time in their own bowls of delicate porcelain, each with a china ladle and a lid to match. In quantity there seemed enough to feed an army, or if not an army, at least a regiment.

"All that for us?" Karl asked.

"You'd be surprised," said Carole. "Tutu or no, I'm afraid I'll forget my diet."

Willie was already busy with the carving knife. He handled it with skill. Perhaps he had also learned to carve from Carole. "The more you eat, the more you want. But if we run shy, Frankie can always fill them up again."

As the waiter moved to the new guests, Karl sampled the food. The delicate flavors and nuances were so delightful he could hardly choose a favorite. Whatever he tried appealed more than the last, even when he had eaten full circle. But the duck was perhaps best of all, with the hint of almonds and tangerine that made it far different from a Thanksgiving bird.

All three were so engrossed in their food the conversation lagged. Willie, for a backwoods boy from Ireland, was far from remiss in his obligations as a host. No one could lower the level of his Liebfraumilch a quarter inch before Willie refilled it to the brim.

They talked about the ballet, about Soho, about America, about Bishop's Monksham. Gradually the bones of the duck stood out clearly on the platter, and the island of lobster balls sunk lower and lower in the pot.

Willie ate with the gusto of a man of the soil, with a hard day's work under his belt, and the robustness of a man who appreciated good food. No less heartily did Carole and Karl follow his example, she with a more dainty reticence, he with the questing search of a crusader too long lost from the mysteries of forbidden food.

As the zeal of the banqueters finally flagged, Willie uncorked another bottle. It had an odd square shape, with green-brown glass, and a look as if it had been buried in cobwebs or wet rope on a Portuguese fishing smack.

"Absinthe," Willie said. "Ever had any?"

"Can't say I have. Isn't that the stuff that makes you go blind?"

"Gin will, too, if you drink enough. No, it's safe."

"It's not bad, really," said Carole. "But just between the two of us, what Willie likes best about it is that it's illegal. Anything hard to get Willie gets. And that's what makes it good."

Karl rolled the oily green liquor over his tongue. It tasted of herbs and mountains, but pleasant enough. He examined the label. Spanish. A firm in Malaga. But wasn't this the stuff Henry James wrote so much about — addicts and alcoholism and blindness and hangovers — that almost every civilized country had outlawed? "Can you still buy it?"

"No, not really. Only in Spain. This came from — shall

we say friends? You know how it is when people give you things." He winked facetiously.

Karl did not mind the taste. It would go well with almost anything, as liqueur, aperitif, even with a meal.

"Ready for a cigarette? Or would you rather have your dessert first?"

"Thanks, I will." He offered one to Carole, then took one himself. He lit both from the candle. It was a pleasant smoke, somewhat too perfumed, like the candy known as Turkish delight.

Karl recalled the Turkish and Egyptian brands at the shops, which were fashionable among the Continental set. You could dream of being a Sartre of Kafka or Lorca or at least smoke their brand.

On the other hand, Turkish had been the fetish at Oxford in the '30s and was still popular out of nostalgia for days gone by, pleasanter days for all that. For Willie, Karl reckoned, the lure of the Turkish was probably the same as of absinthe. Smuggled in through a fishing boat on the Channel, like the watch and who knows what else, and fashionable because it was illegal.

"What's for dessert, Carole? Preserved ginger? Litchis?"

"The litchis, please. Something light after all the food."

Willie kept filling the glasses with absinthe. Karl had not noticed before, but now the alcohol was beginning to take effect. The Chinese horses on the silken hangings seemed to stir and almost to be racing. He wasn't sure it was the absinthe — the Tuborg and the champagne and the Liebfraumilch were equally to blame.

He was not by any means drunk, just pleasantly relaxed. In one of those flashing insights that seem so clear to one in his condition, he remembered his choice of clothes that morning as he left the Cross and Mitre — the business suit versus the clerical collar. What would he look like now, with somewhat too much alcohol under the belt, dining with one of London's best-known hoodlums and an equally well-known ballerina — in a clerical collar? He laughed. The others were too preoccupied to notice.

Frankie brought three bowls of litchis and a pot of Keemun and Jasmine. The perfumed fruit blended with the aroma of the tea. In handleless porcelain Carole poured three steaming cups. Her hand was unsteady, and she made a splotch on the cloth.

Only Willie was still wide awake. If anything, he had consumed far more than the rest, food and alcohol alike, but he gave the appearance of a young bull whom nothing could faze or tire. "Frankie says a pot this size should last an hour. And three people ought to do away with three pots. Let's see, that figures at about three hours. One o'clock. Think we can stay above the table that long?"

Karl was feeling perfectly content. Good company — interesting anyway — the best food he had ever eaten in his life, good and exciting things to drink, even a Turkish cigarette. In most moods he would have preferred a pipe, but this was hardly one of them. He felt as much at ease as a Persian sultan in the comforts of his harem.

With the alcohol flowing so freely, he hoped he might garner some firsthand scoops on the ways of the Soho underworld. He didn't even know what Willie's line was — black marketeering, smuggling, women, gambling, shakedowns, horses, perhaps even drugs. It would make a good story for the next Tyndale Conference. Or for Josie. No, he wasn't thinking straight. He couldn't explain Willie without explaining Carole, and perhaps that was exposing too much dirty linen.

Outside one could hear the occasional mutter of thunder. For Willie the threat of rain seemed a perfect reason to stay inside.

In the doorway the proprietor wagged his finger, and Willie rose. "I wouldn't have bothered you, Willie, but he says it's urgent. It's Paolo. Why don't you take it in the office?"

"Excuse me, kids, would you? I'll be right back." Willie slipped down the hallway with a stride so steady Karl wondered what had happened to the alcohol.

"That's the trouble with Willie. Always on call. Just like a doctor. With his little empire — I don't know how big it is myself — he's always got to be on the jump to keep it from falling apart." Her speech was slightly slow and blurred. The alcohol had released the lines of tension in her face, and she looked radiantly happy.

"Does he own part of the Coolie?"

"Some, I guess. He'd have to, the way they treat him. He's a big man around here at any rate. Maybe he takes care of the passports for the new waiters. Communist Chinese, probably. Not exactly legal, I mean. But they do send him a bill every month. It's not that he eats for free."

Karl kept an eye on the door. He heard footfalls in the hall.

"I'm sorry I've got to break up the party." Willie Gavin threw a grey mackintosh over his arm. He was all business, as if he had had a shot of adrenalin. "It was Paolo. One of the boys is in trouble in Mayfair. Scotland Yard. I'll dig out the solicitor and stand bail. You can't be king if you don't treat your subjects right."

"Don't get yourself in trouble, Willie."

"No fear. Nothing serious. You take her home, will you, padre? Or send her in a taxi. Nice meeting you. I'll call you in the morning, honey." He was already halfway down the steps.

Carole smoothed her dress and brushed away the crumbs a little self-consciously. "I guess I really ought to break it off. But he is fun to be around." Her eyes were not clear, and her voice was unsteady. With all that alcohol, neither of them was in any mood for confessions — making them or hearing them.

"Would more tea do you any good? Or coffee? Or would you rather go home?"

"Let's leave. It'll take more than tea to wear this off."

Karl rose to his feet, more unsteadily than he would have guessed. It must have been the absinthe. He had felt secure enough in the chair, but now the world seemed to reel. His head pounded, and he thought he could feel the blood thumping through the arteries in his temples. He helped her with her wrap and slipped a 10-shilling tip under his cup.

The proprietor was waiting on the landing, a little above the hum and chatter of the after-theater diners. "I hope you enjoyed it, sir. Your first visit?"

"Yes. Everything was perfect. Good night."

"Good night. Good night, Miss Dunning."

They walked out into the freshened air but not beyond the marquee, where the steady drip of the rain echoed monotonously off the walk. For a second Karl was angry he had left the car a block away. But in his present condition it really made no difference. He was in no shape to sit behind the wheel. There was nothing for it but to take a taxi.

A rank of taxis stood waiting all along Frith Street, hovering like bats to snatch their customers from the row of fashionable restaurants. Karl swung open the door and pushed Carole ahead. The splatter of rain felt cooling against his face. The driver turned.

"Where to, sir?"

Carole whispered the address. "Ten Tyburn Mews."

"Right you are, sir."

The square old taxi swung round Soho Square, past the little green Morris where Karl had parked, and into Oxford Street. In six minutes flat they drew to a stop in the mews.

"Wait for me, would you, driver?"

Carole's eyes were half closed. He wondered if he would

have to carry her into her little pied-à-terre. It was a charming spot to live, though she might have done far better to have saved half the rent and taken an ordinary flat.

She leaned heavily on his shoulder and kept a hard grip on his lapel. "I'm sorry it's turned out this way. Can I make amends?"

"Nothing to be sorry for, is there? We were all in it together. Key?"

She fumbled in her purse. After two minutes Karl took the bag and came up with the key. It was one of those double-turn locks and a bit on the stiff side, but he finally swung the door open. Carole still clung limply to his lapel.

"Coffee, Karl? If I can stay on my feet enough to brew it. Better yet, why not spend the night? You're certainly in no shape to go anywhere." She tried to straighten his tie but only made it worse. "There's a spare sofa if that's what's bothering you."

He was not sure what the glazed look meant, but in any case he could not take the chance. "Thanks for everything. I really did enjoy it." He closed the door gently behind him and left her leaning against the wall.

The rain beat relentlessly on his face, and he climbed back into the cab. He slumped into the far corner of the seat, smelling the ancient leather through a haze of alcohol.

"Where to, sir?"

He tried to think. With luck, he might sit out the night in his little Morris, back on the square. On the other hand there was no point in being picked up as a common drunk. Not for the Lutheran vicar of Bishop's Monksham. "Just get me to the nearest small hotel, would you?" He slipped him a pound, with his head resting dizzily on the front seat.

"Yes, sir, guv. Anything you say."

The cab grunted out into the night.

The
King's
Jester

The Royal Dane was the sort of hotel one finds in every country town, catering with a certain lackadaisical care to anyone who needs a bed and breakfast — traveling salesmen, government lackeys, vacationing families, honeymooners. The name went all the way back to the time of the Danelaw, when Bishop's Monksham had lain under the bloody hand of the Norse pirates.

The building proper could not boast so lavish a history as the name. In its first decade it had played host to Prince Albert, but this was no longer a claim to fame. "Prince Albert slepte here" in gold print on the letterhead could be claimed by almost any hotel in England.

The third and fourth floors did have one boast that few hotels in all East Anglia could match — the view. From the rooms at the front, across Colchester Road, one had an exquisite view of the Castle, and from the back, down over the roof of the Guildhall, 20 miles of fenland.

On the plush Victorian carpets Karl Mueller strode to the desk. In spite of his American accent, the clerk paid a proper degree of deference to his clerical collar.

"I wonder, could you please ring Dr. Altschuler? Dr. David Altschuler."

"Sir, I believe he's eating breakfast. Do you know him?"

"No, I haven't had the pleasure."

"A tall sparse man, sir. Sixtyish, I should say. Graying hair, gold rimmed spectacles. Quite distinguished. I'm sure you'll recognize him."

"Thank you. You've been most helpful."

In the intimate room where breakfast was served, there were few diners, and Karl spotted his man at once. It might have been simpler if they had met the night before. That was when Dr. Dennis had phoned, on his way to London, to say they had arrived safely in Bishop's Monksham. The phone call came at ten-thirty, and Dr. Altschuler was tired after a hard drive from Leeds.

Paul Dennis had made pointed queries and suggestions for the care and feeding of Altschuler. Karl knew who he was, certainly, didn't he? Dr. Dennis ticked it all off, so there would be no mistake. The very important churchman from Cleveland who handled the purse strings for foreign missions. Wine and dine him royally, had been the orders, even if he protests. And when it comes to showing him the new mission and the challenge of the New Town, lay it on thick. Gild the lily, and all that. Nothing dishonest of course. But best foot forward.

From Dennis' point of view Karl knew exactly what was wanted. A view through rose-tinted glasses. More men and more buildings and more money. A little empire Paul could call his own. The Lutheran Church of England. Perhaps that was putting it too crassly because basically the motives were honest and sincere. But to Karl it was not so completely simon-pure as to Paul.

Karl moved quickly to an austere man with gold-rimmed glasses. "Dr. Altschuler?"

"Yes. Good Morning. You must be Karl Mueller." He made half an effort to rise but found his legs too far beneath the table. He reached out his hand instead. "Sit down, won't you? Had breakfast?"

"Yes, thank you. Nothing so good as golden kippers, though. Just some porridge and sausage. Did you sleep well?"

"Yes indeed. The best since I've been here. Takes a few days to get used to the change in time, I guess. And then Paul's not let me have a minute's rest. I'm hardly as young as he, you know. I trust *you'll* give me a few more moments I can call my own."

"Whatever you like, sir. Dr. Dennis says you're to be here two days."

"Yes. And then down to London for the weekend."

"Too bad I couldn't have you preach. The people would enjoy it. But I suppose he has you booked at St. James?"

"Yes. He's rather insistent, you know. Besides, I enjoy preaching. Especially in a strange pulpit. A prophet outside his own country — you know how it goes."

"Yes, indeed. We can do whatever you like in Bishop's Monksham. I imagine you'll want to spend your evenings at the mission. Not a great deal doing — a Bible class and a youth club. Then you'll have a better notion of the work. The rest of the time is your own. Of course you really ought to have a tour of the cathedral and the castle and, if you like, an afternoon in the fens or at Cambridge."

"Sounds splendid. Today I'm fit as a fiddle."

The old man filleted his kipper from the backbone. His wrinkled fingers showed the trace of a tremble.

"Tell me, son. How do you like England? Are you happy here?"

"Yes, sir. Extremely. It's not completely new, of course. I had two years here with the army."

"Ah, yes. But what of the work? Are we really getting on as fast as Dr. Dennis thinks? He's so enthusiastic I can't tell what the real picture is. Let's see, how long've you been here?"

"Four months, sir."

"And the mission's growing?"

"Yes, I'm quite happy with it. We get sixty or so for services, and half again that many for Sunday school."

"Splendid. No wonder Paul was bubbling. You'll be another St. Augustine if you aren't careful."

"What is it they say about the dead — *nihil nisi bonum?*

Maybe we'd better let Augustine rest in peace. Percentage-wise he really wasn't so successful, you know. With forty monks to help it took him four generations to Christianize what is now only four shires, and it wasn't a very thorough job at that."

"There. I shouldn't be talking about Augustine when I really don't know anything about him, should I? Maybe church officials are all that way. Especially when we get old."

"Not at all, sir. It was just something that came up at our last Tyndale Conference. Maybe we want success too fast, we Americans. One way or another, the Gospel has been here two thousand years, off and on, and it may not be so simple to reseed it in a single decade."

"Now that should have been my line. The voice of age and experience, you know. Tell me, what's the building on the hill? I awoke early this morning and saw a glorious glow on the battlements. Something to write the wife about. Like fairyland."

"Oh, that. The castle. I'll take you round if you like. An old one from the time of Richard the Lion-hearted. Not very well preserved inside, but worth a half hour anyway. Oh, and we shouldn't forget the Roman Forum either. The hypocausts and the fossa and the amphitheater."

"You sound as if you're right at home. Made many friends? Or have you been too tied up in your work?"

This was a question Karl felt safer to sidestep. "They seem to go together, sir, work and friends. I've a pleasant place to stay and plenty to do and all the friends I've time for."

"Going to get a British wife like Dr. Dennis?"

Karl thought a question so pointed somewhat out of line. Probably the old man was just making talk. "It's fun to look, I like to think. But of course it's a bit tough, being a padre and being a Lutheran."

"I can imagine. A kind of black sheep."

"It's a little like being a Nigerian jazz artist. Everybody wants you over to tea, but no one thinks you're good enough to marry his daughter. Know what I mean?"

"Ah, well, *you* won't have any trouble. With a personality and drive like yours you'll go far."

Karl was not being cynical when his ears winced a bit at the compliment. David Altschuler's reputation for compliments, not always too sincere, had reached to every corner of the Lutheran mission fields.

"Shall I ring for more tea?"

"No, this is just right. In fact, I've so much life this morning, I'm like a schoolboy on the Grand Tour. What say we have a look round Bishop's Monksham, so I can get the lay of the land?"

"Fine. The Morris is just around the corner. But there's really no great hurry. We can do the whole town in three or four hours, and you may want to save some for tomorrow."

"Let's try the castle and the cathedral anyway. And have lunch together. By then you'll doubtless have run the legs off me, and you can tuck me in for a long siesta. How does that sound?"

It sounded practical enough. "If that's the program, maybe we'd better leave the car right where she is. The cathedral's only a block and a half, and the castle not much more. We couldn't park any closer anyway."

"Fine. I've not been out yet, I hate to admit, but from this side of the windows it looks like a perfect day."

"It is. Just a few mackerel clouds high up in the sky. To break the monotony of the solid blue."

"That's the poet in you. You'll go far, lad, you'll go far."

Karl winced once more. They left the room key at the desk and pushed through the hallway. For a market day the streets were rather empty — just the usual shuffle of morning shoppers at the greengrocers.

At the stop light on Shoe Lane, Karl herded his guest

quickly round the corner. "There you are, sir. Bishop's Monks-ham's claim to fame. The cathedral."

In the midmorning sun, with the light circling the towers, the huge bulk of stone loomed up against the bright glare of the heavens. She was still a hundred yards away, across a greensward of gently rising turf. On the side toward the town lolled an occasional tourist or old-age pensioner or gossiping housewife.

"Big, isn't it?"

It was not quite the note of appreciation Karl expected. "The sixth in the land, Dr. Altschuler. In size. It's the details that would put her queen of the hill. The brasses in the crypt and the carving on the priory stalls. But all in all, unless you've grown up in Monkshamshire, it's safer simply to say you'll find things here you won't find in other cathedrals. Not even Lincoln or Winchester or Durham or Salisbury or Exeter."

"Why do they make such museums of them? And graveyards?"

"*Other lands, other customs.* Isn't that how it goes? Nowadays, of course, the cathedrals are getting back to being cathedrals. In Victoria's day they were museums. The only ticket you needed for a tomb was a rich purse and a nodding acquaintance with the dean."

"Still, when I worship, I don't like to be distracted by those tombs and plaques. They take you far from Jesus."

Karl did not reply. Personally, he thought it useful to know that the God of Abraham, Isaac, and Jacob was the same yesterday, today, and forever — the same his grandfather had worshiped, and his grandfather's grandfather.

As they approached the north porch, Karl spotted an old well-wisher, Tom Swopes. On his stumpy leg Tom leaned against the buttress and trimmed a strand of ivy from the molding of the arch.

"Mornin', Mr. Mueller. How be ye?"

"Thanks, Tom. And yourself?"

"Tol'able, thank'ee. These thunderstorms been painin' me in the leg that's not there, but otherwise I be fine. Good to see'ee again."

Karl felt a degree of surprise that he was recognized. Old Tom was getting on now and as a character about town was one whom everybody would know. But for Tom to know Karl, that was different. What was it, anyway, to single him out? Josie, maybe, and the backyard gossip of the vergers?

Karl held the door wide for Dr. Altschuler. "You seem to be well acquainted, Karl. He one of your parishioners?"

"Hardly. He's the chief verger. Retired, I guess, but still active and still emeritus. No, he's as solid C. of E. as they come."

Inside the cathedral the stone walls shut out the clamor of the outer world and the dazzling brilliance of the July sun. The quiet air bore a faint odor of must and incense, of candle wicks and damp linen. A score of tourists ambled softly on their rounds.

Karl resumed his travelog. He enjoyed it, really, especially when his guests could appreciate the cathedral's distinctions. "Part of the structure goes right back to the time of Ethelwold. Ninth century. The crypt at any rate. But of course the main fabric is much later. Fourteenth and fifteenth centuries."

They moved quietly to the base of the west front, where the cavernous height seemed never to end, spotlighted high behind the altar by the rose window. "It's not just the size. It's the loving little details. Those bosses on the fan vaulting. Some of the finest in England if you take Baedeker's word."

"We should, shouldn't we? Wasn't he one of those thorough German scholars? A Lutheran, too, I dare say."

"Don't miss the corbels and the quatrefoils either. The

mason's finest hours went into them. As famous as the gargoyles outside, I'd guess."

There was a certain blank expression on the face of the honorary doctor of divinity that gave Karl pause. He really shouldn't be bitter at the old man. Four months ago Karl didn't know a gargoyle from a corbel, either.

"England's the best in the world for cathedrals. Better even than France for most things. Except glass, probably. Not so many wars, they say, and the churches had a better chance to come through unscathed. Wonderful stone too. Soft. Easy to work, with plenty of water for barges. Take that high altar there and the screen. To duplicate that in Cleveland would take a fortune just for the stone, and twenty sculptors the best years of their lives."

"It's pleasant in an antique way. Not too Catholic for your taste, is it?"

Karl bit his lip. How such blessed ignorance could ever come out of the Prairies and climb to high office in the church was a mystery he was in no mood to unravel. "No, this is about as Reformed as you can get. That upper rank of figures there — the small ones — they're strictly from the Reformation. Cranmer, Latimer, Ridley, Barnes."

In the south transept Karl's zeal began to flag. He took a new tack. Rather than bombard his guest with learned bits of information — not learned, really, unless one took into consideration the state of invincible ignorance of the good Dr. Altschuler — he decided to keep mum. He would answer direct questions but otherwise sit back and keep track of how much his companion noted.

Bishop Hunt's Chantry was one of the glories of the cathedral, as exquisite for its iron gates as for the tracery of its windows and the vaulting of its ceiling. Dr. Altschuler took one quick step inside, glanced swiftly about, and withdrew almost at once. He did exactly the same at the tomb of Princess Ingrid, whose gilded statue lay brilliant on the lid of the sarcophagus, a triumph of the carver's art.

Karl said absolutely nothing. He simply let his companion walk about at his own pace, treading silently across the funeral brasses that half the schoolboys in Monkshamshire gave up their holidays to make tracings of. In the gallery behind the altar Altschuler finally came to life.

"Beautiful, isn't it?" He swept his arm lovingly toward the Lady Chapel. For Victorian work the little chapel was pleasant enough, even if it failed to blend with the rest of the cathedral. The banner of the Mothers Union hung there, and of the Boys Brigade, almost like the American and Christian flags in some Lutheran church in the dusty outskirts of Kansas City.

"What I wouldn't give to have that in the States! Wonderful stonework! But I guess I'd have to be a Carnegie to afford it. And those windows! Marvelous!"

Karl tightened every muscle in his face to hold back a laugh. These were the very windows, said a recent issue of *Chruch Architecture,* that typified every fault of the Victorian era — "sentimental, gaudy, overbrilliant, lacking in feeling, artistry, and reverence."

From that moment Karl knew the tour was a flop. The next two days, in fact, appeared to be doomed. The old soul was pleasant for all that, and Karl had enough of the Hebrew in his upbringing to reverence a hoary head, however empty it might prove. He remembered, too, the warm encouragement of Dr. Dennis, who was not to be let down merely because he felt it politic to kowtow to influence and position. For better or worse, Karl would go on. It might even get to be fun.

They spent a glorious 10 minutes at the chantry stalls, peering beneath the seats. The woodcarver had been in his glory there. The scenes were a bit too secular for a cathedral perhaps, but a social history nonetheless — a catalog of 15th-century craftsmen.

The tanner, the butcher, the hunter, the farmer, the candlemaker, the blacksmith, the wheelwright, the fisher, the doctor, the saddlemaker, the innkeeper, the carpenter, the weaver, the baker, the apothecary, the cooper, the chimney-sweep. All carved into history on the bottom of a folding bench.

There was one corner of the cathedral which was neither public nor private — the old library in the chapter house. Not many visitors realized it was there, for you could reach it only from the tiny stairway that led up from the north transept.

The bishop himself had spoken lovingly of the old volumes in sheepskin and calfskin there and had guided Karl through its loveliest treasures. It was not really advertised as open to the public, but neither was it locked off as private. Every vicar and teacher in the diocese had the use of it at one time or another, and among the scholarly it was a quiet spot to sit and read and meet one's friends.

Karl led the way up the winding steps, so narrow it was safest single file. Along the Norman balustrade they walked 20 feet above the altar, then two steps down to the level of the library. The room was not massive in the sense of size, but overpowering in its atmosphere of learning and tradition.

"At one time this was a center of learning for all England. This same room wasn't here then, in the days of Charlemagne, when English monks were the schoolteachers to all the Continent, but many of the manuscripts were." Karl had forgotten not to be a guide. The leaded windows and the heavy oaken stacks were simply too persuasive.

"Look! They've a chained Bible." Dr. Altschuler was so excited his voice trembled. "Like you read about in Luther. Chained right to the stand."

Karl had seen enough of monasteries and ancient libraries to know that a chained book was nothing unusual. In the days of copying by hand, naturally a book that required the skins of three hundred sheep and the labor of one monk for four or five years, plus all the illumination and binding, was apt to be chained. It was the equivalent of 10 or 20 years of wages.

"No wonder he wanted an open Bible. One that all the people could read. When I get back to Cleveland, I'll be able to say in my sermons I saw a chained Bible. Like the one that started the Reformation."

Karl thought it wisest not to comment. The English really didn't chain their Bibles anymore, nor did they keep the peasants from reading the Scriptures. He refrained from suggesting that the King James version had had as much impact on the Christian church as any other Bible the world ever saw, including Luther's.

He didn't mention that the British and Foreign Bible Society was the great-granddaddy of Scripture distribution, in every tongue on the globe. If Altschuler didn't know this, there was no point now in trying to tell him.

The library desks were not quite so empty as Karl had first thought. At the far wall, where the light was clearest, sat an elderly scholar with steel-rimmed glasses. His jacket was of soft tweed, good cloth certainly, if a bit rumpled. At the exclamations over the chained Bible the scholar peered toward the intruders over the top of his glasses.

Karl thought him a bit annoyed. In fact the old gentleman immediately pushed back his chair, moved toward them, and spoke directly to the point.

"You're the new Lutheran vicar, aren't you?"

"Yes, sir. Karl Mueller."

"How do you do? Could you perhaps step into the hall one moment? I've something you ought to hear." He nodded courteously to Dr. Altschuler but with a tinge of superiority. "Perhaps your friend will excuse us for a moment."

"Certainly."

Karl swung open the door, and they stood in the crossing, where one could peer out toward the back of the rood screen.

"I've heard some excellent things about your work. Mostly from Miss Tarbury at St. Michael's School, who has quite a few of her children in your Sunday school."

"Thank you, sir."

"Who I am isn't so important, but it's necessary for you to know if you're to get the whole picture." He dug into his breast pocket for his wallet and took out a card. George Hopp-Townsend, O.B.E.

"I'm sorry, sir. I still don't place you."

"I shouldn't expect it, really. I'm a solicitor. Law offices in London. Living here in Monkshamshire. Perhaps you know it, the manor house toward Steeple Bumpstead. Woolaston."

"Indeed I do, sir."

"Several years ago the bishop appointed me chancellor of the diocese. I enjoy it, now that I'm well along in years and can afford some spare time for it." He patted a paunch that indicated he had never had any trouble eating. "But it has its problems too."

"I imagine."

"Perhaps it would be wisest if the bishop did not know I am speaking to you. Let me get to the point. St. Swithums, I have it on the best authority, will be placed on the list of redundant churches. This autumn sometime. The Romans already have word of it. Through Anglo-Catholic friends at Lambeth, no doubt."

"Is it because of Mr. Thorkill, sir?"

"Heavens, no. What's one vicar more or less? It's just that St. Saviours is so close and, by the by, much bigger and in better repair."

"Yes, sir. And there's something you want me to do?"

"Well, I've thought about it for weeks. Even prayed about it. And today, here you were! I think by far it's the best solution."

"What's that, sir?"

"I imagine you're paying a pretty penny to rent the old Community Hall. Three hundred pounds a year, I should guess. For about the same you could have St. Swithums. It's not a bargain, mind you. As you can read on the posters, she's got deathwatch beetle in the timbers and dry rot in the floors. She'll cost you a bit for cleaning and for heat. All the same, I'd love to see you have her."

Karl stood speechless. It was an idea he had only dreamed of but a challenge that struck to the very marrow.

"What about the terms, sir?"

"The commission on redundant churches is rather new. Headquarters at Lambeth Palace. Three bishops and an archdeacon and an architect. The final decision still rests with the local bishop, of course, who gets his legal advice from the chancellor. Me. But even when the bishop doesn't like it, he usually goes along. The real problem, you see, is manpower. We've got more buildings than vicars, and of course we ought to put them where they'll do the most good. In the New Towns. Like Thamesborough for example.

"Now the details. I'd like you not to mention your source of information. Just write to the commission. The Romans want to buy it outright, I understand. That's probably out of the question, though of course if they go to forty thousand, they'll have friends in court. But selling, that's out, I think. For reasons of history. Make us an offer for renting. Say four hundred a year. Promise to keep the fabric in reasonable repair, but of course don't obligate yourself for anything like new lead for the roof or a replacement of the timbers. Better talk it over with your solicitors. You have some, I suppose?"

"Yes. The Lutheran Church of England, that is. A London firm."

"Good! Get together with your people. See what you can do. I'll venture you can do more with St. Swithums than anybody else. And cheaper than a new plant would run you, by three fourths."

Karl was taken aback. "This is extremely kind of you, sir. I really don't know what to say."

"Saying isn't needed. Doing is. As I mentioned, perhaps I can continue to serve the bishop best if you are discreet about your source of information. Can you manage that? If you need anything further, perhaps you could ring me at London. Tuesdays, Wednesdays, and Fridays. Better not use your own name — say something like Hunter-Jones. Will that do? Mind you, I can't promise anything, but it's certainly worth the effort, don't you think? You will excuse me now? Your friend must think I'm quite a boor, leaving him stranded so long."

"Thank you indeed, sir. I feel a little like the Israelites with their manna from heaven."

"I'm not Jehovah, mind you. You still have to stay in His favor. God bless."

"God bless."

The chancellor buttoned his single-breasted tweed and disappeared round the parapet. Karl's mind turned cartwheels of joy as if he had discovered a whole new world. Thirty feet away, across the open vault of the choir, he saw the mighty rood screen. Even from the back the stone likeness of the Son of God moved him as he had seldom been moved. It was as if he were a man sick of the palsy and Jesus had said, "Thy sins be forgiven thee. Take up thy bed and walk."

He was triflingly annoyed to think of Altschuler waiting for him in the library, the man who would doubtless have a large say in the plans for leasing St. Swithums. But Dr. Altschuler would be no block. This was too important.

Karl would place a call to Dr. Dennis. The first minute

he was alone. Paul was the diplomat. Paul was the builder. Paul could have the glory if glory there would be. St. Swithums they must have if there was any chance of it. Karl's mind swam from cloud to cloud, with a chorus of heavenly hosts for company.

Altschuler was not leaving till tomorrow night. Dennis would need an hour to drive up. The three of them could look at St. Swithums together. This afternoon maybe, or at least tomorrow.

In six months, if the Great Jehovah of Israel was kindly with His quail and manna, Karl would be the vicar of St. Swithums.

A
Woman
Spurned

The ancient gargoyles of the Guildhall looked down over the marketplace just as they had for centuries. Except for the cathedral, 200 yards down the highroad, nothing had changed so little in Bishop's Monksham over the last 500 years as the market.

The ancient stalls were heaped high with the vegetables of September: potatoes, carrots, cabbage, marrows, Brussels sprouts, turnips, beets. Against the back of the Guildhall the market smelled of vegetables and the good earth, but as one moved about the square, there were also the scents of haddock from the North Sea, of chrysanthemums from the hothouses of Norfolk, of bananas from Jamaica, of flitches of bacon from the farms of Essex.

Just to see the countryfolk and townfolk was as enjoyable as a good play in the West End, Karl thought. Dressed in their farm clothes or straight from another week of work in London, these people seemed to be what made England so great — a proper blend of city and country, of stability and progress, of ignorance and education. Every Saturday he managed to stop by the market, even if it were only for a half dozen oranges, just to see and hear what was going on. Perhaps he'd even find a good thought to include in the morrow's sermon.

He had just stuffed the last of his oranges into the bag and paid the two and threepence when he caught sight of Josie three stalls up the row, examining the plaice and skate. The chocolate tweed of her suit made her honey-colored hair seem almost ashen. Almost at the same instant she looked up from the fish and recognized him but quickly pivoted and moved away.

In a minute Karl had threaded his way through the shoppers and bounded toward her. "Morning, Josie. Had a good week in London?"

"Yes, thank you." There was a coldness in her eye and a curtness in her voice he had never before noticed. She turned as if to go. "I've got to be getting home."

"Can I drive you? I'm parked just behind the Guildhall."

"It's just two turnings. Besides, I'd rather walk."

She was obviously giving him the cold shoulder, and he did not know why. He'd seen her six or seven times, in the months at Bishop's Monksham, and their relations had always been so cordial he did not even recognize this side of her personality. She seemed to be looking at his tieless shirt and sports jacket, which made him seem rather American. Perhaps she was too annoyed to face him.

"What is it, Josie? Is it something I've done? I wouldn't want to offend you, not for the world."

She flung her head back like a young mare sending its mane flying. "It's not very ladylike to tell your friends why you don't like them. Especially when you'd always thought so well of them." In her voice there was an overtone of anger.

"Tell me, Josie. What've I done?"

Even though their voices were low, one or two of the shoppers had stopped to stare. This time she almost whispered. "You don't think I'd tell you right here in the market with all those gargoyles staring down at us!"

"I'm not sure you'd tell me at all. But let's not make a scene about it. Come along." He took her by the elbow, just firmly enough to show he was the master, and led her across the High Road. Four hundred feet from the market a path started to wind down one side of Forum Hill towards the ancient ruins of the Romans, sticking up starkly from the sod.

He parked her on a bench, a favorite haunt for those

who were elderly. "Now out with it! In England I'd always heard a man was innocent until he was proven guilty."

Her eyes were red and she could hardly get the words out. "It's Carole Dunning! She's got one of the worst reputations in town, ballerina or no. And you've been squiring her all over London. And then you come traipsing back to me as if nothing's happened."

"Nothing *has* happened, Josie. Nothing."

"It has." She stomped her foot and burst out crying. "Don't try to deny it. My roommate from the hospital saw you. At the Chungking Coolie."

"OK, so she did. But there's nothing wrong with that." He tried to keep his voice calm. "It was the night of the Founders Day Tea, that's all. You had to go to the formal dinner at the hospital. I'd even asked you if you'd like to see a play with me. Remember?"

She was now completely in tears, and Karl handed her his handkerchief. He sat nervously at the far end of the bench, not quite understanding what was happening.

"You've been at her house too. Cocklesfields. Often. Mr. Fyffenfield says he's seen your car there half a dozen times. Any time of the day. He's the beadle at the cathedral. Lives right next door to them, and as far as I'm concerned, his word is as good as the Bible's."

Karl faintly began to realize just how upset the girl really was. "Now listen, Josie," he began, trying to be as objective and as soothing as he could. "I know she's no angel, but I don't think she's a fallen one, either. Maybe I shouldn't have gone out with her. Not even once. I did. But there was nothing wrong with it. We were with Willie the Knife. He's her real beau. I wouldn't even have phoned her if I hadn't been a little jealous. After all, you were off banqueting with dozens of dukes and doctors, all far more eligible than Carole Dunning."

"You can't deny she's attractive. Handles herself beautifully and, if one cares for eye shadow and mascara, uses it as well as anyone in London." There was still the sound of jealousy and anger in every word. "And what about Cocklesfields?"

"That one's easy. That's not Carole. That's her mother. An arthritic. She's been coming to us Lutherans ever since the mission started. When she's well enough to get out of bed. If she can't, I pay her a sick call. She needs *me* too. Doesn't have more than a few years to live. Besides, she's worried about her daughter. The only time I go near Cocklesfields is during the week, when Carole's in London. Ask your Mister Fyffenfield about that, beadle or no beadle."

The handkerchief was now crumpled and damp, and Josie was once more getting control of herself. "I just don't know, Karl, I just don't know. I thought I was getting to know you and even to think well of you, and then all this had to happen."

"I know it's not very easy, Josie. Being a bishop's daughter. Having to live your whole life in the public eye. Running around with a Lutheran padre, and an American at that. In a little market town like Bishop's Monksham. It's not easy. Not for me, either. But I honestly thought the Dunnings needed me. As a man of God. Both of them — mother and daughter too. I still think they do."

Down along the Aublin rose the ancient hypocausts. Not even the houses of modern Britain could boast such fine central heating as the ancient villas of the Romans; in fact very few of the modern ones had any at all.

Just to look out over the fens, beyond the fields of St. Maudlin's College and the ruins of the Roman town, reminded Karl of the wonderful afternoon he had spent with Josie there, his first month in Bishop's Monksham. They'd wandered through the amphitheater, walked through the village streets, examined the hypocausts, looked at a tomb or two, and dawdled through the museum.

There for the first time he had really come to know Josephine Ellingston-Harte and to realize how much they had in common — their love for children, their dislike for pretension, their appreciation of classical music, their preference for independence, their deep-rooted faith.

For hours they'd wandered through the ruins, as oblivious to time as if they had been living 2,000 years earlier and had been some Roman soldier and his girl. They'd taken their tea on a shaded little dock jutting out into the river behind the Fighting Cocks. Only the tolling of Big Tom from the tower of the cathedral had reminded them of the flow of time.

Looking at Josie, Karl did not know quite what he ought to do. In her present mood, however calm she had become, anything he said might be used against him. Yet he hated to see so pleasant a friendship — and perhaps even more than a friendship — go swirling down the drain.

"Can I see you tomorrow, Josie? After church? For a walk along the river?"

She put the handkerchief on the bench beside him and tucked the shopping basket on her arm. Her eyes were still red, but she spoke as if she had regained complete control. "I don't think so, Karl, thank you. No. I need to think. Thanks all the same." She rose to her feet and started off toward the high road. "See you," she called over her shoulder with as much flippancy and spriteliness as she could muster.

"See you," said Karl glumly, looking out over the fens.

Defender
of the
Faith

Against a blue-damask sky the larks sailed valiantly
into the gale, like tiny wasps attacking a giant. The
yellowing leaves of the linden skittered about the garden,
swirling headlong before the breeze.

"It's not really a day for gardening, Karl. I shouldn't have
let you come. To garden, I mean." Sarah Ellingston-Harte
moved with a spry step among the roses. In the steel-gray
sweater knitted with her own hands, matching the color of
her hair and eyes, she could have passed for 60 as easily
as for 77.

"That's the only fault I can find with living at the Cross
and Mitre. The greatest flower country in the world, with no
chance to get my hands on a garden."

"As I said on the phone, you're welcome here any time.
But I can appreciate you best when I don't have to share you.
Old people get lonely, they say. Bet you read in the Monks
Watchman that Alred would be in York this week, and
decided you'd better come while he was gone. On a week-
day, too, while Josie's in London."

"If this is confession time, I'll have to admit you're right.
But it was the weather too. A glorious day in spite of the
wind. The BBC put out a small-craft warning."

"St. Martin's summer we call it. It's a French notion.
What is it you Americans say — 'Indian summer'? Properly
I guess it's still real summer. St. Martin's shouldn't count
until we're well into October or even November."

"It's a glorious day anyway. Makes you want to be a boy
again with a kite or sailboat."

"You just tend to the clippers. We'll stand for no sky-larking when you're working for me."

"Maybe you're right. Besides, if I don't get the job done, you'll have to invite me back. And of course it would hardly be fair to an Anglican bishop to make him look out his study window and see a Lutheran vicar digging among the roses."

"There now! You're exaggerating. Whoever makes them grow best, he's the best gardener. Alred always did love roses. Lately he's been too busy. All these committees and commissions. The local diocese wouldn't be so bad. It's all the other jobs. Tom Swopes, he used to help too. But with that peg leg of his digging holes in the turf, he does as much damage as good."

"You're quite a gardener, I hear."

"I used to be. Still like it. But there's a limit."

With gloved hands Karl snipped at the roses. The bushes still bloomed lustily. With luck they might not peter out until the first Sunday in Advent.

"It's a nice time of the year, autumn. Most people my age pray to see another summer. Me, I pray for another autumn."

"The garden's lovely then. At home we'd be having frost now."

He looked once more at the lush grass and the holly and the laurel and the boxwood and the ivy. The geraniums still stood red as a cock's comb against the snowy blanket of alyssum, and a row of asters highlighted the floribundas clambering over the garden wall.

From the pillars of ancient brick he trimmed a strand of ivy. It was laced so thick with hoary vines he wondered whether the brick held the ivy, or the ivy the brick. The whole garden was pleasant, sandwiched between the gate-house and the abbey. About an acre, he would guess. It was just wild enough to be personal and intimate, without the vast expanse of lawn and garden that reminded one of Hampton Court or Hampstead Heath.

"There's something enticing about a garden, Sarah. Keeps your hands busy and your soul out of mischief."

"Yes, indeed. Keeps right on growing even if you neglect it. Wish they'd make the Foreign Office take a course in gardening. Cut down the number of wars, it would."

"Now, Granny. You're exaggerating."

"Am I? Maybe so. But you take someone like Josephine. Just like the Foreign Office. Out to change the world. What's worse, she really believes she can. One little social worker in one little hospital in one little corner of one little world. A drop in the ocean. If she were a gardener, now, like her father, she'd know it comes and goes. You can't change good and evil any more'n life and death. They go on forever."

"Don't you think people ought to try? Changing the world, I mean, if they think there's something really wrong with it?"

"Try, yes, but realistically. With enough experience to know the odds. Then they don't get discouraged and go blowing their brains out."

Karl gathered an armful of cuttings and carried them to the far corner of the wall, behind a holly, on a heap of compost. Alfred the Great gamboled along at his feet. It was almost as if the little dog had been out chasing cats and was disappointed not to know his mistress had company. Or maybe his legs were just so short an hour's worth of cat chasing was all he could take.

"Think in terms of the church, Karl. A young vicar like you is apt to think God's kingdom stands or falls on what one man can do. That's good, that kind of devotion, but it's not realistic. What I like about you is your realism. Down to earth. Maybe we shouldn't even talk about St. Swithums, me being the bishop's mother. But you — you'll win either way.

"Get it, and you'd be the happiest vicar this side of

heaven. Lose it, and your work'd still go on. You'd still visit the sick and teach the young and preach the Gospel, there or elsewhere. And that, I think, is one of the lessons that comes from gardening."

"You should write a testimonial for a seed company, Sarah. No, I'm just joshing. But with those sentiments and with your name it'd be worth fifty quid."

"I really shouldn't bother you with all this. Not when you're so kind to help me with the garden. But I do like to talk and have someone listen. So many of the folk who come here, of course, are the kind one can't speak to. The prebends and the canons and the theological bods. To some of them it makes more difference whether you swing a censer than whether Christ was God."

"I'm enjoying every minute. I'll work all night if you'll keep up the conversation."

"Take this business of Evangelical and Anglo-Catholic. With their newspapers and books and pamphlets and feuds they spend more time fighting than preaching. And yet, when you get right down to it, the living Gospel still goes on. If not from the vicars, at least from the plain folks."

"What is it *you* read, Sarah — the *Church Times* or the *C. of E. Newspaper?*"

"I read 'em both if Alred hasn't used them for kindling. Summertimes it's pretty safe."

Overhead a long wedge of waterfowl flew southward for the warmer climes of Africa. You could hear the faint mewing and honking above the rush of the wind. Sarah watched them in silence until they were far down the horizon.

"In a job like yours, Karl, doubtless you hear a great deal about the C. of E. People who have grievances, people who look back with fondness to the days of their confirmation and their ties with the village parish."

"It's one of the glories of a preacher, seeing the Gospel at work."

"No one really gets to know the C. of E., not even someone like Alred. It's too big, too complicated, too many facets. But it's an intriguing experience, and for me at least, an unending one."

"I always have to smile, as a Lutheran. Sure, I know something of Anglican history and doctrine. But not much more than a kindergartener, really. Some odd little quirk where Lutheranism and Anglicanism happen to touch. Say the Augsburg Confession and the Thirty-Nine Articles. The same subject matter and the same sequence, as if the English had found it simpler to start with Melanchthon and then revise or reword where necessary."

"I didn't know that."

"Oh, and then there's that bit about the *Defensor Fidei.* I think of it every time I spend a coin. The initials D. F. Old Henry won his title from the pope for his articles against Luther. But now Defender of the Faith has come to mean just the opposite. Not a loyal Roman, as opposed to heretics, but a loyal heretic, as opposed to Rome."

Karl spotted the little patch of vegetables along the north wall. Three or four tomato plants, marrows, cucumbers, lettuce, parsley, carrots, peas. They were half hidden beneath a low hedge of holly as if they were necessary for the kitchen but not quite in place at so honored an establishment as the garden of the Abbey Gatehouse.

"There're stories and stories about the church if one could only remember them. When I was a girl in the Cotswolds, there was a big fight between the vicar and the churchwardens. No one ever quite knew why. In the end the vicar had to resign."

"How was that?"

"Well, almost every pew in the church had a pew holder, with annual rents. There were only a few in back that were free, mostly for laborers and maids and servants and folks of servile status. The pewholders refused to come, and locked their stalls to keep out the rest. In the end they even pad-locked the church. For a while the vicar preached from the lich gate, and the few odd who worshiped sat on the tomb-stones. But come winter, there was nothing for it but resign."

"Now that's the sort of thing I miss. Spending all this time in England and not really getting to know the C. of E. People just don't talk about it, knowing you're an American and a Lutheran to boot. And of course I can't very well visit the local parishes, with my services the same time as theirs."

"These country places, they're the ones to visit. That's where the dead still die in the Lord and the infants still get their christening. There's many a faithful shepherd in the land despite the prophets of doom."

"Why is it the bishops keep talking about spiritual malaise?"

"Whistling in the cemetery, I imagine. They need man-power and income, and they're short of both. Somehow we've never really recovered from Pusey and Newman. The Romans have been making great strides, and not merely, as someone like Alred is apt to say, because there're so many immigrants from Ireland."

"Why then?"

"A power vacuum. Since the faith of the Victorian Age had so little to offer, something else stepped in to fill the void. That's part of the reason, at any rate. But we're re-covering. I just wish I had another decade to live, to see how some of these modern touches work out. Slum evangeliza-tion. City missions. New Sunday schools. New Towns. Stew-ardship of money. Missions to students."

"That's what an American misses. Money and stewardship. We aren't blessed with magnificent old churches from the faithful forefathers. We have to pay for them ourselves. We don't have trust funds and lands. They're nice to have, but they make a man feel religion is free. That he needn't dig into his pocket and support it."

"That's a sore point all right. Nobody denies it."

Alfred the Great spotted a squirrel among the limes and made a great to-do. He raced round and round the trunk, clawing at the bark. The squirrel jumped from tree to tree, then onto the greensward of the cathedral.

"Sometimes we Americans worship organization. That's what our German friends charge. Congenial churches, with social uplift and massive societies. Women's groups, men's groups, boys' groups, girls' groups, even babies' groups. Organization for the sake of organization and not for the sake of the Gospel. In a way they're right. But stewardship helps break into the real meaning of faith. Envelope systems and sealed pledges and tithing and record keeping. Even if the methods are wrong, they at least ram home a man's obligations. If God doesn't cost anything, He's not worth much."

"We're getting there. It takes time, but the tide is beginning to flow."

"Sometimes the Free Churches are too hard on the C. of E. Even us Lutherans. Want to know my favorite sport? Know these little tally cards the smaller churches post after the Sunday collections — so many pennies, so many thruppences, so many sixpences, so many half crowns? Well, look at them sometime on the bulletin board. Forty worshipers and an offering of seven bob!

"That works out at maybe tuppence a head. Since there're a couple of half crowns there, half the people don't even contribute a penny. Among us, if we didn't average a shilling or two a man, we simply couldn't afford to operate. Salaries and heat and light and rent."

"It *is* a shocking state, isn't it?"

"Mind you, if the money were really needed, you'd get it. But no one is going to throw money in the plate because he sees a sign urging him to preserve a historic fabric or to stamp out the deathwatch beetle. If that's a motive for Christian giving, he might just as well contribute to the British Museum."

"Alred hates those signs."

"But he's a tiny minority. Where there's real need, of course, and God's people have a chance to give, they do. Look at all you've done in the field of mission work and Scripture distribution: the British and Foreign Bible Society, The Society for the Propagation of the Gospel, The Society for The Promotion of Christian Knowledge, The Student Christian Movement, and The International Missionary Council. They're the envy of all Christendom. Even Rome doesn't have anything to match."

"I've been underestimating you, padre. Here I thought you were a babe in the woods — knowledgeable, of course, but a little green about us Anglicans."

"Oh, I am, I am. A man outside his country is always a great prophet. To himself at any rate."

"No, the insights are right. Deep, too. It's just that one doesn't see the forest for the trees."

The great clock of the cathedral struck four. Sarah Ellingston-Harte dropped the handful of cuttings. It was as if the striking of the tower clock triggered some Druidic impulse.

"Four o'clock, and the saints be praised. I haven't even put on the kettle for tea. But that be your fault, Karl Mueller. Keeping a pious old believer from her work by your magic spell. Just when I'd dug out the best Darjeeling in the house, too, and a fresh batch o' cakes. But we can remedy that fast. Come along, Alfred! Here, Alfred! Time for tea."

The
Commandment
on Poaching

The cool drizzle of October drifted off the fens. It was so persistent Karl swore it would pierce the very walls of the Cross and Mitre, bricks, mortar, plaster, woodwork, and all. The thermometer registered in the lower 40s, but with a bleak sky and a wind off the Channel it might as well have been snowing.

He thumbed through Cruden's looking for a text which might give new insight on the doctrine of justification. To *make just* in the legal sense, to absolve, to remit, to find not guilty — what was the legal term in English anyway? For once the Greek was clearer than the Anglo-Saxon. Maybe it would be clearer from the pulpit if he described a scene at the Old Bailey, with a Crown Prosecutor and a Queen's Counsel and a bewigged judge.

He looked out over the landscape. The larch across the way was still not bare of its yellow needles, and the turf looked as fresh and green as in a spring rain. Little gusts of wind sent the drizzle scurrying into the farthest crevices, more like a fine mist or a penetrating fog.

He stuffed his pipe once more with a tobacco he did not really enjoy but one which bore a noble ecclesiastical name — Canon's Delight. A bit too raw for the taste, with too heavy a dose of burley and a bit light on the rum. Even if it didn't burn well, it was at least exhilarating. This morning, even by nine o'clock, he needed somehow to keep from dozing over his sermon. He made a mental note not to buy a second pack of Canon's Delight.

There came a sharp knock at the door. The maid probably.

"Mr. Mueller?"

"Yes. Come in."

"It's the telephone, sir. A trunk call."

"Thank you, Millie."

He tramped down the rear stairs and took the call at the bar. "Karl Mueller here."

"Good morning, sir. This is the Rev. Mr. Camthorne. The vicar of Edgecomb St. Mary's. Since you probably don't know East Anglia too well, it's not far from Huntingdon."

"Yes, sir." As a matter of fact, he did know of Edgecomb St. Mary's. One of the minor churches off the beaten path, a little architectural gem that made all the guidebooks, like Long Melford and Devizes. He thought it wiser not to waste the vicar's money discussing architecture.

"We're having our harvest festival on October Twentieth. A bit later than usual, I know. The Bishop of Ely's speaking at the morning service, and the Archdeacon of Norwich at matins. We had hoped to have the Suffragan Bishop of South Africa for evensong, but he's been taken ill. Maybe it's the British climate." There was a hearty laugh in the receiver. "I know it doesn't give you a great deal of time, but perhaps you could make yourself free to substitute. Of course there'd just be the sermon. I know you're not Anglican, and of course we couldn't expect you to do the liturgy."

It was not often that a Lutheran, of all people, was asked to fill an Anglican pulpit, and even rarer when he substituted for a suffragan. "Are you sure I wouldn't try to steal your sheep? I'm not C. of E., you know."

"Tommyrot. You just preach the Gospel, and we'll listen. Besides, you have good recommendations."

"The twentieth of October, is it?"

"That's right. At six in the evening."

"It's a bit sticky, what with a service of my own. I'd love to, of course, and I suppose it wouldn't be altogether impossible to fill my pulpit. Could I check my diary? Will you hang on, or shall I phone back?"

"I'll hold, thanks."

Karl did not even reach for his shirt pocket though the brown leather notebook was there beside his heart. He tried to conceive what Paul Dennis would think. 'Lutheran preachers for Lutheran altars,' the slogan of generations of Lutherans.

But for some queer reason, theologically, Lutherans in non-Lutheran pulpits were not so heretical as non-Lutherans in Lutheran ones. Besides, there was the precedent of Paul and of Luther. Preach the Gospel to those who will hear, and let the chips fall where they may.

"The date looks fine. I'd love it. I can't give you a final answer at the moment until my own pulpit is filled. Tell you what. I'll get busy on the phone. Let you know for sure tonight. At the latest, tomorrow. Would that suit?"

"Excellent. We certainly hope to have you. Shall I ring back?"

"No, it's easier if I ring you. Camthorne — was that the name?"

"Yes, indeed. Edgecomb St. Mary's 19. You have to go through the operator at Huntingdon."

"Yes, sir. I'll be phoning as soon as I have an answer."

He rang off. Karl grinned sheepishly. His eyes glanced at the bottles behind the bar, not put away properly as the licensing laws required. Had he put his foot in it? For himself he didn't think so, but some of the other Lutheran bods might consider him a heretic.

Well, that was the chance one took. Whom could he get to fill the pulpit? Without going through Dr. Dennis. Milt Howeisen? Milt was a good bet. No evensong of his own, and a good man when it came to going out of his way.

Karl tripped up the stairs to his room, forgetting the darkling skies of October. Somehow the room seemed brighter and warmer, even without a fire, and the rain outside

no longer depressed him. How'd they heard about him anyway? Josie? Sarah? The bishop? He'd give a silver thruppence
to find out.

It was 17 days to the day of the phone call when Karl
Mueller rolled his little Morris to a stop in the broad lane
outside the church of Edgecomb St. Mary's. The day was
bright, with the sun still well off the horizon, and the rolling
fields of the valley littered with stooks of grain and ricks
of hay.

His sermon was down pat — the glories of the Creator,
the bountiful harvest, the obligations of those who shared
these blessings, the proper blend of material gifts and spiritual ones, the coming of the Christ as a firstfruit of the
Harvest. It was a good sermon, touchingly worked out to appeal to a countryman. For once in his life Karl had blotted
out the faint touch of nervousness the pulpit usually brought,
and stood eager to proclaim his message.

The church lived up to its reputation. The west porch
was clearly Norman, and there was no doubt at all about
its age. The bell tower and the chancel struck one as later
additions, with a glorious touch of light tracery, in the best
sort of Perpendicular.

The whole east front glittered dully with ancient glass
and spidery stonework until one wondered how so little structure could support so vast a sea of glass. The windows
must have been as early as 13th century, not with the rich
colors of a guild church in wealthy Norwich but with the
delicate blacks and whites of a monastery sworn to austerity.

The church rose on a little hillock 20 feet or so from
the floor of the Vale of Monthup, where the Cistercians had
once trained their white-robed monks for all England. Besides the church there was not much else in the village of
Edgecomb St. Mary's. The brick-and-thatch cottage across

the lane would surely be the New Rectory, and two turnings on, the old vine-covered structure was probably the pub.

Beyond that the houses were scarce. Three or four, maybe, buried behind copses of elm and lime. What looked like an oast house boasted a wide flue at the top to take the moisture off the hops. And farther up one side of the valley stood an abandoned windmill, the arms long rotted away, but with bins and racks that served as a storehouse for sugar beets.

Karl Mueller had promised to come at five and take high tea at the vicarage. After the service, Mr. Camthorne had said, several of the young folks would take him to dinner.

There was a flurry of ancient crones about the south porch, carrying all the necessaries for a harvest festival — marrows, carrots, loaves of bread, onions, sheaves of grain, armloads of chrysanthemums and ivy. He was still early, and he thought it best to dawdle in the car, or along the lane, lest the vicar's wife be caught in the midst of tea making.

"Hello, there." He heard the voice before he heard a footfall. "I'm Shirley Camthorne. I expect you're Karl Mueller."

"Yes. You've taken me quite by surprise."

"Did you have any trouble finding us?"

"No, not really. Your father gave good directions. I turned too soon, but that was easy to correct. Once in the valley, you can pick out the church two or three miles away."

"That you can. The old monks discovered a really glorious site. Too bad it didn't develop into a town."

"No, it's nicer this way, don't you think? If the valley were stuffed with medieval slums, you couldn't appreciate the church."

"It was really quite a monastery in its day. The Cistercians were never good showmen like the Dominicans, and the records suggest it was falling apart even in the time of

Wycliffe. Not much support from the motherhouse apparently. By the time of the Dissolution there wasn't much left to dissolve. A whole country of rich farmland, but that's about all. Now the buildings have fallen apart, and the church's all that's left."

"Do I get a Cook's tour?"

"Love to. After tea. Mum's got the things on the table. Me, I'm like you. Just as soon show you the church as take tea. Maybe there'll be time later. Father's best at it anyway. He can tell you where the abbots are buried and why they knocked off St. Joseph's head in Wat Tyler's Revolt."

She wore a black woolen dress so simple and classic it caught Karl's eye — something French about it, or even American. No fringes, no flounces, no pleats, just plain fabric, cut tastefully and relieved by the whiteness of the collar and the cuffs. Her hair was nearly as dark as the cloth, almost Spanish.

Her eyes seemed to flash continuously, and but for an angular face, especially the pointed nose, she would have been strikingly beautiful. She certainly knew how to make the most of her attractive personality — there was no doubt about that.

The flagstones that wound to the door of the New Rectory were exactly the shade of those that formed the walls of the church, and it would be a safe bet to say that someone, sometime, had gathered them from the ruins of the priory.

"For a couple of years after the Dissolution, the vicar lived in the house that's now the local. Then King Henry gave it to one of his friends, with the land it's on. So they built this one. You don't often find a New Rectory in a monastic foundation, where there's no need even for a rectory. But Edgecomb St. Mary's does everything different."

"Do you live at home? Is it a little dull, so far from town?"

"No, not really. Last year I was graduated from Girton,

and now I'm teaching. Seven-year-olds. How to sketch stick men and dabble in finger paints. Over in Edgecomb proper, across the ridge."

"It's a wonderful old house. Been here long?"

"Eight years. Father was out in Jamaica most of his life. Then the tropical agues got him. We had to come back to England. Making friends of preachers always was his specialty, and he's put it to good use. Knows half the bishops in Crockford's by first name, and the rest by face."

"Is that how he got here?"

"Yes. I was just going to say. He and the Bishop of Ely were at school together. Edgecomb's a good spot for him. Historic, well thought of, highly endowed, with not too much work."

"Looks like a pleasant house too."

"A wonderful place. Right out of Sir Francis Drake. Sliding panels and hidden stairways and Elizabethan fireplaces, with built-in warming benches. A little small, but now John's off and married, there's plenty of room."

"Weatherproof?"

"Perfect. Not so warm as if there were central heating, but you can't have everything. With two feet of thatch you've got good insulation. Warm in the winter and cool in the summer."

The lintel of the door was dangerously low, and Karl ducked. "Want to wash up?"

"No, thanks."

"Bath's just down the hall if you need it."

Camthorne and his wife stood waiting in the parlor. "Father, this is Karl Mueller. And this is mother of course."

"How do you do? It was gracious of you to come."

"No, it's I who am honored. Thank you for inviting me."

"Perhaps you'd like to eat right away. Then we can take our time and chat as we eat."

"Fine." They drew chairs round the table. Like the

benches built into the chimney, the furniture was of simple cottage style, built of solid oak and showing the wear of generations. "If we're through a bit early, Shirley promised me the Grand Tour. The priory ruins and the bell tower and the monastery gardens."

"No, I'd better help mum clear up. Dad's the better guide anyway."

"Pshaw. We'll just let the dishes sit. No flies this time of year anyway."

The high tea was extremely high — a full meal rather than tea. To see the array, Karl wondered whether the hint of a later dinner might have fallen through. The food was so varied, he didn't see how he could sample it all and then sit down two hours later to dinner.

With bread and butter for basics, there was everything else you might imagine: jelly tarts, marmalade, gelatine, cream, savories, hot cross buns, honey, treacle, marmite, cakes, pickles, smoked ham, preserved apples. It was almost as if the vicar's wife had emptied her pantry and moved it en masse to the table.

"Won't you have another cake?"

"No, thank you. I couldn't."

"P'raps we should have a look round if you like. It's still half an hour, though the people are already beginning to straggle in. They do, harvest festival, you know. Only time in the year we can be sure of standing room only."

"Would you want me to wear a preaching stole, or a cassock and surplice?"

"Preaching scarf, eh? Yes, if you like. They're still quite common. Whatever you like, really. As soon as they hear you, they'll know you're an American, and then of course they'll be tolerant whatever you wear. Wear what you'd wear at home. I'll put on a cope. With us a stole is just for the sacraments. Holy Baptism or the Eucharist."

"I can just as well leave it off?"

"No, wear it. The people need a variety of experience. Besides, it'll set them to thinking, and the more they think about garb and liturgy, the more they appreciate it."

As it worked out, the men made their tour alone, starting from the back door of the rectory. "Doubtless it'll be too dark, once the service is over. But you can get a fair view even from here. Through the apples there. What's left of the priory house and the refectorium. In its day, as you can guess by the fish pond, it was quite an establishment."

"How many monks were there?"

"Near as we can tell, from the old documents, the peak was a hundred and eighty. That's counting the novices but not the lay brothers or those at the outlying farms."

"That's good sized, isn't it?"

"Yes, it was. The church seems to have been built solely as a monastic chapel. Then for a hundred years or so the brothers also doubled as parish priests, and the building became a parish church."

They walked through the churchyard and the little cemetery where the monks lay buried. "The most noteworthy thing about the fabric is the chancel window. Inside it's glorious. Floods the whole nave with never a glare. The east light, that's what does it."

The Rev. Mr. Camthorne appeared to be in his late 50s, with the composure of one who knows exactly what he's doing, and enough experience of men and the world not to concern himself with what others might imagine. That, mused Karl, was doubtless why they had a Lutheran in the pulpit tonight.

"How the architect ever came up with the stone tracery still baffles every engineer who sees it. Logically, with all the glass and so little stone, you'd think the roof would come tumbling down. But it's stood for eight hundred years, more or less. The only other churches as old are the little wooden ones in the Weald. Like East Grinstead."

The crowd for evensong grew thicker by the moment, though there was still a full 20 minutes before the service. "Maybe you'd like a look at the pulpit while we can still move about. Normally, if I'm ten minutes early, there's no one here but the organist and the verger."

"Yes, I'd like to. Then I won't feel so strange."

"You'll sit behind the *prie-dieu*. The sidesmen will be just behind you if you need anything. I'll be opposite with the acolytes."

The sacristy was in the north porch. Once the service started, the vicar had to pass through the whole congregation and sit it out in the chancel. But it was a good arrangement, for it brought the pastor close to his people, a man among men, or at one time a monk among monks.

The minute he stepped into the nave, Karl gaped. He had never seen a church quite so glorious. Even apart from the decorations of the harvest festival, the church was worth more than a casual glance, with its intricate angel roof and the simple tile floor and the open stonework to the bell chamber.

Every sill and lintel bore signs of the harvesttime, and across the arches hung garlands of laurel and ivy. With baskets of chrysanthemums and asters, the altar rail and the altar were decked out in a vivid bank of color. Even the heads of the pews boasted clusters of the flower and fruit, tied by a length of golden ribbon.

In each window, against the slightly bluish glass, stood a pot of tobacco 3 or 4 feet tall. From the flowers Karl thought it was nicotiana, not real tobacco, but a second look and a whiff of the blossoms told him he was wrong. Real tobacco.

The vicar watched him closely. "It's an old custom in the Vale of Monthup, growing tobacco. With the hills on either side, we're protected from the weather. And with two and thruppence a pack on fags, it saves a good bit of tax. When I first came, I thought it scandalous, bringing tobacco into the church. But it's always been done, and so long as it's a part of the people's lives, we can turn it to good advantage."

"This'll please my father. He's a keen gardener but a nonsmoker."

"It does add a bit of interest. Maybe I'm too lax. If I were in China, I might even be tempted to let them bring their poppies into the church. The ones for medicinal purposes, I mean."

"Did you see that little squib in the last *Expository Times,* about poppies? The *papaver,* I think, in Latin. Professor Hamilton up at Edinburgh mentioned it to his students. The tares among the wheat. In the Vulgate the word for tares is the same as poppy. The Chinese Communists are claiming Christ encouraged the growing of opium and that it was commonly used among the Canaanites."

"Now I've heard everything."

"It is far fetched, but at least the connection between the poppies and the tares seem to have an element of truth."

They finished their look at the chancel and pulpit, weaving their way along the aisles between the apples and the marrows and the yard-long loaves of bread.

"The nave's filling quickly. Maybe we'd best get back to the sacristy and robe."

"Fine."

Beneath the bell tower the choir wiggled into their red cottas, a bit faded and musty with age. Off in the sacristy the clergymen donned their cassocks, with the help of the sidesmen and the verger and the crucifer and the acolytes. All wore cassocks and surplices, even the laymen, and in effect Karl was no more gaudily decked out than a mere altar boy.

The green stole, with flowered embroidery, gave him at least some symbol of rank. But it was nothing compared with the vicar's cope, whose green brocade and gold handwork might have made the Cistercians turn over in their graves, in their vows of poverty.

The crowd still surged into the country church like the waters of a flood. Many waited outside, perhaps for a glimpse through the windows, perhaps to take up the standing room the choir would leave vacant. In the vestry the vicar asked his little group of assistants to join him in prayer. He spoke with depth and affection, in a way that even the youngest altar boy might know that he too was in the house and service of God, not to please or serve himself but his Maker and those who had come to worship.

With the crucifer leading the way and the choir in full song, they marched triumphantly down the aisle. The cross shone gently in its burnished silver, reflecting the glow of the sun through the west window. The voices in the pews joined those of the choir until the whole world seemed filled with a band of "Onward, Christian Soldiers."

As they reached the chancel, Karl did just as the others, the verger and the vicar and the acolytes. He crossed himself, genuflected, and took his seat behind the *prie-dieu*. He was not particularly strange to Anglican evensong, for he had attended often back in his Army days. In fact it had been a favorite way to spend Sunday evening.

Still, that was a long way in the past, and there in the chancel he had to stay on his toes. He was screened to some degree by the pulpit and, when he was seated, by the heavy garland of fruit and leaves interwoven into the rail. He watched the acolyte fill the censer with charcoal, light it, fan it into a bed of coals, and load it with incense.

He had a strange feeling, sitting there, as the vicar swung it toward the altar, then toward the other officiants, then toward Karl, then toward the parish. It was just a symbol, he knew, a symbol of God's blessing upon men and of man's prayers to God. But unaccustomed to it, he had his doubts. Somehow, in spite of the serious atmosphere, it was not unlike the magical aspects of the worship of Baal and Astarte.

The prayers moved all too quickly, the Old Testament and

the Epistle and the Gospel. He took a firm stand in the pulpit, as sure of himself as a canny old Prime Minister before the House of Commons at question time. He started well. About God as the conductor of a great orchestra, with man and creation as the players, coming to life and playing their parts even as God directed.

He was proud of himself. He could almost feel the Holy Spirit at work. The words poured out with warmth and feeling, and he could sense the eyes of the people upon him and their minds following his every word. He began to look directly from face to face, to establish an even stronger tie.

Four rows from the front, under the windows, were familiar faces. Shirley Camthorne. Beside her sat Josie Ellingston-Harte. Karl stumbled a moment in midword, finally regained his train of thought and finished the paragraph.

His notes were the briefest kind of outline — mere starting phrases — no more than a dozen words on the whole card. Without knowing it he skipped two paragraphs. He couldn't quite forget Josie's face with the cynical grin of a Cheshire cat. Sitting side by side with the Camthorne girl. And a chap on the aisle who also seemed to belong.

He forced himself back to his sermon. It took another paragraph until he was master again, in full charge of his voice and thoughts. Way back in the organ loft he could see an intent and wrinkled face, a pensioner, cupping his hand to hear every word.

In fifteen minutes he had finished his say. He blessed them in the fashion of Moses and turned the service back to the capable hands of the vicar. Another prayer or two, a hymn, the offering, the recessional, and finally the blessing, with the vicar not in the chancel but in the midst of his people, halfway down the aisle. "The grace of the Lord Jesus Christ, the love of God, and the fellowship of the Holy Spirit be with you this night and forevermore."

There were just traces of daylight in the sky as he stood with the vicar in the south porch, greeting the worshipers on their homeward way. They were interesting folk, aged tillers of the soil, factory folk, gamekeepers, schoolboys, office girls, young marrieds, war widows, pensioners. Just to look them in the face and to shake their hand and to exchange a kindly word gave added pleasure to a pleasurable evening.

The last to dawdle out were Shirley and Josie and the chap on the aisle, whose name proved to be Tony Ruttock. It was Shirley who spoke first.

"I hope we didn't surprise you." She winked at Josie. "And the sermon, it all turned out so wonderfully. We're glad we could start the evening so well."

Karl didn't quite know what to make of the word *start*. "No, I wouldn't be surprised to see Josephine anywhere. Or not see her, either." He thought he was joking, but there was the least bit of satire in his words.

"Daddy did mention about the dinner, didn't he? We didn't want to make it too official. Just a half dozen of us. At the Hunter's Arms in Trumpington."

With two sermons under his belt for the day, one at Bishop's Monksham and one at Edgecomb St. Mary's, Karl was pleasantly relaxed. He was not tired, and yet he was not exactly in the mood to drive across the countryside. "Sure. Sounds good." He tried to make his answer enthusiastic.

Apparently Josie had come with Tony, and the two were going on ahead in the Hillman. He was to bring Shirley and make his good-bys to the Camthornes. Another couple, apparently from Cambridge, was already at the inn, supervising the dinner.

As they drove out of the valley with the slightest trace of daylight still on the horizon, Karl switched on the headlamps. From what little he could guess, Josie had been the instigator of the evening. Of this he could not be sure, though there was not much doubt that the invitation to the harvest festival was tied in somehow with the Ellingston-Hartes.

He did not at all resent Shirley's company. It was a fine chance to learn something of English schools. Even so, his mind was unsettled. He wondered whether Josie was cutting him off publicly, in her friendship with Tony, as an easy way to let him down. Troubled and with his eyes on the road, he was hardly at his social peak.

"You mustn't mind Fran," Shirley was saying. "She and Ted are on the wild side. He's an interne at London Hospital."

"Anything else I should know about them?"

"He and Tony are cousins. Wealthy landowners from Hereford. Brought up too strictly, I imagine, and like to give the impression they can be as naughty as dukes. Champagne, caviar, all-night parties. Tonight, I imagine, will be a little quieter. Maybe that's where you fit in."

"I'm a chaperon, is that it?"

"Well, a brake, anyway. That's it on the left. Next turning. And there're the Hillman and the Humber."

Karl piloted the Morris beside the massive Humber and helped Shirley climb out. He felt the least bit odd, squiring a girl he had met only hours before, into a remote pub, in his double-breasted suit and clerical collar. In the dim light of the Hunter's Arms his suiting looked dead black, without the minute flecks of blue and red one could spot in the sunlight.

A buxom waitress nodded from the bar. "Your party's upstairs. Way up's in the corner."

Like most inns on the fringe of town, the Hunter's Arms doubtless had a lively history. An old coaching house maybe, or a rendezvous for hunters and woodcutters, or a headquarters for highwaymen. It had the faintly ramshackle look of the days of Queen Elizabeth, with open beams in the ceiling and a half-timbered wall that showed wood even on the inside. The huge planks on the floor slanted at odd angles, with boards sometimes a foot wide.

The room upstairs might once have been a dormitory, in the days when a dozen travelers shared the same loft and roof. The boards creaked, but in the flare of a dozen candles, which was the only light, the creaking sounded in character.

Shirley did the introductions. Ted Hallman and Fran Tollefson. Anglo-Saxon names, both of them, with just a trace of Nordic. Anglo-Saxon faces too, with the fair skin and red cheeks and prominent features of people close to the soil. And Anglo-Saxon heartiness, if the boisterous level of chatter meant anything.

" 'Bout time you're here," thundered Ted Hallman, whose face appeared flustered. "We're hungry enough to eat an elephant." He clasped Karl and Shirley so heartily he spilled three drops from a nearly empty gin and lime.

During the introductions two waitresses scurried back and forth to the table. It was simply three long chunks of timber, roughly joined, and matching benches that seated one or two on each. Without so much as a cloth, the scarred surface of the beechwood reflected the scrubbing of hundreds of maids, some perhaps as far back as George II.

Together the girls bore a steaming bird on a massive pewter platter so heavy it took two to manage. As the diners watched, Fran brought Karl gin and It, and Shirley gin and tonic, in a vain effort to catch them up to the others.

On the planks of the table the platter stretched nearly from edge to edge. In fact, it was so huge they would have to crane to see round.

"What do you think of our swan, Shirley?" Tony asked. "Big enough?"

"Swan! But aren't they protected?"

"That depends whose pond you hunt. The Queen owns

those on the Thames of course. We wouldn't think of borrowing hers. This is the Squire of Audley End's."

"It looks young enough. Smells good too," Josie said.

"How would you know, Joze? Bet you never saw one in your life. In the raw I mean." Ted clapped her boisterously on the back.

"You should have seen the one that got away," Fran went on. "Not swan. Deer, I mean. The boys sat out in Epping Forest two whole nights. With high-powered air rifles, to keep down the racket. But the herd was holed up. Didn't see hide nor hair. But that's all right. Think I like swan better anyway."

"You didn't?" From Josie's voice Karl couldn't tell whether it was surprise or shame. "Shoot one of those deer, and they'd give you five years. The Queen's, they are."

"Well, if you get caught for poaching, you might as well hang high. On the law books a deer's no more than a hare."

"Law books are for the ashcan." It was Tony now. "You know bloody well what a magistrate'd do. A year or two off, if you're upper class, on the grounds you're entitled to special consideration. But he'd probably sock you with a big fine anyway."

"Well, she looks all set." Ted flailed a foot-long carving blade against the steel. "I nearly forgot. With a padre we'll have to have a blessing."

"Think I really ought to pray over a stolen swan?" There was not enough room to put his glass on the table, and he had to hold it. Karl didn't trust himself with an ex-corde prayer but chose instead one they had doubtless all learned from their nannies. Maybe it would bring back a streak of childish memories and responsibility.

"For that which we are about to receive, Lord, make us truly thankful." He felt the least bit sacrilegious, not so much for praying over a stolen swan as for praying with a glass of gin in his hand.

To give Ted carving room, they pulled their benches away from the table. With the kind of rough skill one might see in a countryman who dresses out sheep, the lumbering interne pried back the drumsticks and thighs and whittled away. There must have been enough meat for a platoon. Ruin as much as he did, there was still a mountain remaining.

Ted's hands trembled from gin, and Josie gave what help she could, securing the bird with a fork on either side. It did not do a great deal of good. With a shudder Karl wondered what these same hands, sodden with alcohol, might one day do to a human torso with the scalpel of a surgeon.

Meanwhile Tony had assumed command of the banquet. He raised a bottle of wine from the sideboard, examined the label, dusted it off, peered at the cork, and opened it. A touch in his own glass, a smell, a taste, all done with the skill of a buyer for Gilbey's in Oporto.

"Montrachet. A little expensive, even for French tastes. But worth the extra." He poured glasses all round, emptied the bottle, and immediately opened another.

Fran took her eyes off Ted. "To the hunters!" Six glasses were raised, including those of the hunters. "Makes you feel like a cave man, doesn't it, Josie, old girl? Or at least like a cave man's wife. Having your man go out and put meat on the table."

The swan did not taste at all strong. A little oilier than turkey but not so greasy as goose. There was no hint of fishiness, which was a little odd in terms of a swan's food. Perhaps the squire had kept them fed on bread and barley, and easy on the minnows.

The food tasted far better than Karl had imagined. Naturally he resented even the smallest share in the crime, the eating. But with a glass of gin in his stomach and one of Montrachet in his hand, the sin appeared venial rather than mortal. He was pleasantly tired, after a long day, and too relaxed to be more than a casual and uncomplaining guest.

The roast potatoes were done to a turn, with a hard coating where they had been basted. For vegetables there were fresh sprouts, doubtless straight from the fens, and lush green artichokes, with little pots of melted butter for dipping.

As a man's supper, planned and paid for by Tony and Ted, it was delicious. What they had saved on meat they had more than tripled on trimmings. Tony opened the third bottle of Montrachet. Fran passed the tray of savories — melon rind, pickles, cinnamoned peaches, preserved apples, orange peel.

With the plates empty as quickly as they were filled, the conversation lagged. Karl did not know quite whether they were all as sleepy as he or whether it was merely his imagination.

Sitting behind Josie, Ted gave the impression of annoying her. Begging her pardon, of course, he regularly reached in front of her, and on the return trip, when his hands were empty, lingered a while at her shoulder or breast. She did not openly object or resist, but neither did she encourage him.

With the fourth bottle of wine Tony announced that the party was just beginning. Karl looked at his watch. It was already ten. "Got to finish this one off before we start the drambuie. It's bad luck to leave one full."

There was a flurried conversation between Josie and Shirley. Karl caught only inklings here and there. With the alcohol flowing so freely and with everyone acting as host, rising from the stool to play waiter, no one really noticed Josie as she left her seat to whisper in Karl's ear.

"Would you please take me home, Karl? I'm sick."

"Sick?"

"Yes. And dizzy. I just can't take any more."

"What about Shirley? We can't just desert her."

"That's the way she wants it. She said so. Tony's not so

bad. He'll sober up and see she gets home safe. Besides, she can take care of herself. Better than I, maybe. She'd have set that oaf Ted straight. Without hurting his feelings too."

Karl rose to his feet and pushed the bench from the table. He pounded mockingly on the beechwood with the heavy end of the knife. "Knights of the Round Table to the rescue!" It was an odd pose in his clerical collar. "A Lady in Distress. Josie's not well. Would you think too horribly of us if I took her home?"

"The caveman's mate? Never!" Ted Hallman was on his feet, pounding his fist on the table. Fran dug her elbow hard into his ribs, bringing a faint gasp.

"But not before the shortcake. Fresh passion fruit, straight from Jamaica." Tony rose to make his point.

"Sorry. Chivalry and all that. A lady's whim, you know." Karl helped Josie into her jacket. Her face was ashen, and she trembled. The paleness made her even prettier, like a little puppy with a hurt leg. "Nice meeting you. See you all in Avalon."

"God go with you, Sir Galahad." It was Shirley. Karl took it as a compliment.

"Will you be OK, Guinevere?"

"Lancelot'll see to that."

"Good. Night, all."

Josie leaned heavily against Karl's shoulder as he half lifted her down the steps. In the sparkling air of the night she breathed deep.

"Does that help any?" Karl was glad he had scarcely sipped his wine. With a heavy meal the excitement of the gin was long gone, and though he was tired, he no longer felt the alcohol.

"Some, yes. It's a beastly headache, Karl. Stomach too. Psychological, I suppose." He opened the door and helped her to the seat. With his raincoat he made a pillow for her head. "I'm really sorry about tonight, Karl. They've never been so bad before."

"Oh, them. No need to apologize."

"I want to. I'd hate to have you think I'm like them."

"Just trying to show off, don't you think? They're really good kids at heart, except maybe Fran and Ted."

"Thanks for saying so. As I said, maybe I didn't choose my friends too knowingly."

"Come now. That'd include me."

"Silly! Don't make me talk. It hurts."

"Don't fret. Just close your eyes and relax." With a gentle hand he touched her brow. With the coat for a pillow she leaned half against the door, half against the seat.

The little Morris pulled into the highroad and rolled toward Bishop's Monksham.

The
Mouse in
the Garret

Shoemakers Lane was one of the few medieval streets in all Bishop's Monksham. Boasting a score or two of half-timbered dwellings, of the two- and three-story sort where the shopkeepers had lived in the days of the Pilgrims and the Commonwealth, the narrow street meandered from the market down to the goods yard of the East Anglian Railway.

For decades the town fathers had considered it a relic. That it still existed at all was a wonder, when most of the medieval quarter had long been torn down and rebuilt in the Victorian style. But it stood near the railroad tracks, with all the soot and grime and whistle-blowing that one would expect in the 19th century, and it had simply been ignored. In the 20th it was saved for qualities that might best be described as picturesque.

John Betjemann, for example, had written lovingly about Shoemakers Lane for one of the London papers. The leaky old tile, the steeply pitched roofs, the half-timbered facades, the handmade glass, the cobblestoned paving, the chimneys slanting at every conceivable angle did provide the sort of atmosphere one might expect in an ancient painting by Duerer or Brueghel.

But for those who were doomed to live there, with no facilities and no repairs, the housing was not much better than that of a gipsy. Most of the tenements did have running water, and usually there was at least one toilet per building, though for a bath the good folk who lived there had to traipse mostly to the town baths, on the far side of the castle.

Karl Mueller did not really know which position he ought to support when it came to Shoemakers Lane. The alley certainly was a picturesque one, but when he thought of it in terms of the little ones who still had to grow up there, with almost no light and air, with gutters that often reeked of stale garbage, he was not quite so convinced of the splendors of Medievalism. Great cathedrals those people of the Middle Ages certainly knew how to build, but whether the magnificence of their churches was excuse enough to allow youngsters to go on living in squalid houses was questionable.

Number 17 seemed as if it might once have been a house or perhaps a shop, or a little of both, squeezed tight between two other half-timbered places that were larger and in considerably better repair. It could hardly have been more than one room wide, with a narrow hall and a staircase, and two rooms deep.

He remembered the instructions and cautiously felt his way up the shadowy stairway. The dust of centuries assaulted his nostrils, and the treads were so worn he thought at any moment the old timbers might give way and send him crashing in a shower of dust and splinters.

At the landing a shaft of light filtered in through an opening high in the face of the plaster, like some lookout or airhole. He had little trouble finding the room he wanted, of the two there, for it bore a rather crude and yellowed piece of pasteboard with the name Mrs. F. J. Nickerson. The heavy oak timbers of the door were warped and cracked with age, with never a smidgeon of varnish, and of the sort one might expect in a stable rather than in a house.

Karl knocked at the door. The taps echoed almost like those of St. Michael on Doomsday. From within he heard no footsteps but only a high-pitched and rather broken voice.

"Come in, please."

He did. Within, the room was clean and bare. The flooring was of odd widths of pine, 8 or 10 inches across. At one side of the room was an ancient window with tiny panes of hand-made bubble glass, off-white and not very transparent, admitting just enough light to make the place bearable.

A withered old lady sat rocking near the window in a chair that seemed as ageless as she. Rather straggly curls fell down over her forehead, mainly gray but with hints of dirty blue and yellow.

"Mrs. Nickerson?"

"That be me."

"I'm the Lutheran vicar. Karl Mueller. I think your grandson Timmy has mentioned me. He said he would. At any rate it was he that told me about you, and I've just come by to see if there was anything I could do for you — read a psalm, offer a prayer, even help with the shopping. Whatever you need."

"That's kind of you, vicar. Do sit down. It's not a very comfortable chair I've got to offer you, but it's the only one and better than the floor, an't it?" There was a lively twinkle in her eyes despite the 80-odd years.

"Timmy's a captivating little one. Comes to our youth club without fail. I envy him his smile and head of hair."

"They all takes good care of me, vicar. The grandchildren, especially, even though there's only five. I can't get about much any more, not even to buy some eggs or potatoes. And my eyes are failin'. If it's a real nice afternoon, Timmy sometimes comes up and helps me across the highroad — I'm deathly afraid of those big lorries — and we sit on a bench in the Cathedral Close. In the sun. It's about the only enjoyment I have these days."

The room was singularly bare. It contained almost nothing at all — a narrow wooden bed in the corner, the two chairs, a rather decrepit chest of drawers, a little stand that held a hot plate and a few dishes. The walls were of rough plaster, with the timbers showing through. Overhead the wooden laths of the roof were stained with the rains of centuries, and so low one could easily touch them. A single shadeless light bulb hung from the rafters.

"That's one of the blessings of old age, Mrs. Nickerson. The age and the experience, and the opportunity to help mold the lives of one's grandchildren."

"Thank you, vicar. That's the kindest thing I've heard in a month. I'll take you up on that Scripture reading. I still try to do a bit of it myself, but my eyes just aren't good enough. The type's too tiny. For the moment, though, let's just talk. An old woman gets lonely up here, especially when the young ones are in school all week, and I hanker for somebody to talk to. I can't get down to the shops much and do my gossiping, but the neighbors are quite kind about looking in on me."

"Fine. What'd you like to talk about — your husband — the old days — your children? Anything you like."

"That's all pretty far in the past. No, I'd rather find out what's going on now. Haven't had a vicar here in years. Tell me, what's this business about being a Lutheran? And where's this church of yours?"

"That's a long story, Grandma Nickerson. I'm not so sure you'd be interested."

"Try me." She cocked her ear and loosened the shawl about her neck. "Is it anything like the Mormons?"

Karl didn't know what to say. He thought he saw a mischievous grin but could not be sure. "Surely you've heard of Martin Luther? He was a monk in Germany who lived at the time of Henry VIII and Archbishop Cranmer. In fact, Cranmer got many of his notions —"

"Come, I'm just joking. I know who Luther is. I was just trying to wave a red flag and egg you on. But tell me, how's the mission going? Timmy keeps me posted, but then his little eight-year-old brain still works a little slower than mine. Thank the Good Lord for that."

Despite her years she was so lively Karl couldn't help

wondering how she had been in her teens — certainly attractive, to judge by her face, which still boasted a kindly smile and delicate features. "Rather well, thank you. We've half a dozen Lutheran missions in England, and this one seems to be taking off like a skyrocket. Any kind of church work is slow of course, unless you're a Billy Graham, but we'll have a good, solid congregation in another year."

"Timmy says you have the best tea and cakes in town. For free too."

"We do have a fine old German baker as one of our members. From the Thuringian Forest, where Hansel and Gretel are supposed to have lived. He's not rich, but he is generous. We try to keep the little ones happy, especially when they don't get many treats at home."

"Bribing them with cookies and movies, that's what it is." Except for the grin on her face Karl might have thought she was not joking.

"Anything's fair in love and war. And in making Christians, too, according to St. Paul."

"Don't take me too seriously, vicar. When I was young, they all thought me a horrid tease, and I still haven't outgrown it. Too bad I seldom get the chance to try nowadays. But tell me. Why couldn't somebody else do what you're doing here — the Church of England or the Methodists?"

"I wish I knew, Granny Nickerson. I do think they could if they wanted. It's not merely the Old World versus the New. We don't do anything they couldn't. Show Christian films, concentrate on those without any church, organize our members to go out and make calls. The preacher has to be busy, too, of course. Calls, hospital work, public appearances. The American image doesn't hurt, either. All the little tykes think this is their chance to see a real cowboy."

On the roof the patter of rain and the drip of the eaves dulled the sound of their voices. "Odd," said the old lady, "how often it rains on St. Simon and Jude's. I'd swear it hasn't missed in ten years. Time of the year maybe. But I've a hunch it's also the good Lord trying to remind us that this would be a rather gloomy place if we didn't have Him to bring us the sun and the flowers. Now, vicar, I think it's time for the Scriptures. I don't want to steal all your day. How about the one where Jesus says He is going to prepare a place for us? It's in John, I think."

"Yes. The high-priestly prayer. It's a fine one. Let me see. It's John, all right. Starting in the thirteenth or fourteenth chapter, I think."

Outside the rain was falling more heavily, and inside the light had grown fainter. With his back against the window Karl could still make out the letters, though he could also understand how old Mrs. Nickerson might have troubles. He read steadily and easily. He had finished the 14th chapter and was just getting into the 15th, to the verses about Jesus being the Vine and his Father the Husbandman, when a sharp rapping sounded from the door.

"I wonder who that can be," said Mrs. Nickerson. "Maybe Mrs. Dunsmore. Ask her in, and she can listen too."

Karl swung the door wide. In the dimness of the hall he could make out the vague silhouette of a man, but he needed most of a minute to realize that the newcomer was the Rev. Lancelot Evans. Little trickles of water dripped off his black raincape, and on the cuffs of his trousers he still wore a pair of bicycle clips.

"Hello, Mr. Evans. Come in, won't you?"

The newcomer shook his cape in the hall. "Thank you. I see I've come just in time to catch you in the act of sheepstealing. By the way, you don't address all Anglicans by the name of *Mister,* you know. You've still got a lot to learn about England. Some of us use the proper title of *Father.*"

"Do come in," Granny added, when she learned who the

new guest was. "I've been looking forward to your coming. For a long time."

"I've only been at St. Michael's for three years, Mrs. Nickerson. I guess I should have called sooner. Somehow I always thought you were Methodist, like the Nickersons with the fish stall."

"No, I'm C. of E. Not related. Still like to give my Easter gift, though of course it's been years since I could get about. I'm sure if you looked over the list, you'd find my name. It's only three quid I give, but then my pension's only thirty bob a week, and there's not much left to keep body and soul together."

Karl did some fast calculating. If this old soul could give two weeks' pension as an Easter gift to the vicar, she was doing far better than most of those who were still able to get about and worship there.

With his cape and hat hung on a nail Father Evans sat gingerly at the edge of the bed. "Mrs. Nickerson," he said, "I've brought you this little medallion of the mother of God. Perhaps you will want to hang it on your wall to remind you that the Virgin is still concerned with the welfare of your soul and is still praying for you."

Mrs. Nickerson took in a gulp of air and sighed it out again. *"Father* Evans," she said, "I'm glad you've come. I've got a good many things to say to you, and if you hadn't come, I'd have missed my chance. From what I hear, you'd be far more interested in praying my soul out of purgatory after I'm dead, than praying me back to stronger faith while I'm alive. You and your incense and your holy water and your scapulars! I'd as soon take my chances with the Old Nick himself as with you!"

Lancelot Evans jumped to his feet. Even in the shadows one could see his face violently angry. "Some of you just don't know the proper way of salvation. Ignorant peasants." His clerical collar was perhaps two inches high and seemed to be choking him. "This upstart here, for example. Jumps right into the Church of England like some starry-eyed billy goat and wonders why he's resented. Why doesn't he stay home in America or wherever he's from? We don't go stealing members from him!"

Karl forcibly stopped himself from too hasty a reply. "*Father* Evans, if that's what you prefer to be called, I came to this house at the request of this woman's grandson. To read her the Scriptures. She can't so much as walk a block from this room. I'm not here to make her a Lutheran; I'm here to bring her the Gospel."

"And to get her three pounds?"

"I didn't even know she had it to give. Did you — until she said so?"

It was now apparent that the vicar of St. Michael's and All Angels was fighting a losing battle, and since it appeared he had little to gain, perhaps he also assumed he had little to lose.

"Don't try any of your American sarcasm on me, young man, even if you do presume to hide behind a clerical collar. I can have Mr. Fyffenfield jerk that tin shanty you're using for a church out from under your feet on a month's notice. That's what the lease says. We were just discussing it the other day. Why they ever let you have it in the first place I'll never know! Soft in the head, all of them."

It was Granny who stopped him. "Vicar, I won't have you talking like that to a guest in my home! Theological differences you may have, and you can talk about them like a civilized gentleman, but there won't be no threatening or name-calling in my house!"

"House! You call this a house? Serve you right if the rain washed it right down the drain. As for this man, I'm not even sure he's a Christian. Outside the mainstream of Christianity. From a sect. Wouldn't even know the meaning of a word like apostolic succession or the laying on of hands or bishop." Though the words were still fierce, the old lady's warning had quieted him.

"Mr. Evans," said Karl, "Lutherans do have bishops — in Denmark and Sweden. But most of us don't consider them essential, one way or the other."

"No tradition, no history, no creed. Modern upstarts, these Lutherans. Pushing their nose inside the tent till they push us out. Like the Jehovah's Witnesses or the Seventh Day Adventists."

"Mr. Evans, did you ever hear of the Thirty-Nine Articles?"

"Of course. I swore my loyalty to them when I was ordained. Of course."

This time Granny broke into the conversation again. "You wouldn't know it, vicar, you wouldn't know it."

"Of course there's far too much of the Reformation about them," Evans continued. "But that was an accident of history. Henry VIII and Queen Mary and St. Thomas More."

"Know where the Articles came from?"

"Naturally. Cranmer."

"Yes and no. If you'll have a good look at the Augsburg Confession, you'll find that Cranmer simply condensed and revised what was written by Melanchthon and Luther. All the same points and all in the same order. It's too close to be mere coincidence."

"Now you're trying to tell me that the Anglicans stole the Articles from the Lutherans?"

"In a nice way, yes."

Evans stomped his umbrella on the floor. "This is too much. I'm leaving. Insulted in my own parish, calling on one of my own parishioners."

Mrs. Nickerson struggled to her feet. "Mr. Evans, I'm glad to see you go. I'd hate to have it on my conscience that I threw a man of God out into the rain, even if he was already all wet. This young man was nice enough to come and read the Scriptures to me. And you've done nothing but insult him, and me too. And as for me belonging to you, why'd you have to wait so long to visit me? Was it because you saw his car standing out front?"

The vicar of St. Michael's and All Angels stood menacingly in the door. "Just you see if you have a roof over your head in another month, Mueller! I'll get you out of that hall if I have to tear the boards down with my own hands." In another minute his shoes were scraping their way down the stairwell.

From the roof overhead the steady dripping of the eaves seemed almost to wash away some of the unpleasantness, and occasionally a drop of water worked its way between the laths and came splashing onto the floor. Almost as if there had been no interruption Karl resumed the reading of the high priestly prayer:

"If a man abide not in Me, he is cast forth as a branch and is withered, and men gather them and cast them into the fire, and they are burned. . . . Herein is My Father glorified, that ye bear much fruit; so shall ye be My disciples."

In the
Waters of
the Aublin

An Arctic night, Karl supposed, must be like an English fog. Too dark to see through, and with no hope of ending.

Actually the fog was not dark, not if one considered the hour. At seven in the morning, even on a bright November day, the sun would just be piercing the horizon. What light there was the little droplets of water seemed to diffuse everywhere. Beneath the massive yews and the sturdy oaks of the Cross and Mitre there was for once as much light as anywhere else.

The quiet air was scarcely above frost point. Karl pulled his cap tight about his ears and wrenched the scarf above the collar of his mac. The damp cut through to the very bone. At any rate the snap in the air would bring out his appetite, and old Ma Huggins would have a plate of cakes and bacon waiting for him when he got back to the inn.

Fifteen minutes earlier he had been dozing beneath the warm comforter when for no reason he awoke. He could not fall alseep again and chose to walk instead.

Once one cut across the Little Wealdstonebury Common and the London Road, he would be a hop, skip, and jump from the Aublin. Another ten minutes would bring him to the Abbot's Bridge and the abbey fishpond. Across the stream lay the playing fields of St. Maudlin's, always a spot to stir the soul of a boyish heart.

Whenever the mood struck, Karl walked. Mornings, usually, when the first thrushes chanted the dawn in. Night-times, too, when the bats dove about one's head and the birds of prey were on the wing.

A boy at heart, Karl loved the river, even as the Celts and Romans had loved it before him. If he could spare a whole hour, he liked to walk to the Roman forum, or a half hour, to the Bishop's Meadows. St. Maudlin's and the fishpond lay halfway between.

For once Karl enjoyed the fog. It was expected this time of year, when the warmth of summer yielded to the frost of winter. First there was ground mist, and if the air was really quiet, there'd be a pea-souper lasting for weeks.

Karl crossed the highroad with considerable care, knowing how the lorries sometimes barreled through the fog. He could make out the landscape only about 10 feet ahead or, where there was a clear spot, sometimes 15.

He resolved to stay strictly to the path. That way there was no chance of losing his way, and what was worse, missing the cakes and bacon. Besides, this morning he did not really want to look. He just wanted to think.

Even the most athletic of the Maudlin boys would still be in bed in this weather, not out practicing the mile. The old-age pensioners would not sit fishing along the Aublin, and in such a fog even the housemaids would not venture out to do the morning marketing. He would have the path to himself.

For Monday morning Karl was keyed up, but for no particular reason. There was not the usual mood of Monday relaxation after a couple of sermons and youth clubs and Sunday school the day before. He sang as he walked, knowing he was completely alone. In bright daylight he would have hesitated, in a country where people simply did not sing as they went about their work. In Italy or France it was different.

"A mighty Fortress is our God, A trusty Shield and Weapon." The words brought a whole string of ideas. He remembered the apocryphal story of Luther and the pious *Hausfrau.* Almost like the Paul Revere thing of two if by land and one if by sea. For her the hymn was just an egg timer. Luther had complimented her for singing a hymn before breakfast. Oh, no, Dr. Luther, she had said. It's two stanzas for soft boiled and four for hard.

Yesterday the congregation has sung it too. For Reformation Sunday. According to the editorial in *Church Times,* you could tell an Evangelical from an Anglo-Catholic by his singing. "A Mighty Fortress" if he were Evangelical, and the "Te Deum" if he were Anglo-Catholic. That, and incense, seemed to be the touchstones.

Of course, in a literate age, a rector who was charged with being Anglo-Catholic might combine the incense and the hymn, just to confuse the issue, so you couldn't be absolutely sure.

Karl grinned to think of Paul Dennis and the Reformation. Paul was forever running about the bylanes of East Anglia, digging up a bit of Lutheran history. Thomas Bilney's house or Robert Barnes's birthplace or an English version of a Luther sermon in the Chapter House at Norwich.

It was fascinating to Paul. No wonder so many vicars at St. James had spent so many weeks running down Lutheran books and sketches and manuscripts! No wonder they sought out the White Horse Inn at Cambridge, where Cranmer, Latimer, and Barnes had met to discuss the writings of Luther!

Karl recalled other items from the English Reformation: the stories of Henry VIII and his theses against Luther, his sudden courtship of Wittenberg under the threat of a Spanish invasion; the adventures of William Tyndale, moved to translate the Scriptures into English from his stay with Luther; the book smugglers of Norwich, who imported religious works concealed in bolts of cloth.

It was an odd subject for reflection, there along the foggy

banks of the Aublin, even on Reformation Day. And yet it was an understandable one. Even the people of Israel, scattered among the pagan peoples of Babylon, gloried in the days of their past — the wanderings in the desert, the Passovers, the temple of Solomon.

The thought of Karl's little parish always brought him a good deal of joy. Evensong and matins had grown more than he could hope, and he counted it a poor day when there were not at least three score for each. What was best of all, among his people there was a contagious enthusiasm. Yesterday, as if the Reformation were somehow more Lutheran than Anglican, there had been 65 in the morning and 82 at night.

The success was in part embarrassing. A gallant little minister of a Free Church, struggling to hold his own, might be on the best of terms with his Anglican brethren, but one who was so conspicuously successful was to be envied.

Karl was undoubtedly a success even among the vicars of the Lutheran Church of England. Already his yearling flock was as healthy as the four- and five-year-olds. Despite his social connections with the bishop, he did not feel guilty about the loyal circle of churchgoers who had gathered round him like chicks round a hen.

They had never really been members of someone else's flock, not really. They may have been baptized and confirmed, to be sure. The Congregationalist from the furniture factory who gave up church when he was married. The Scotsman who came south and, not finding Presbyterians very handy, simply gave up his ties with the kirk. The Anglican grandma who couldn't stand a vicar who smoked and, not knowing about Karl's pipe moved over from St. Saviours.

When he could, Karl tried to send them where they belonged. He leaned over backward not to offend. He wanted their souls of course, and he knew God wanted them too. But he didn't want them for their shillings and pence, and above all, he didn't want them simply because they had tired of churchgoing elsewhere. Still, if they insisted they didn't belong to someone else, he was most happy to count them his.

Through the fog he could hear the cathedral clock strike seven-fifteen. The still air made it sound just next door. Somehow it reminded him of Josie, for a reason he could not lay his finger on. He had not seen her for two whole weeks, since the disastrous night of the harvest festival.

It was not that he did not want to see her. It was not that he felt in any way guilty. It was just a matter of soothing her feelings, she who had felt so apologetic about the whole affair. He must remember to ring her. The last thing in the world he wanted was to make her think he was no longer interested.

He well remembered that night, the taste of the swan, the levity of Fran and Ted, Josie's getting sick, the long ride home under starry skies. He had had trouble rousing her on the lane beside the Abbey Gatehouse. For once she had appeared really helpless and troubled, as if she needed him.

Half asleep, she had groped her way along the hall as Karl watched from the doorstep. It was an odd look on her face, with the upturned nose, like a girl who has betrayed her own grandmother. He had to smile, remembering. Poor little thing. Not so grown up or sophisticated as she liked to pretend.

He wondered what the outcome would be in a year or two. Just another friend? How much did they really have in common? Education, background, religion, nationality, age? Five years' difference, he knew, may not have been much, but at a sheltered 22 he wondered if she were really old enough to know what she wanted in the way of a husband.

The religious difference was toughest of all. Not so much the actual doctrines as the way of life. He had seen too much of it in the case of Paul and Audrey Dennis. Lutheranism versus Anglicanism. Even a little thing like a christening became a problem, whether one poured the water from a ewer or simply from the cupped fingers.

There was no doubt of Josie's faith. She would have had no trouble with the Apostles' Creed or even with the intricacies of the Athanasian. The real question was one of background. Harvest festivals, the blessing of the crops, rush bearing, Perpendicular architecture, crucifers, acolytes, sidesmen, vergers, archdeacons.

Was it fair to take all that and bury it in a little parish at an Iowa crossroads? Or would Karl spend his life in England?

Four, five years was all most of them spent in England before the strain of the climate and the burden of child bearing and the difficulty of educating their children on an English salary of $1,800 a year became all too apparent. Except for Paul Dennis, when the excitement of the new country and the new sphere of work had dimmed, the younger clergy usually returned to their homes — America, Australia, Canada.

Could Karl really expect Josie to consider him at all, she who could have her choice of dukes and marquises and landed gentry? Could he even consider marriage until he had a few thousand in the bank and some notion what he wanted from life? Could he ask her to think of him, for better or worse, whether in England or America, till the ties of their families did them part?

In the dank air of the fog the thought of Josie was warming. It was funny, these first inklings of love. There was not much doubt what it was. He wondered whether she felt it too. He wondered whether she felt she needed him, for the first time, at the swan feast or whether it was merely his imagination.

The ancient cobblestones beneath his feet snapped him out of his pleasant dreams. It was the Abbot's Bridge, the rough-hewn blocks of limestone that dated to the time of William the Conqueror, pictured in all the guidebooks.

It was a pleasant sight, on a summer's day, with the tender

boys of St. Maudlin's sitting on the stone railing, joshing with their friends on the river beneath, punting along the banks in the sluggish current. In their own little way, three or four years too early, it was practice for the years to come. Boating on the Isis at Oxford or the Cam at Cambridge. Then the girls would be serious, and the boys no longer shy.

In the dampness Karl could hardly hear his heels tapping against the cobblestones. He looked at his watch. He had been gone for 20 minutes. A quick turn about the old mill, and then back to the Cross and Mitre. Couldn't delay too long, or he'd miss the cakes and bacon.

Though he could see not more than a few feet, there where the mists from the stream made the fog even denser, he knew the mill lay just ahead. It was a landmark of considerable pride. One could still see where the millrace ran, though weirs closed both ends to the flow of the current.

Built of flint and mortar, the mill now housed the school chaplain. On three sides it was shut off by a hedge of holly and hawthorn, carefully interwoven by generations of gardeners. On the fourth, across a gated bridge, ran the ancient millrace.

From the neighborhood gossip the mill might have been more useful to St. Maudlin's as a museum than as a home. The old milling chamber would draw hordes of tourists at sixpence a look. Besides, the structure wasn't really livable. Too damp and decrepit.

There'd never been a wife of the last three chaplains who could say kind words of it, and the turnover, according to the local chatter, was more the fault of the housing than anything else. For a family with toddlers, of course, the millrace was an open temptation, and some said it should be filled up like the moats of medieval houses.

Out of the half light of the fog Karl heard the muffled sound of running. He took two steps off the path. From the direction of the school an odd shape loomed out of the darkness. A Maudliner, in his red tie and gray pants and navy blazer, with a straw boater tight to his head. Probably some lad who had idolized Roger Bannister and wanted to do the mile in four minutes. He flashed across the bridge and out of sight.

Off the path Karl felt the nip of the air. He shivered. He couldn't believe there had been no frost. He left the path a dozen steps to take a closer look. From the rains of October the river overflowed and reached a foot or two into the grass. There was no sign of ice nor any crystals of frost. Maybe if the night had been clearer. Sometimes the fog acted as a blanket, shielding out the colder air above.

Through the mist he noticed a dark blob floating on the stream. It gave him a start when he peered closer, for it looked oddly like a man. Probably just some schoolboy trick. The effigy of a favorite don, or a tackling dummy from the rugby field.

Karl sought to pierce the haze but with little luck. He sought out a stick and cast it at the form. There was a sodden splash. Whatever it was, it was heavy. The stick landed square, but there was hardly a ripple.

On a warm day Karl would not have hesitated. Take off his shoes and wade out. Now he was not so sure. He looked again. He sought out his conscience. With gingerly steps he edged into the water, shoe high, then ankle high.

It was no dummy. The flecks of water on the hair looked perfectly real. And he saw a costly pair of brogans that wouldn't wind up in the middle of the Aublin, not as a stunt. He rolled his pants to his knees and stooped to grab at the collar.

Whoever the man was, he was big. Fifteen stone, likely as not, and over six feet. The waterlogged clothes made him heavy as a beech log. Even a man the size of Karl had no chance to lift him, there on the gravelly bottom. He clutched the collar with both hands and dragged the sodden form shoreward. The face scraped against the grass.

Half by instinct, half by common sense, the vicar did what had to be done. It was as if he waded into the Aublin in the middle of every pea-souper, pulling lifeless bodies from the weir. His mind was two jumps ahead of his feet. He would have to summon the authorities, naturally. Make a full report of the circumstances.

The nearest phone, of course, would be the chaplain's. Better wake him, seeing the circumstances. No point in running all the way to St. Maudlin's. Not in the fog.

He tugged harder, now that the body scraped against the turf. A good 15 stone. Two hundred pounds or more. He'd have to get it free of the water.

With both hands he reached under the body and caught the lapels. One last roll. He flipped the still form on its back. The face was discolored with clay, and the curly black hair straggled over the temple.

He caught his breath. He thought he recognized the face. No, it couldn't be. He looked again. It was. There was no doubt. It was Willie the Knife.

The
Wake

On the wall behind the sergeant the oaken clock
struck eleven. Watching the steady swing of the pen-
dulum, Karl grew almost sleepy in spite of four cups of
sugary tea. The police station was spanking new, with a smell
of soap and plaster in the air, but the furniture — the dock
and desks and swivel chairs were still the battered chunks of
oak from the old one.

Karl thought wistfully of the cakes and bacon he had
missed at the Cross and Mitre. After he'd gone out and bought
a sack of buckwheat too, which gave them a flavor all their
own. Hard to find in England, but it kept him from being
homesick. For the thought of breakfast he half apologized,
as if it were sinful to think of his stomach on so tragic a
morning.

Two or three hours later the sharpness of each event
began to take on a haze in his memory, as if the fog had
soaked inside and clouded it. Sgt. Fredricks had been a great
help, knowing exactly what to do. The sergeant had come
on duty early that morning, to see if he could catch the schoolboy who regularly put wax on the shop windows of the High
Street, and Karl's phone call had gone right to Fredricks.

Despite the fog, within five minutes the big, black Humber
bumped slowly across the cobblestones of the bridge. The
flashing red of the spotlight glowed pink through the mist, as
reassuring as the sight of land to a water-logged Noah.

In his dressing gown the school chaplain had stood there
beside the Lutheran vicar, gazing speechless at the cold corpse.
There was nothing the two clergymen could do or say. Sgt.
Fredricks, more accustomed to violent death than the padres,

who were not strangers to the bedside variety, took the matter in stride.

"I'm Sgt. Fredricks. Remember, we met at the cricket match at the Limes."

"So we did. I'd nearly forgotten."

"Tell me, now. Just where was it you found him?" He did not wait for an answer but proceeded to examine the face of the victim.

"About ten feet out. Against the weir, where the millrace used to empty."

"You'd expect that, I guess. There's an eddy there. Either o' you seen him before?"

"Yes, as a matter of fact." It was the chaplain who spoke. "Seen him quite often on the streets. Weekends mostly. Horrid dresser, with those silk ties and Italian shoes."

"How about you, Mueller?"

"Oh, yes. That's what made it such a shock."

"Know his name?"

"By a roundabout way, yes. It's Willie Gavin."

"Right you are. Willie the Knife. King of Soho. But tell me, how does a padre know?"

"Well, it's a long story. A mutual friend."

"Carole Dunning, eh? Her saintly old mother'd tan her hide if she knew the girl was running with the likes of 'im."

"But, sergeant, how did *you* know him?"

"Me? That's like asking the Prime Minister how he happens to know the Queen. He's top dog in Soho — rackets, women, dope, even the barrows boys. But nobody could ever make anything stick. Won't make much difference now. Every other month he'd get a summons. Speeding, reckless driving, under the influence. But he'd never show before the magistrate. Just send a solicitor in to pay the fine.

"In Bishop's Monksham?"

"All the time. Besides, Scotland Yard's been on us. Think he may have a fence this way. In a country town, where the heat isn't supposed to be so tough. Not heroin, I think. Probably Swiss watches or Irish whiskey."

"Ever find anything?"

"No, can't say we have. Nothing that would hold up in court."

"How do you think it happened?"

"Hard to say. Competition, maybe. He's big time. Perhaps even the Mafia. Hate to stick my neck out without an autopsy. But hold on a minute. I'm supposed to be asking the questions." The sergeant's face had one of those milk-and-peach complexions a painter like Gainsborough always painted, countrified but full of vigor and character.

"I came out this way for a walk. From the Cross and Mitre. Often do when I can't sleep. About seven, it was."

"You needn't go into it, padre. Plenty of time for that when you've had your tea. Now, let me make some notes."

On the radio the sergeant's companion called the station. First they'd need a hearse, and as soon as possible the coroner. Better get the Yard too, Fredricks ordered. Willie was big. Too big for the county.

He took a notebook from his pocket and began to write. He examined Karl's footprints in the grass, fairly far apart where he had walked into the stream, and much closer and deeper where he had dragged the body ashore. "What'd you say the visibility is, Marlin?"

"Twenty feet, sir."

"Right. That's about what I make it. Changeable, though. Not too important anyway. He's been dead for hours."

Fredricks made some sketches of the coat, the face, the position of the body. He reached inside Willie's breast pocket, feeling for a wallet. "This'll give us something to work on at the station till we can go through the clothing."

"Yes, sir."

"You get Toby on the wireless?"

"Yes, sir. Just called back. He's gotten through to the

Yard. Night man there. The hearse will be down from Brown's as soon as the driver can find his way. Doesn't know the river in the fog, he said. Will come across at Maudlin's and then drive over the playing fields."

"Right. You stay here with the body. Better cover it with a blanket. Chaplain, you'd better get in out of this fog. Freeze to death in that dressing gown. We'll get in touch when we need you. Mueller and I, we'll take the scout car to the station."

Thinking back on it now, Karl remembered it as a dream. The shock, the fog, the utter quiet, the rigid lips of a face locked in death. That this was the same Willie of Chungking Coolie, the boisterous Willie, the domineering Willie, the thoughtful Willie! The paths of glory led but to the grave. Except for cultured England, Irish Willie might as easily have wound up a normal life and been quietly buried in a country churchyard.

On the wall behind the desk hung a huge clock of the age of Victoria. It did not have the exquisite lines of a grandfather's clock or even the delicacy of a carriage piece from France. It was totally utilitarian, in an austere frame, like the things a clockmaker once might have given to the town fathers as advertising.

It had just gone eleven when tires squealed against the pavement outside. "That'd be Scotland Yard," said the sergeant. "Nobody else'd drive like that even if the fog's thinned out."

He was right. A motley collection of five men piled into the station, looking a bit like the galley crew of a Panama tramp steamer. The early emergency had given them time neither to shave nor to wash.

Inspector Wintergren was clearly the boss, if only by the clarity and strength of his gait. A second man, with a shorthand pad, was obviously his aide. The other three introduced themselves as members of the vice squad.

Karl was rather glad he hadn't gone home. It would have meant an early trip back. Besides, sipping tea with the sergeant, in his present state of shock, was far more attractive than the thought of sitting alone at the Cross and Mitre, with the specter of a corpse staring him in the memory. Besides, the Yard men had come quickly.

"What've you got, Fredricks?" Inspector Wintergren sat heavily on a swivel chair, peering out through the fog at the shadows in the street.

"Not a great deal, sir. Body was found about seven-thirty this morning. The chap here — Lutheran padre — Mr. Mueller — out for a morning walk. Snagged against the weir at the mill."

"Cause of death?"

"The coroner's still working. A sharp gash on the forehead, but probably not the cause of death. No marks of violence, apparently. Gun or knife or anything like that. They're sending some of the tissues to the lab. Take another hour or two, we reckon."

"Good. Never did like a cold murder. Sooner you get the corpse, sooner you get the murderer." It was a proverb every constable in England was ready to quote, and a kind of trademark of Wintergren.

"Mueller says he knew Willie. Through Carole Dunning. Think she's involved?"

"Hmmm. Worth a check." He whispered instructions to an aide. "Johnstone and Biggins are going to the mill. Can I send them with your man Marlin? He knows the details, I take it? Good. If they can use one of your cars, Maitley can take ours to the Dunnings. If you've got a spare man to go along, so much the better."

For the dozenth time Karl scoured his mind for every little detail of what had happened. The fog, the bridge, the mill, the striking of the cathedral clock. This time, he even recalled the schoolboy, out for track in that odd getup of school blazer and boater and plimsolls. He talked about the night at the Chungking Coolie, about the other nights he'd seen Carole Dunning, about the saintly old mother who'd been coming to the parish.

"What do you know about Carole, Fredricks? Local girl? I grabbed Willie's file to read in the car, and it's she that keeps popping up. Nothing much, really. Just that she's been seen here and there."

"Good girl, basically. With the Sadler's Wells. The local folk are rather keen on her. Takes fine care of her mother, who's nearly an invalid. Still, she bears watching. An odd one. Had her in once for driving under the influence. A little red MG. Don't think she did it, do you?"

"Don't think anybody did it, really. Little blue men with red wings, from a flying saucer." The inspector watched Karl fill his pipe, then took out his own. "Can I try some of your Canon's Delight, son? Heard wild things about it, and I won't believe them till I test'r m'self." He tamped a load into the bowl and lit up. "It *is* a little like church incense. They were right. Good thing I didn't bet."

With half his force scouring the countryside, Sgt. Fredricks had no one left to cover the phone. From time to time it rang incessantly until he finally lifted the receiver. Somebody'd rammed a plate glass at the greengrocer's. No one hurt. And was the police magistrate holding court today, or would it be canceled by the weather?

This time the phone rang even longer. Fredricks looked annoyed. He took it from the cradle. "It's Maitley. For you, inspector."

"Thanks. Maitley? Yes, go on — The Monksham County Hospital. Room 233. Too hysterical, eh. Right. Will do. Right away." He rang off. "It was really for you, padre. It's Carole Dunning. At the hospital. She's hysterical, apparently, and sobbing for Mueller here. Been pregnant several months, the doctor says, and chances not very good. Infection."

"When was she admitted?"

"Three this morning."

Fredricks crinkled his eyes in a frown. "Did she do it? Bash him in the head and push him in?"

Karl was pulling on his mac. "Got a car, sergeant?"

"Righto." It was Inspector Wintergren. "I'll take you round myself. Not that I want to ask her anything. Not if she's hysterical. For the time the church can have her, padre. You bring her out — then maybe we'll get some answers. Meanwhile I'll just have a talk with the staff."

The Monksham hospital lay halfway across town beyond the station, on the rise behind the East Anglian Railway. The reception room looked like an ancient manor, and the wings, which were new, showed the sloppy kind of brickwork dating from the war. A RAF hospital, likely as not, for the abandoned airstrips over the hill.

Karl made his way through the covered walkways to the surgery. He found Carole in a room to herself, attended by an intern and a sister and swinging her head wildly from side to side. Against the white of the pillow her face shone gastly and colorless, and the eyes, usually so bright, rolled listlessly. She did not appear to recognize him.

"Carole, it's me. Karl Mueller. The Lutheran padre. Remember? You wanted me." There seemed no mark of recognition, though the eyes fluttered and quieted.

"Karl." The word was muffled and indistinct. "At last."

"You needn't try to talk, Carole. Don't try, please. Whatever happened last night, don't try to think of it. Think of your baby and all the pleasure it will bring."

"Don't let them take it. Don't. Don't. I'd rather die. That doctor. He wants to take it." She swung her arms wildly against the coverlet.

"Think of your mother. Think of your memories of your father. Someday you'll marry too, have a family. Like them. Even if you have to lose the child. Remember that night you played the liturgy for us? You can't say the Lord has passed you by, can you?"

She was quiet again now. Under the pressure of the moment Karl felt self-conscious. Ministering to a hysterical ballerina, unmarried, pregnant. The preacher wore only a woolen shirt and sweater under his mac, without even a shave. This wasn't the kind of thing they taught in pastoral theology at the seminary.

He asked the sister if she could find a Book of Common Prayer. She hustled off. The intern leaned over and whispered in his ear. "She's failing quickly, padre. No will to live. We had to remove the fetus. It was long dead. She doesn't even realize. Infection. Chances aren't good. Better prepare her for the end. These young ones, though — sometimes they pull through."

Karl nodded. "Just relax and listen, will you, Carole? I want to talk to you about God's love and His forgiveness. Sometimes He gives us great problems so we can understand Him better. You've seen that with your mother. Your father's death and the arthritis."

He was not sure he was getting through. She was quiet, with her eyes closed and a glazed expression. He began to recite the Twenty-third Psalm. *"The Lord is my Shepherd, I shall not want. He maketh me to lie down in green pastures.* You've had green pastures, Carole. A name on the stage. And talent — talent to become great. But you must consider Him, too, not just yourself. *He leadeth you beside still waters. Yea, though you walk through the valley of the shadow of death, you will fear no evil."*

The sister came with the Prayer Book. Karl flipped it open to the Office for the Dying. He finished the psalm.

Her face flushed and she choked. "I didn't mean to do it, I didn't mean to do it."

"Do what, Carole? Relax. It'll be all right."

"Push him. Push him. He hit his head on the railing. Just lay there in the water, not moving. Like he was dead."

"Did you know what you were doing, Carole?"

"I did, I did. I didn't want to marry him. Not even for the baby. I didn't want to. He wasn't good. Had a gun. Said he would shoot us both if I wouldn't marry him."

"Really, Carole, you mustn't get excited. You mustn't. The doctor wants you to be quiet. You have to rest, so you can get well."

"I don't want to, I don't want to. Not without the baby. Don't let them take it, Karl."

"Sometimes God's ways are hard to understand, Carole. Sometimes we argue too much when He knows what's best. Let me pray with you again, to reassure you that God loves you and forgives you, whatever you feel or do." He stood over her and began to read. She seemed to follow only in patches, as if her mind were far away.

On the opposite side of the bed the intern unlimbered his stethoscope. He put it to her chest. "Nurse, would you fetch Dr. Wogly, please. She's slipping quickly."

Karl looked at the shapely features — the slanted eyes with a touch of the Oriental, the dark locks that made her so distinctive on the stage, the doll-like nose and mouth, pallid now with the touch of death.

"Any chance doctor?" he asked in a whisper.

The intern did not answer. He shook his head.

"Karl!"

"Yes, Carole. I'm here."

"Can God forgive — even me?"

"Even you, Carole. Remember the woman at the well who had six husbands? Remember the water of life and the loving Jesus who poured it for her? You can have it, too. That's why Jesus died."

"My baby, my baby. Can they —" Her voice trailed away.

The doctor strode into the room, listened to the stethoscope, and looked into her eyes. He turned his face to the wall and shook his head. "The syringe, sister, quickly." He put the needle into her arm, with a speed that indicated he was already too late.

"The water of life is here for us all. All you need do is drink it. Drink as freely as He gave it, to wash away sin."

"Karl, the well, the well."

He took her by the hand. The fingers were without sensation and clammy to the touch. She did not respond. The doctor sought her pulse without finding it. He used the stethoscope once more; then he placed her hands on her lap, taking the limp fingers from Karl's grasp. Without so much as a word he stood at the window, gazing out at the fog.

With shaking fingers Karl made the sign of the cross. In the still of the room he saw the others cross themselves as well — the doctor, the intern, the nurse. The four walked silently into the hall.

Renouncing
the Devil

As the door of the Cross and Mitre closed behind him, Karl patted the huge stone lion that lay couchant outside. Touching Leo was a sign of good luck, a totem. Karl often wondered, half jokingly, what Paul Dennis might think if he were to know. Was it the act of a schoolboy who runs a stick across the picket fence, or was it a bona fide superstition, buried even deeper in his nature than his faith in Jehovah?

The lion was cold to the fingers, with the same coat of frost that whitened the grass and the gravel. Karl swung off onto the path leading toward Sevenoaks Hill and St. Swithums. It was seven in the morning, the day after Carole's funeral, and he had found his sleep troubled. Maybe a walk to the grave would help now that the crowds of balletomanes had faded into history.

The whole *affair* of Carole and Willie had been gory and earthy. Even after the inquest, even after Bishop's Monksham had swarmed with reporters, even after the Yard had dug deep into the background, the strands were still twisted.

Old Doc Wogly's best guess was that there had been an attempted abortion. Not a successful one, by any means, for the fetus had still been there, though dead some weeks. Apparently that's what had caused Carole to go so quickly, hemorrhage and infection. In her last delirium doubtless she'd forgotten all about the abortion.

But what about the baby, and what about her hysterical cries not to let them take it? Did she really think it still alive? Had she been completely out of her head? Was it a kind of guilt complex, a plea for forgiveness? Was she perhaps trying to undo the wrong she knew she had already done?

Willie's death was as mysterious as Carole's. Sure enough, Fredrick's men found a Luger on the bed of the Aublin, below the railing of the bridge. One shot had been fired. Nobody had heard it, nobody had seen it. The blanket of fog saw to that.

But who was shot, and why? The fingerprints on the gun were Willie's, not Carole's. Had he threatened to shoot her if she did not marry him? Or himself? Or both? And why did he miss? Had it been a fight over the unborn baby when the abortion had gone wrong, with Willie voting for another try and Carole against?

The Yard had combed out Willie's friends with a fine-tooth comb, and to a lesser degree Carole's. Yet their private relations lay masked, and even the manager of the Chung-king Coolie, who was as helpful as anyone, was stymied.

The coroner labeled Willie's death as accidental drowning. The gash on the forehead was negligible. If Willie had been sober, there'd have been little problem. The water was scarcely chest deep. But his whole system was loaded with alcohol, as if he'd gulped down 10 or 12 ounces of gin. The eyes and the blood showed faint traces of opiates.

With a waterlogged overcoat he hadn't stood a chance. In that condition he probably would have had difficulty staying on his feet even on a cobblestone pavement.

What concerned Karl, now that the two were dead and buried, was the publicity. The yellow rags of London had had a field day with the scandal. "Rising Ballerina Consorting with Underworld." "King of Soho Murdered." "Dancer, Mobster Kill Baby, Die Themselves."

It was juicy enough to last a month, and the press boys were digging up all the dirt they could find. Willie's henchmen, Carole's mother, the attending doctor, the Lutheran padre — anyone who could give them a lead was fair game.

Karl had not been very cordial with the gentlemen of the press. But then the gentlemen were really not gentle. In fact, he'd refused to talk about his previous contacts with the girl, and as a result the *Daily Sun* had hinted he might be the child's father. If he hadn't been a parson, with a mission to worry about, the story could have been actionable for libel. But that would only give credence to an obvious lie. This way he had to ignore it.

The details of Carole's last moments never did make the papers, except for what Karl said in his sermon of her acceptance of Jesus. The hospital was as discreet as Karl. He'd told one or two people, of course. Carole's mother, who certainly deserved to know, and Geoff Thorkill, the parish parson who conducted the funeral. The hospital scene would have shed a whole new light on the account, but as yet, though the coroner and the police and half the clergy knew, no reporter ever stumbled onto it.

The funeral, the burial, the sermon — these were all somewhat delicate. Karl would have had no scruples at all about taking the whole funeral. From every indication she had accepted the Savior. But he would still need leave to bury her and the churchyards were all Anglican.

Old Geoff Thorkill in his steel-rimmed glasses and his patched coat sleeves suddenly appeared on the doorstep of Cocklesfields as a knight in shining armor, just as Karl was comforting her mother. Carole had lived in Geoff's parish, and even if her mother had deserted to the Lutherans, Geoff would still not shirk from offering comfort and help at a time of trouble. Bless his Bach-loving soul!

As it worked out, Geoff took the service and the burial and Karl the sermon — chiefly because that's the way Mrs. Dunning wanted it. It was a little odd for a Lutheran to share the Anglican pulpit.

The little medieval church was packed to the quatrefoils. Half of Sadler's Wells was there, to judge by the modish styles and garb. In the pulpit Karl spoke of the love of God, of the eternal life Christ had promised, of the deathbed faith of Carole Dunning.

He was not in the pulpit long — nine, ten minutes, maybe — but long enough to see the questing for God in the 200 faces there in the pews. He hoped they were a trifle readier to meet their own deaths after thinking of hers. He hoped he had made them reconsider their allegiance to Christ. And just in passing, as he closed his sermon with the votum, he wondered if he would ever again stand in the pulpit of St. Swithums.

But all this had been a part of yesterday, and this was a new day. The cold bite of the air brought him back to the present. On one side of the pathway lay a fence of hawthorn, and across the way the sprawling houses of the New Town. Just off the path, hardly in keeping with the new glass and aluminum, rose a decrepit row of King's Houses. Nobody knew for sure just which king had long ago given them his name. Charles II, maybe. Or even William and Mary, though then they should have been "Queen's Houses."

At five shillings a week, including water, they sheltered a score of pensioners. No more than individual rooms, they were a shade too large to be the cells of monks but a shade too small for real apartments. The single room served as bedroom, kitchen, and sitting room.

In this kind of weather, even with a pleasant little fireplace, one room was enough. It was pleasanter to freeze in one, even a small one, than in three.

The lower level of the houses was of masonry, the upper level of half-timbered plaster. They made a pleasant attraction for the tourists. The photographers loved them, for you could frame them against the shining façades of the New Town as a contrast in the modern and the ancient.

Of the hardy characters who were his closest neighbors in the King's Houses, Karl could count only one as an old acquaintance. Tom Swopes. It was the Tom Swopes who came from a long line of vergers, the self-appointed chief of those who tended the cathedral. The Tom Swopes who had won his wooden leg at Ypres, who knew when the first cuckoo would sing, when the first frost would kill the nasturtiums.

At the far end of the row, in the King's House that Tom called home, the battered door swung open. Sure enough, out came Tom in his brown Harris Tweed jacket, his sole outer dress whether in winter or summer. The calfskin patches on the elbows guaranteed an extra 20 years of service, though it was a little hard to understand how even the tweed itself would ever wear out.

In the sharp air Tom pulled his cap tight and wore a huge shawl over his cheeks and ears, like a grandmother with a babushka. The black walking stick stood out clearly against the frost. Karl was a little glad to see him. Fifteen minutes ago a quiet walk to Carole's grave had been appealing. But now he was wide awake, and old Tom's company would be equally pleasant. A good way to find out what the town was thinking.

Karl hastened his step and was about to call out. But the door swung open again, and out walked a dumpy little woman who must have weighed all of 200 pounds. Her complexion was dark, dirty looking. The raven hair hung haphazardly beneath the broad brim of her hat. Her coat fitted too loosely, with a cheap pattern of purple-and-brown checks no mortal woman would have been seen dead in.

The padre stopped in his tracks and subconsciously crept back into the hedge. Old Tom Swopes consorting with a woman! And a woman like that, of all sorts. Old Tom who was a lifetime bachelor, Tom, who had always insisted over his half-and-half the whole country would be better off without women. A misogynist he called himself, the one word of four syllables he could call his own.

The woman had every appearance of a gypsy. Farther down the highroad, in sheltered nooks, you could often spot their caravans. South for the winter they were, to help with the sugar beets. Summers they liked the Midlands, with the range of Pennines to remind them of their ancestral home in the Tatras.

Between them, Tom and the gypsy carried the oddest collection of bric-a-brac Karl had ever seen. A hundred yards away, he was not sure of the individual items. The woman bore a market basket, full, to judge how she hefted it. You could see all sorts of oddments sticking out — branches, bottles, cloth, a palm frond.

Tom appeared ready for a year's safari in Tanganyika. He hadn't a pocket that didn't bulge, in coat or trousers, and he carried not only the familiar rod of iron but a 3-foot cross of polished beech. It was the iron probe that caught Karl's eye — the one he had once seen in the Bishop's Meadows, probing for the bones of the dead.

The parson faded into the hedge. He was so fascinated by what he saw he did not want to frighten them away. This would be worth his whole year in England. Tom and the gypsy went about their business as if it were an everyday event. They talked in normal tones and moved naturally along the path, with the wooden leg tapping ominously against the gravel.

Whatever they were doing, they needed a lot of gear. The weight of the basket gave several hints. The gypsy shifted it regularly from arm to arm, to tire first one, then the other.

Many an evening in the pub Karl had chatted with wrinkled countrymen about their folklore and folkways. When to plant crops, how mistletoe protects oaks from lightning, what makes a well go dry, what to do when thunder frightens the cattle, how to keep evil spirits out of the sheep. And now, for the first time, he could watch primitive folklore in the raw.

One didn't have to read far to get a rough notion of English superstitions. Whether Celtic or Nordic, they reached so far back into the mists of time no one quite knew where they came from. According to the county histories, it hadn't been four generations since there was a needfire right there in Bishop's Monksham. The seat of a bishopric, no less.

The story made good fun now, but a century earlier it was serious business. The cattle had been dying like flies, of a plague no one had ever seen before. What to do? The vicars didn't seem to be able to exorcise the demons responsible, nor even the canons or bishop. So there was only one alternative. A needfire.

Douse every fire in town, to freeze the spirits out. Take a fire drill of ash and kindle new sparks, because anyone knows a fresh fire is better to frighten spirits than an old and friendly one. Scrape up a windrow of wet hay, and set it afire, to make their eyes cry from the smoke.

Drive every cow and sheep and horse through the smoking windrow. That'll kill off every sprite that ever lived, or at least frighten them away. Then take the fire and spread it from hearth to hearth, so the home fires can also witness to the power of the Highest.

Karl wasn't at all sure he would see a needfire. True, there was something over Tom's shoulder that might be a fire bow. But it could be many other things as well.

The probing rod was a giveaway. The path led only in one direction, and that was toward St. Swithums. If one took into consideration Tom's game leg and the heavy basket of the gypsy, the pair moved along at a quick gait. More youthful and unencumbered, Karl tagged behind, to give them a good start.

When they passed through the lich gate, screened by tombstones and yews and ancient oaks, Karl quickened his pace. By their heading he knew they sought the fresh grave. He reconnoitered. If he crawled through the hawthorns and came up behind the church, the stone wall would screen him as he crept along on hands and knees. The ground would be cold if he lay behind that fringe of low junipers, but it would be worth it.

The thorns caught at his face as he pushed the branches aside and slipped through. He could hear their voices plainly, and he could only hope the stirring of the grass as he inched forward would be drowned out by their chatter. On knees and elbows he crawled to the junipers and peered through.

The basket lay on the ground now, its contents spread on a half circle of tombstones. Tom had unlimbered the iron probe and poked it searchingly into the fresh mound of earth. Already he had scraped off the covering of ivy that hid the brown soil till the rains of spring would bring forth the grass.

"Have to be sure we kill the incubus if it's still there." He jabbed hard with the sharp bar, breathing heavily. "Sometimes one will even sleep with the dead."

"Do you think there really was one? Couldn't it have been a human father?"

"Could have, Sadie. Doubt it. Who? Willie? She wouldn'ta slept with him. The padre? Not likely. But somebody had to be the father. Who? The incubus! They's still about. Heard of one in Frothingham last year. Came at midnight, when she was asleep, and brought a baby on a farm girl. The infant weren't natural, they all said. Couldn't'a been a human father. A monster."

He slammed the iron hard until one could hear the cracking of the wooden coffin. "There, that got him. He won't sleep with her no more."

"Could've been another kind. Have to make sure." The fat gypsy tucked sprigs of mistletoe and ivy and oak into her hair. She jumped twice on the head of the grave, once each at the foot and the middle. All the time she beat upon the earth with a handful of branches. "Twig of apple, twig of pear, Drive away the bugabear." She drew the sign of the cross on the fresh earth and filled it with a white substance Karl guessed to be salt.

The cold earth caught at his elbows and knees, but he was so fascinated by the proceedings he could not bear to risk getting comfortable. The soft red orb of the sun bobbed from the horizon, as secretly and as furtively as the goings-on in St. Swithums churchyard.

Where'd the old gypsy come from anyway, Karl wondered. Couldn't Tom have done the job himself, or were ghosts frightened by numbers? Or was it just a matter of companionship?

"Shouldn't've buried her in the churchyard, at all. Wasn't fittin'." His leathery cheeks looked red with the cold in spite of their age. In the quiet air the puffs of breath were as white and large as those of a race horse.

"Where else? Put her in the open field, and the ghosts'd have'er for sure. In holy ground she's a fighting chance. With a little help, of course."

Tom piled a pyramid of yew twigs on the grave. What he used for kindling Karl could not quite see — rotten punk, perhaps, or the shell of a puffball. On a flat tombstone Tom hunched over the bow and drill, sawing violently back and forth. The firepan lay caught between his foot and his stump. With one hand he twirled the bow and with the other pushed hard on the drill.

A tiny puff of smoke poured from the wood. He breathed gently, till he had a healthy flame, and touched it to his pyramid of twigs. With pitch-dry speed they burst into flame.

Gypsy and pegleg began a common chant. Karl could not at first hear the words. They danced clockwise round the grave three times, then counterclockwise. With his face to the east, Tom leaped across the flames. So did the woman. They both jumped back to the west. They tried the same from north to south and south to north. Once each.

Now the words were getting faster and louder. "Fire burn

and kindling twinkle, Burn the home of Evil Incle." The chant seemed never to end, a kind of low moaning to scatter the ghosts to the mountain of Walpurgis. It was scary, really — scary and pathetic. If it were not for their dead seriousness, Karl would have laughed openly. Imagine — a one-legged 70-year-old leaping over graves and dancing round a pyre.

"Fire burn and kindling twinkle. Burn the home of Evil Incle, Fire burn and kindling twinkle, Burn the home of Evil Incle, Fire burn and kindling twinkle, Burn the home of Evil Incle."

"There now, Sarah. Time to purge it." Old Tom found a seat on a stone, breathless. He looked aged and tired, as if he were not used to the rigors of an exorcist.

The ancient crone, still a good deal younger than Tom, shook with frenzy. Her conduct and bearing would have passed her for some ancient priestess at Delphi, but the purple-and-brown coat and the dismal orange scarf, in a frosty churchyard in England, were ludicrous.

With a flat tombstone for a table she mixed powders and liquids in a tiny crock. Karl peered intently from his observation post. What were they — anise, chicory, lizard eggs, nightshade, cummin? He would probably never know.

With a shock that disturbed him he focused more attentively. The crock was no crock. It was too uneven, too unstable. It was the cranium of a human skull.

As she mixed, the woman paused and threw a powder into the fire. The puffs of smoke ascended almost like a prayer to Baal or Wotan. Karl sensed the aroma of incense as if he were in a catacomb.

Meanwhile old Tom watched intently. Once, briefly, he rose to his feet and stuck in the soil the cross of new beech wood, sanded white. In the morning sun the crosspiece cast a hazy shadow on the earth. Atop the steeple of St. Swithums the old stone cross also stood contrasted against the early sun, and the two symbols, though both the same, seemed different.

As he watched from the junipers, Karl's mind wandered among all he had ever heard of necromancy and demonology and wizardry. Where did all this come from anyway? Saxo Grammaticus and the Norse eddas? Or was it from the age of Hengest and Horsa, from the lowlands of Frisia and Jutland?

The gypsy took five candles and arranged them in the form of a cross, stuck into the soil. With a brand from the fire she touched each one into flame, chanting all the while. "There came two spirits out of the East, One brought fire and one brought frost, In, Fire, Out, Frost, In the name of the Heavenly Host."

She sat quietly beside the skull, stirring it from time to time.

"Will it hurt if I smoke?"

"Yes! It'll confuse the spirits, having two sorts of smoke." Tom looked downcast, as if a warm pipe might take off the chill.

The woman had taken the skin of a snake from her basket and wrapped it twice round her throat. With a wand of willow she began a regular drumming on the stone, with an odd rhythm of the Congo or Haiti.

"That's to gather *all* the spirits," she said. "Make sure they're here, then kill them. So she can rest in peace." The gypsy rose to her feet a trifle heavily and poured the potion drop by drop into the sizzling fire. "Wine of Mosel, Lye of oak, Menstrual blood and Eye of newt, Banish goblin, ghost, and fewt."

The frost of the earth worked deeply into Karl's knees and thighs, and he was so numb he shivered. He shifted to a new position, in a sitting crouch. Beneath his shoe a twig cracked. He watched the sorcerers closely for fear they had heard, but they seemed absorbed in their task.

Tom took two dolls from the basket. "Time to finish up before someone comes."

The dolls were of cloth, perhaps 8 or 10 inches long. Even from the junipers, 40 feet away, they looked remarkably like Carole Dunning. The hair was dark and long, and the pale skin and narrow eyes had a faint touch of the Orient.

The clothes they wore were clearly from the ballet. A white bodice with sequins, and a black tutu beneath the skirt. Oh, and wings! Swan wings. The costume was right out of Swan Lake.

Tom and the gypsy crouched over the fire with the doll. They huddled so close it was difficult to see. First they tore off the wings and the clothing and dropped them piece by piece into the flames.

The old verger took a penknife from his pocket and rammed it through the doll's breast. He cut off the head and the legs and the arms, consigning them one by one to the fire. The torso he quartered. Each piece he cast straight into the air, facing in the four directions of the compass, and then burned.

"There, that should do it."

He stuffed the other doll into his pocket and took out a trowel. On top of the loose earth he dug into the soil, making a grave for the second of the dolls. He measured her length against the size of the hole.

"I think we've done it, Sarah. There're plenty of spirits about. Methinks I can even hear 'em in the brush." The old man paused a moment and looked squarely toward the junipers.

Karl knew the jig was up. In the sunlight surely his coat was too bright to merge with the dark green of the foliage.

"You there, whoever ye be. Ye en't no spirit. Come out, and quit yer mucking about."

Karl rose to his feet. With frozen knees and ankles it

was scarcely easy to stand. His face bore the sheepish look of a 10-year-old who has been caught in the cookie jar.

"Padre! A padre! Ain't ye no sense at all? Di'n't ye know a ghost can't be queered when there's a man o' God aboot? Skeers 'em every time!"

The gypsy cringed behind Old Tom. She was honest enough to realize that it wasn't the preacher who was in the wrong. After all, it wasn't legal to desecrate graves or even build fires in churchyards.

"Damme, vicar, yew get! Yew get! Now we's got to do it all over again. And don't come mucking about again either."

In Tom's state there was no use saying a word. That could come later if need be. Besides, Karl was too mellow and too full of fun to put up a fuss. Without a word he walked along the path, this time in full view of the cemetery, and out through the lich gate.

Knowing Tom, he realized the morning was not so serious as it looked. More like a mock-heroic scene from Gilbert and Sullivan. For Tom was still a faithful old Christian even if he hadn't shaken off his pagan forebears.

As Karl strode out into the highroad, he grinned mischievously. And if the good Lord was watching over Bishop's Monksham that morning, and St. Swithums' churchyard, as He doubtless was, Karl'd have bet his last shilling the good Lord was grinning too.

An
Overbid
in Hearts

When Karl braked the Morris outside the rectory on Kensington Walk, he was not altogether sure what to expect. Charming as she was, Audrey Dennis was not always explicit. Vaguely he realized only he had been invited to dinner and the theater, in company with Paul and Audrey Dennis, and what was more unexpected, with a girl from the American embassy.

Audrey had rather a penchant as a marriage broker, but her tastes were seldom equal to her enthusiasm. Say what you would, her matchmaking was intriguing. In nine months of England, Karl had been invited, at Audrey's pleading, to meet a doctor of botany at London University who specialized in the flora of the Lapland tundra, an Italian model whom Audrey's mother had met on the Riviera, and a Hungarian nurse whose English was limited to a hundred words.

As he pushed the rectory bell, he wondered what it would be this time. He hadn't minded the rush-hour traffic, though he had had to buck it nearly all the way from Bishop's Monksham. Now, when the December sun sank below the horizon soon after four, he didn't even mind driving in the twilight. And the play, according to the reviews in *Punch,* was worth seeing.

It was not Audrey who answered the bell, or Paul, or a two-headed calf, but a sprightly American who might have stepped straight from the pages of *Vogue.* She seemed strangely out of place in England, in a Victorian house with a common lawn in the rear, and a rectory doorway of ornate brickwork and limestone.

"I'm Norma Ruppert. Paul's not back from the hospital, and Audrey's seeing the last of the youngsters to bed. Do come in, won't you?"

Her American sense of knowing just what to say and saying it directly seemed almost foreign, now that he was nearly a year away from the New World. "Hi. I'm Karl Mueller. Has Audrey told you all about me?"

"Hasn't had time yet. I just arrived. Five minutes ago. Can I take the coat?"

"Thanks. I'll just hang it in the hall." He had been on the point of stashing it there before she asked. "Been in England long?"

"No. Just came over on the Mayflower. Three weeks ago. The Dennises have been insisting I come to dinner, but it took too long getting settled. Apartment and job and clothes and all that." There was a chic and groomed look about her that Karl missed in the British. The trim, black suit with its natural-linen blouse was probably what she had worn to work, though the gold-and-garnet earrings were a shade too ornate for daytime.

Karl felt almost as much at home at the Dennises as at the Cross and Mitre. There were always differences of opinion, in degree, between Karl and Paul. But there was so much in common in their love of the Gospel, their outlook on the British, their sense of fun, their liking for Worthington's light ale, that he stopped almost every time he came to London.

"Audrey says you're at the embassy. Something interesting?"

"A kind of flunky. But interesting. Girl Friday. The aide to the first secretary, if that means anything."

It did mean something, though he didn't put it into words. GS level up in the clouds. Her living allowance alone was probably twice his salary. "Good boss?"

"So far not a complaint. Career type, married, three kids. From Baltimore."

"How'd you ever get into the business of diplomacy?"

"Wanderlust, I guess. In French class at Smith we'd read too many *policiers*. Spent a year with an advertising firm on Madison Avenue while I was waiting for the call from State."

He could imagine her as a kind of receptionist-office manager, with two or three British girls doing the typing. As they made their way across the Indian carpets to the living room, he felt the least bit uncomfortable. Her grooming, her polish, her conversation were a shade too sprightly. Though he had worn his best suit and knotted his tie with supercilious care, he still felt outclassed.

A roaring fire blazed on the hearth, the only light in the room. At the windows the last trace of twilight was glimmering away, and the ancient lamplighter paused beneath the street lamp. With a long pole he pulled the switch of the globe, and the soft glare of the gas flame flooded in through the panes of the window.

The girl watched with a touch of awe, as if she had never seen a streetlighter before. Ah, well, probably she hadn't. Give her another two months, and the novelty would be old stuff. That careful American grooming, likely as not, and the rush to get things done might be dulled too.

Audrey appeared in the doorway. "Glad to see you're getting on. Sorry about not being at the door. The little horrors are stored away. For the night, we hope." From the buffet she brought a tray of glasses and a bottle of Bristol Cream. "Paul just phoned. Says he'll be along in five minutes. You learned to drink sherry yet, Norma? If you stick with the Americans, you'll get martinis, but in the proper corners of England, this time of day, it's sherry or nothing."

"I'm still a bit green, but one's got to learn. It's certainly a step up from those horrid French *apéritifs*. Can I help?"

"Yes, would you? Hildur's not home from class yet, and Ilse's in the kitchen."

Knowing Audrey, Karl grinned. It was Audrey's proud old ancestry coming out, with the simplicity of a girl from Devon. He liked her in spite of it: mentioning the fact that she had two maids, preacher's wife or no.

Not maids, really, if one were truthful. German exchange students. With the children and the cooking they were a real help. Because of Paul's friends on the Continent, one could get a *Haustochter* for practically nothing. Fifteen, twenty shillings a week plus board and room.

The mention of the maids had its proper effect. Norma knew exactly what was expected. She wasn't wanted in the kitchen, with a maid at work, and could stick to the sherry and the appetizers as her effort. She filled three glasses.

"Norma comes from an exceptional family, Karl. Did I tell you? The Cleveland Rupperts. Her grandfather was president of the synod, and her father and uncle — they've the big machine tool company."

"Yes, I've heard the name. They donated a dormitory to the seminary, didn't they?"

"Did they? You're getting beyond my depth. That's all Paul told me. Is that true, Norma?"

"Yes, that was uncle's doing. He made his before the days of the income tax."

"Ha. Bet you Americans still don't have to pay nine and six in the pound." It was a subject any Englishman could spend hours on.

Karl preferred not to talk of income tax. The girl's words had helped to characterize her, with a background of money and Smith and gentility. In an American kind of way she was wealthy, not gaudily perhaps, but far beyond the stage of having to work.

As the flickers of the fire played against the walls, he wondered whether life with a girl like this might not be somewhat like life with Audrey, with class and culture. Certainly it had made Paul's life pleasant and gave him the amenities and leisure to build a little ecclesiastical hierarchy all his own. Without Audrey he might never have had St. James. He might have been simply a Doug Harting or Ted Gruber or Gene Bratlich, or even a circuit rider in the outback of Australia.

In the soft light, Audrey's hair shone with the color of honey. She moved graciously about the room, lighting the candles of a sconce. The dull brass caught the flickers and cast them back into the room. The solid mahoganies and upholstered tapestries spoke of a comfortable way of life, though Audrey was perhaps fondest of the pair of wing chairs on either side of the fire, finished in natural leather.

The front door banged to, and Dr. Paul Dennis strode into the room. "Sorry I'm late. Hello, Norma. Hi, Karl." He pecked his wife dutifully on the cheek and wriggled out of his overcoat. "It's old Mrs. Halbfleisch. Doing rather well, really."

Norma poured another glass. "Nothing like sherry by your own fire."

"Thanks, Norma. Karl been telling you all about Lutheranism here? He's doing a spectacular job, you know. Too spectacular when he tries to convert Soho and Sadler's Wells." There was a mischievous twinkle in his eye, and the Australian accent betrayed his enthusiasm.

"No. We were talking about me, I'm afraid. He's too polite to talk of himself."

"When was it you came, Karl? April?"

"Almost. End of March."

"In less than a year he's got the boomingest little parish in England. Not as wealthy as St. James, of course, but you should see the enthusiasm. Cockneys from the East End, mostly, who've moved up to the New Town to better themselves. And he's got them eating out of his hat."

"Sounds exciting."

"It is, really. Dr. Altschuler was here during the summer,

from Cleveland. You should have heard him rave about Karl's work! If all the missions were going so well, we could either knock out the subsidy from the States or triple the number of missions."

A neat girl of 15 appeared in the doorway in pigtails and apron. "The meat is near cooked, Mrs. Dennis. Would you care come see?" She spoke slowly and with a heavy accent.

"Thank you, Ilse. I'll come help." From the doorway she turned back to her husband and guests. "Don't get too involved. We eat in ten minutes."

Audrey ran a careful household. The German girls provided her time and leisure to do what she liked, to entertain lavishly, to cultivate her Devonshire acquaintances, in spite of her marriage to a padre — a Lutheran and an Australian at that.

The draperies were neat and dustfree, the furniture polished to perfection, the hearth scrubbed spotless. It was a house one would have liked to live in, clean, well run, orderly. No wonder Paul could devote his energies to St. James and the Lutheran Church of England, with so competent a home front.

"Karl's pulled off one coup no one else has managed to tackle. Not pull off, I suppose, but at least the foot's in the door."

"How's that?"

"Usually — perhaps you recall reading in the booklet I gave you — we try to rent a hall in the New Towns, build up a mission, and then construct our own little plant. Parsonage and church hall. Nothing fancy, mind you. Eight, ten thousand pounds' worth."

"For parsonage and house, you'd never do that in Cleveland, would you?"

"Hardly. Maybe not even house these days, from what I hear. That's what makes the program so attractive. In terms of salaries and buildings we can start three missions in England for the price of one in America. Of course, we could do it in Australia, too, maybe five for one, but the theological climate there isn't so ripe."

"How does Karl's differ from the others?"

"He's dickering for an Anglican building. They've two old churches just a few minutes apart, and of course one is enough. Fifteenth century and showing signs of age, but a charming little structure. St. Swithums."

"Sounds exciting."

"It is. Karl's the real expert, of course. For a few hundred pounds a year we'd have a proper church. Much better than a hall. And of course if we save the cost of a church in Bishop's Monksham, we can build another elsewhere."

Karl had said little, but a look from Paul pulled him into the conversation. "The Archbishop's Commission on Redundant Churches meets this month. Our proposal went in twelve weeks ago. Chances may not be better than fifty-fifty, but it's an exciting possibility. In the past, the C. of E. has sometimes pulled down a building rather than sell or rent. Too much competition from the Romans and the Methodists."

"Horrid, really. Not very democratic, is it?"

Karl laughed. "No, but we Americans sometimes consider money more important than faith. That's why the Continentals call us materialists."

"This is an exciting guy, Norma. Listen to that. Kirkegaardian existentialism, and he's still on his first sherry." Paul's enthusiasm was catching. Surely this was one of the factors that had pushed him to the top of the Lutheran Church of England, as it had once made him a champion swimmer and a star at inside right.

"I really ought to warn you, Norma. If you want to see the Established Church in action, you'll have to sample their services. Not the Abbey or St. Paul's. That's strictly for the tourists. An evensong in the suburbs, or better yet, in the country."

"Here, now! Can't go stealing my parishioners like that, Karl." There was a mocking touch in the voice.

"No, I'm serious. The more I see of the Anglicans, the more I understand them. Basically I admire them. Of course we Lutherans have a right to care for our own and for those nobody wants, but all the same you've got to admit the Anglicans do a good job. As good, I think, as the Lutherans in Denmark or Sweden."

"They're established churches, too, aren't they?"

"Not so strongly established, from a legal standpoint, but it comes out the same. They were never quite so tough on nonconformists as the English if you wanted to enter the universities or take public office."

"You mean you can't go to Oxford if you're a Methodist?"

"Now, yes. But not in your great-grandfather's day."

Just how Christian the Anglicans really were was always an issue when Paul and Karl sat down at a pub over their Worthington's. Paul slyly brought up his own side of the issue. "You mustn't think they have anywhere near the level of Scriptural background or Sunday schools or confirmation requirements as Lutherans. Matter of fact, I heard a good one the other day. About the wedding at Cana."

In his Australian naïveté he blushed noticeably at the word *wedding*. "There was this Sunday school teacher at St. Peter's in South Kensington. One of the youngsters asked her about the six waterpots that held two or three firkins apiece. What was a firkin, anyway? Well, she wasn't absolutely sure, she said, but wasn't it a kind of pickle you ate with your dinner, like they would probably have at a wedding?"

Paul always had a clever way of driving home his point. There was no denying the Anglicans didn't shine at instructing the young, but so long as one had parochial schools and courses in Bible history, maybe Sunday schools weren't so essential.

Paul sipped his sherry and pushed the frames of his glasses tight against his face. He toyed a moment with his pipe and pouch, as if he would really like to light up, but thought better of it and slipped them back into his pocket.

"Has Karl told you about his publicity? Or was it notoriety?"

"Aha! Ze cat, she slips from ze bag!" Norma hunched her shoulders and looked furtively in the corners. "Matter of fact, I did read his name. Straight out of Eric Ambler. That dancer and the underworld king, wasn't it?"

"Johnny on the spot when they both passed out of the world. The girl, anyway, though he was a bit late for Willie. What papers do you read, Norma?"

"*Telegraph* mostly. Sometimes the *Guardian* or the *Times.*"

"Then you didn't get the best parts of the scandal at all."

"No, I s'pose not."

Paul hesitated, as if for once he thought the water was over his depth. "You'll have to ask him when he gets in a talkative mood. With all the innuendos it's fairly dramatic."

Karl was not in the least embarrassed by his ties with Carole and Willie. On the other hand, he didn't think it diplomatic to confront Norma with the whole rigmarole the first time he set eyes on her.

Perhaps that's why Paul had not pressed the issue. Preachers who made friends with mobsters and unmarried mothers did not grow on every street corner. Knowing him better, she might understand, but on first acquaintance the subject was delicate. In fact almost confidential.

It had been a good 15 minutes since Audrey's disappearance, and no one was reluctant to hear her announcement of "Dinner." The aroma of roasting lamb and the tickling warmth of the sherry had had ample time to stir the appetites.

The two padres flanked Norma en route to the table. Karl was glad to see a place for Ilse in case the conversation lagged. She was a sweet girl, a real gem with the youngsters, and to judge from Audrey's comments, developing into a real cook. She'd been with the Dennises nearly as long as Karl, and in another few months she was scheduled to finish her stay and go off to school at Heidelberg.

The table shone as Audrey's table usually did, with white linen that was the pride of Ireland and sterling silver that did honor to the craftsmen of Sheffield. She'd even dusted off the heirloom Wedgwood with its floral blues, no doubt to impress Norma. The tempting brown of the mulligatawny wafted trails of steam from the tureen.

With Karl seating Audrey and Ilse, the dinner began. Paul took the prayer, a prayer not exactly English but distinct and meaningful. "Be present at our table, Lord, Be here and everywhere adored, Be with us now and grant that we May feast in paradise with Thee."

"It's pleasant to have the youngsters in bed. An hour early too."

"But they *are* fun. In fact they'd be nice to have up." Apparently Norma was being independent.

"We'd never make it to the theater on time. With company they're little show-offs."

"Good for them!"

"Now that's where we differ from the Americans." Her tone was one of fun, not argument.

Ilse was taking the soup bowls away in the mellow light of the tapers. From the sideboard Paul retrieved a bottle of wine and a corkscrew. He wiped the bottle ceremoniously. Knowing the Dennises rather well, Karl would have given three-to-one odds that it had just come that very day from the shop around the corner and really needed no dusting, as if it had been laid up for years in a nonexistant wine cellar.

The bottle boasted the long, swanlike neck of a Rhine wine, and the label clearly indicated Johannisberger. A closer look, however, was revealing. It was from Johannesburg, all right, but in South Africa. What a fraud! Doubtless just as expensive as the authentic. But it was characteristic of Paul, who thought the Commonwealth could supply man's every need far better than America or the Continent. A wonder it wasn't Australian.

With Ilse and Audrey serving, the next course was a steaming platter of dover sole. It was a dish too English to be universally loved, but in this case it was so beautifully done that it would have been ungrateful to find fault. The butter brown flakes of flesh peeled off the backbone as sweet as lobster and twice as tasty. Sprigs of parsley gave a nice contrast.

"Tell me, Ilse, about this *Haustochter*-ing? Is that how you say it?"

"Most German girls do it. After their last year of school. Then, if they want to become secretaries or go to the university, they've learned another language. They do it all over the Continent, but in France and England preferably."

"It's really quite a system, Norma," Paul broke in. "Often you'll find two families trading. *Au pair,* as the French put it. You take our daughter, and we'll take yours. It's a cheaper and more thorough way of making a Grand Tour."

Karl peeled the sweet flesh of the sole from the bone. It tasted so light and appealing he would not have objected to a whole meal of fish instead of a single course. As the fish service disappeared, the table groaned with a massive joint of lamb.

With all the ceremony of Ko-Ko, the Lord High Executioner, sharpening his snickersnee to do away with Nanki-Poo, Paul Dennis rasped his carving blade against the steel. Ilse carted in steaming bowls of roast potatoes, sprouts, and carrots.

It was a feast one would more likely find at a harvest dinner in Devon than a rectory in Kensington. Karl looked it over hungrily. "You must get to Devon, Norma. That's Audrey's home, and this is a sample of Devonshire fare. Mind you, don't believe them about Devonshire cream. It's not the cream that's fattening. It's the whole menu."

"From the looks of it, I'd better stay in London. How do they ever keep their figures on this?"

"Tonight we don't worry about figures, Norma," Audrey said. "Just proving the English aren't such bad cooks as they're claimed."

"Oh, but you've got Australian influences, Audrey," Paul broke in. "And if everything tastes as perfect as it looks, we can give Ilse credit, too, for a touch of the Continent."

"Oh, no, Dr. Dennis. Mrs. Dennis teach me all I know about the kitchen."

It was the kind of dinner everyone enjoyed, the toast to Norma's stay in London, the ceremonious slicing of the meat, the passing of plates from host to guests, the refilling of the wine glasses, the pleasant flow of the conversation.

Karl, who prided himself on his English style of eating, without shifting knife and fork from one hand to the other, noted Norma admiring the technique. He was really rather skillful now, after nine months, and could do it as well as a native. From the corner of his eye he noted her try it too. A squib of mint slid off the bite and landed in a bit of juice, though without a splatter. She did not try it a second time.

To a bachelor and a spinster the homey dinner had an especially appealing touch. Paul cut a fine figure as head of the house, managing the pleasure of his guests in terms of meat and wine with a polish one did not often see in an Australian. Even with the youngsters tucked safely in bed, the scene was one of loving domesticity, where there was still time for the individual in spite of diapers and school and measles.

As a matter of fact, Karl Mueller admired the scene with more than a little envy. Would he ever manage as well as Paul, in terms of a wife and earthly goods and social know-how? He was speculating about this when the thought suddenly exploded. This is exactly what Audrey had planned, had worked for.

Sherry before the fire, a pleasant exchange of conversation, the kind of meal one could remember with pleasure, a diverse little potpourri of guests, and later an amusing Restoration comedy. Congreve, wasn't it? *The Way of the World.* Was it just another sociable evening for Karl and Norma, or was it a baited trap?

"The meal's so appetizing we're not much good on the chatter, Audrey." He made it sound lighthearted.

"It *is* good. You've proved the point about English cooking."

"You're too good a guest, Norma." It was Paul this time. "The people of Devon, you know, aren't really English at all. Celts. What is it, P-Celts or Q-Celts, Audrey? I can never keep them straight."

From his waistcoat Paul took out the monstrous gold watch that had come to him through four generations of clergymen. "It's twenty to seven, dear. We'll have to have the apple charlotte, of course. But is there time for the coffee?"

"It's ready, Mrs. Dennis," said Ilse.

"What about you, Norma? Would you like a quick cup, say five minutes' worth? Or shall we wait and have it when we get home?"

"I'll vote for postponement."

"Karl?"

"Hear, hear. If we change our minds, we can always get some between acts."

"It's my fault," said Paul. "Shouldn't have been late, and

then there'd have been loads of time." He played longingly with the bottle of Courvoisier on the mantel. "Missing the coffee's not so bad as missing the brandy. How about a cigar, Karl? Anyone mind if we smoke?"

"No, do," came the chorus from the women.

He passed over a Havana panatela, obviously an American brand. With half the Lutheran diplomatic corps in Paul's parish, Karl wondered whether the cigars arrived by the box or by the mere handful. With a shilling or so on each, the tax was too expensive for anyone but a managing director or a board member.

He rolled the cigar gently in his fingers and clipped the end with a knife. It was a bit dry, but the smell was light and appealing. He bent over one of the candles. "You'll have to come here oftener, Norma. Only preacher in England who regularly offers a stogie."

There was a twinkle of merriment in her eye. "Not me, he didn't." Karl passed her his. Surprisingly, she accepted, took a ceremonious puff, and returned it. "So much for the peace pipe. I'll stick to apple charlotte, thank you."

They worked quickly at the dessert without doing it justice. "We'll be at the Shaftesbury, Ilse," said Audrey, "in case there should be an emergency. Hildur said she'd be home about eight. You might keep a plate warm if it's convenient."

"Yes, mum. We'll manage fine."

"I'm sure you will."

In the press of time there was no chance for the leisurely settling of appetites or even a prayer of thanks. Karl was rather surprised. Perhaps a concession to America. Get things done here and now.

With Paul he adjourned to the hall to wait for the ladies. "She'll go far, that girl," Paul was saying. "Arrived in London on a Saturday night and was in church next morning. Without breakfast. The kind of repartee you expect from the wife of an admiral or ambassador."

"She does seem fun to be around."

"Saves a deal of difficulties, marrying one of your own. Audrey and I had the very devil of a time. Australian outback mixed with Devon society. All in the same Commonwealth too."

The remark amused Karl. The big difference, he reasoned, was religion and money, not background. "We had a good chance to talk in the living room. School, embassy, church, Anglicanism."

"Good show. She's worth getting to know." It sounded almost as pointed as if he meant "worth getting to marry." "Audrey wanted especially for the two of you to meet. I understand she gets enough embassy invitations to be quite the social butterfly."

The women stormed the hall, and the men stood waiting with their coats. Without really thinking, Karl grabbed Audrey's, and Paul, Norma's. They fled quickly down the steps.

Paul strode quickly to the driver's seat while Karl handled the curbside doors for the ladies, then crawled into the back beside Norma. "The Shaftesbury, if you please, James," said Karl.

"Yes, milord," said Paul.

Karl sat back against the leather upholstery of the Consul. With a good meal under his belt, a pleasant companion at his side, a job that challenged him, he could ask nothing more.

The lights of Kensington High Street flashed by. In 20 minutes they would be in the comfort of the theater, watching Congreve's old farce. Some nights he might have been annoyed by Audrey's matchmaking.

But tonight, like the actors in the play, he and Norma would play at Millamant and Mirabell. What pleased him most, in the mild exhilaration of the dinner and the Johannisberger, was his sense of maturity. For once, he felt he could lick his weight in tigers, even human tigers with names such as Audrey Dennis and Norma Ruppert.

A
Gift from
Lambeth Palace

"Morning, Karl. How goes it?" Paul Dennis set the hand brake in the drive of the Cross and Mitre.

"Fine, Paul. You?"

"Good, thanks."

There was a warmth in the two voices that belied the force of the wind and the snap of the December air. Karl swung open the door and piled into the leather seat. The black Consul sped out across Little Wealdstonebury Common and turned up the highroad toward Cathedral Hill.

It was nine in the morning, with an overcast sky. Flying scuds of cloud whipped across the landscape and dropped an occasional flurry of drizzle. The water reminded him not so much of a summer rain as of the salty spray of the sea, driven before the gale.

It was a Thursday morning and market day. A week before Christmas, the market stalls boasted a holiday atmosphere — Jerusalem cherries and poinsettias, holly and ivy, laurel and bay leaves, mistletoe and chrysanthemums. There was the flash of glassy ornaments from the hills of Slovakia, the soft greens of spruces from Scotland, the glittering boxes of snowflakes from a factory in Japan, the brightly painted toys from the foothills of Bavaria.

As they drove quickly up the highroad, too quickly for the hordes of shoppers who skittered recklessly across the pavement, Karl was strangely quiet. This was the day of the great decision. This was the day when they were meeting with Sir George Hopp-Townsend, O.B.E., Chancellor of the Diocese of Bishop's Monksham.

For a solid week they had pondered the cryptic note of the chancellor. It was written on an odd piece of foolscap, brief paper probably, where a solicitor wrote his notes as he sat in court.

The message gave almost no information. "Dear Mr. Mueller," it began, in a bold chancery hand that spread from margin to margin. "Could you and Dr. Dennis meet us at the Chapter House at about nine-thirty on the nineteenth to discuss St. Swithums? Perhaps you could ring my London secretary to confirm the time and place. Hopp-Townsend."

More than once Karl had held the sheet against the light. It was almost as if he were looking for an unwritten text, but all he saw was the wire lines and the monk's head of the watermark.

For nearly a week he had discussed the note with Dr. Dennis, and for nearly a week they had speculated on its meaning. He was certain, from an account in the paper, that the bishops had been meeting at Lambeth just the week before. To save travel funds, what could be more normal than to hold a session of the Commission on Redundant Churches at the same time?

As they whisked past the crowds of the market, he was not at all sure what the decision might be. If *he* had been holding the reins, as an Anglican, and the Lutherans wanted St. Swithums, he would probably have temporized. Postpone the decision for a year or two until the Lutherans were no longer interested. It was more diplomatic than a forthright no.

Paul and he had discussed the possibilities at considerable length. They were countless. The decision might well be indefinitely postponed. The leasing fee might exceed all reason. The rental might be on a yearly basis to keep the Lutherans under thumb. The building might be sold to the Romans or even torn down on the grounds the dry rot and deathwatch beetle had made it unsafe.

There were some considerations in the decision which were beyond all fathoming. Karl could make no logical guess just how seriously the wishes of His Grace the Bishop might influence the decision.

On the one hand, no bishop under the sun would willingly give up a building, especially one so historic and with such architectural value. On the other, the bishop's conflict with the rector and his long fight to gain the advowson might have embittered him enough to be glad to be rid of St. Swithums. For his daughter's sake and her obvious interest in the Lutheran vicar, the bishop might wish to be more congenial. For exactly the same reason he might not.

The Consul swept up beyond the north door of the cathedral and drew to a halt a hundred yards away. In the brisk wind a trio of pigeons took to the air, beating wildly to make headway. Watching, Karl wondered if the day would prove as difficult as the flight of the wind-blown pigeons.

They strode across the cathedral close, with the Channel wind whipping scraps of paper about the lawn. They were not yet inside the porch when they heard, above the roar of the wind, the sound of singing. It was "O Come, O Come, Emmanuel."

"Is there another way into the Chapter House? We don't want to be late."

"Yes, Paul. If the grills above the crypt are unlocked." They paused a moment in the shelter of the entry.

"Ah, there you are!" Sir George Hopp-Townsend smiled casually. "We thought we'd best wait in the porch. I'd quite forgotten it was Ember Day and there'd be a service. I'd like you to meet Mr. Toner. Mr. Horatius Toner of Norwich." The chauffeur stood just behind.

"How do you do, sir?"

"Can we all crowd into the Daimler, Fred? I should think it much more amiable than taking two cars."

"Yes, sir."

"Good. Then it's settled."

The huge, black car stood before the house of the dean, 200 yards across the wintry lawn. The driver seated Toner first, then Dennis, then Hopp-Townsend, whose ample girth filled what was left of even the broad expanse of a Daimler. Karl climbed into the front.

The car purred to life and rolled eagerly along the moat of the castle onto Christchurch Road. Even so genial a man about town as Paul Dennis was somewhat at a loss for words. What he really wanted to discuss was St. Swithums, but he dwelt instead on the sharpness of the frost and the possible damage to the sugar beets and the sprouts.

It was almost as if these were countrymen discussing their manors, not churchmen deciding the fate of a house of God. As they rolled toward St. Swithums, Karl deliberated. At first he had thought a meeting at the Chapter House was a bad omen, and now he wondered about the switch to St. Swithums.

Was it merely a quiet spot out of the storm, where Geoff Thorkill could be counted on to have no service on Ember Day? Or was the move rather the mark of a genuine field marshal who could adequately command his troops only when he stood on the field of battle?

The Daimler halted 10 feet from the lich gate, and the men braced themselves against the wind, scurrying past the ancient tombstones. The south porch was open, as one might expect, and with Karl holding the door, they filed solemnly past the piscina to the semidarkness within.

"How about the alcove near the font? That's what the vicar uses for confirmands, they say, when he last had them." Not far from the bell chamber, where the servants once stood as they came to worship, the little group unloosened scarves and gloves. In their midst stood the ancient chunk of limestone that was the font. Carved in relief, the worn faces of the disciples proudly stood as godparents to the children who had come to God in its cleansing waters century after century.

Hopp-Townsend pulled gently at his heavy overcoat with the help of the chauffeur. Beneath he wore a dark blue suit that appeared to be of melton, with a waistcoat to match and a heavy gold chain that clinked softly with insignia.

"I've asked Mr. Toner to join us because he's had considerable experience in this sort of thing. Perhaps I didn't mention, but we were classmates at Winchester. He is the chancellor in the diocese of Norwich."

Dr. Dennis helped make the party comfortable. Around the font, against the stones of the wall, stood a scattering of heavy oak chairs, without arms but with kneelers attached, that could be strung together when necessary to make a kind of pew.

Paul offered a chair to Hopp-Townsend, then ranged a little semicircle about him. Toner did not remove his coat, a small man with a sharp gray touch of mustache, who appeared as dapper as Lincoln's Inn Fields and the Law Courts.

Each of them seemed to sense the atmosphere of the moldy stone and the aged font, as if they were really here to meditate. Karl in fact was reluctant to think of St. Swithums at all, though it closed in all about him.

He was so moved, on the one hand, he loved the old structure almost with a physical love. He wanted it. But he was so aware, on the other, of the personal involvements that he did not know if the goods were worth the cost. St. Swithums, when the cheese was binding, frankly wasn't worth his friendship with the Ellingston-Hartes or his growing interest in Josie.

From the gallery in the transept floated the soft echoes of Palestrina. Geoff Thorkill was busy as usual on the organ that had once been a *cause célèbre* with the bishop.

"Perhaps we'd best get to business. It's nippy here, and there're many details." In the face of the chancellor's comment, Paul Dennis appeared the soul of wit and grace. He had not lost the charm that once made him a board member of the English Speaking Union, nor the native ebullience of Australians. He leaned forward intently, quite at ease.

"Whatever you prefer, sir."

"Perhaps I should begin by stressing the words *in principle*. The Commission approved your offer *in principle*. They also insisted the details were a concern only of the local see and not of the commission."

Karl appeared somewhat agape but at the same time mystified. Paul sat back comfortably against the sturdy crosspieces of the chair. Toner examined the two of them with the practiced eye of a man who has long searched out the faces of men in the dock, to catch the slightest flicker of guilt or innocence.

Hopp-Townsend continued. "The matter has been discussed at quite some length with the bishop, and at his request, with the dean and canons. We have decided to let you have St. Swithums."

The aplomb of Paul Dennis flew to the winds as he rose excitedly to his feet. "Wonderful! You won't regret it, sir, I assure you."

Karl was startled but kept his seat. A broad grin spread from cheek to cheek.

"You will recall the terms of your offer. A leasehold of four hundred pounds per annum and a reasonable attempt to maintain the structure and the grounds. In our opinion this offer appeared unnecessarily generous in terms of the bad state of the masonry. His Grace has authorized me to make a counter offer of two hundred and fifty pounds. The additional one hundred and fifty he would prefer you apply to maintenance. Of course we cannot expect you to make drastic repairs, such as the damage to the woodwork by the deathwatch beetle. Just keep out the rain and snow — that sort of thing."

Paul Dennis had taken a wild new interest in the bulk of stone that grew around him. The odor of burnt candles and of molding linen, the squint, the hammer-beam roof, the funeral brasses, the Perpendicular tower — all these would be his. With all his churches, this was the first he could call a real church — a kind of cathedral, if you will, of the Lutheran Church of England.

Karl was happy, too, but in a different way from Paul. He liked the simple lines of the pulpit — the pulpit where he had preached the funeral for Carole Dunning. Now it was to be his, where down through the centuries the Word of God had stirred thousands of hearts. It was a challenge, and he hesitated, wondering if he were up to it. At least he would try. That's all God asked.

"Of course there will have to be an agreement in writing, to protect both parties. Horatius has had a good deal of experience there, and that's why he's with us. Who are your solicitors, Dr. Dennis?"

"Laughlin and Desmond, sir."

"Fine. We can work out the details with them. First we'll want to talk them through, however. The church will be available at the beginning of Lent. The fifteenth of February. The vicar has applied for retirement in January." He nodded toward the sound of the organ in the gallery with a knowing smile. "I understand you and he are on excellent terms, Mueller. Two people who respect Bach, they say. That's what we like. In the agreement we want to make special arrangements for the organ. These will not interfere with the services, of course, but they will give Thorkill the right to play the instrument when it is not otherwise in use. Since it is an historic organ by baroque standards, we trust you will also make it available to other musicians on a valid request."

Karl was dreaming about old Geoff Thorkill there on the bench, leaning his hunched shoulders and wrinkled fingers over the manuals, pushing the steel-rimmed spectacles up over his nose.

"The rectory, as you know, is not owned by the diocese but remains the property of the squire."

Horatius Toner noted a slight pause in the conversation. "At Norwich we felt a detailed contract with clauses and subclauses was not wholly necessary. It's not as if you were leasing the Savoy. On the other hand, as I'm sure your solicitors will advise you, some kind of legal understanding is in the best interests of both parties."

"Of course, of course." Paul Dennis still glowed with excitement. He appeared as eager as a schoolboy at a picnic.

Hopp-Townsend drew the huge watch from his waistcoat and examined it with care. His pink cheeks and healthy color made him appear the kind of country squire one saw on old hunting prints, with a full face and a mop of unruly hair.

"We felt a twenty-year lease would be ample. On your part, you could always withdraw on a year's notice. And of course the lease could be renewed if both parties desired."

The damp air felt cold to the fingers, and Karl dug his hands deep into his overcoat. "Sir, if it is not indelicate to inquire, is His Grace quite happy with the decision?"

The chancellor's face rolled with laughter. "No fear on that score, Karl. You know the longstanding — how shall we put it — *entrechat* — between him and the squire, or for that matter, him and Thorkill. As His Grace phrased it, if it's a choice between the Gospel à la Luther and no Gospel at all, he'll vote for Luther. Besides, this will free the endowments for use elsewhere. To work among the New Towners and salary another assistant at St. Saviours. You see, the deeds of gift restricted the money solely to St. Swithums so long as the *locum* was held by an Anglican."

"That certainly makes us feel considerably better. As men

of God, we'd certainly hate to feel like the camel who pushed his head inside the tent and then couldn't be pushed out."

"No fears on that score, Mr. Mueller." Horatius spoke concisely. "I attended all the commission's sessions. Eight or ten churches were involved. And mind, the C. of E. doesn't give up something just to be nice. It's got to be to mutual advantage. The endowments and the rent in this case."

"But isn't it rather novel, granting a church to another body?"

"No, not so unusual. Not this decade anyway. The war changed all that. Besides, the Lutherans have always had a foot in the door. Through the royal family. The Hanoverians. Rather good Lutherans once."

Paul was quick to add a sixpence worth. "George I gave us St. Magdalene's way back in 1732. But of course that was a long time ago."

"Not so long as you'd think, Dr. Dennis. Most of the Scandinavians have held Anglican churches ever since they've been in Britain. On long-term lease. Maybe we're still afraid of the Norse raiders, or maybe they're so much a part of our blood we consider them kinfolk."

Hopp-Townsend rose to his feet and struggled into his coat. "Consider these embassy churches in London and the port towns. That's a case of Lutherans in Anglican buildings every time. With the Swedes, of course, it was easy. They're as insistent on the Apostolic Succession as any Anglican. That it belongs not just to the *bene esse* but to the *esse.*"

He stopped to rub his hands. "The Danes, they managed to keep their bishops even though they didn't feel them absolutely necessary. And the Norwegians, they're about like you in the New World. Take 'em or leave 'em, whichever seems most practical." He smiled in a way which reflected a knowledgeable insight into the character of Lutheranism.

Hopp-Townsend was on his feet now, the heavy brown coat squarely on his shoulders. Paul and Karl stood up quickly.

From the organ loft the soft music of Sweelinck and Buxtehude wafted out over the stillness of the nave. It was a wonder their conversation had not disturbed old Geoff up there on the bench.

Karl looked at the church as a bridegroom might examine his bride. The 11th century apse was really the pride of the whole structure, setting the tone and mood. The gray of the stone boasted a patina of centuries, and on the arches below the clerestory one could still detect the traces of an ancient fresco. The Christ of Golgotha, the guidebooks described it, with the sorrowing women weeping at His feet.

Hopp-Townsend took a dozen strides toward the aisle as if he were inspecting the property for the last time. "Could I make the suggestion you make no announcement of the decision until the bishop has done so? There are always faultfinders about, you know. The sort who think Anglicanism is dying merely because we give up a church. You and I, we know this isn't true."

"Of course. In fact, perhaps it would be wisest to make no announcement at all. On our part, I mean." Dr. Dennis had found the old diplomacy, the kind that made him so effective among the Anglicans.

"Excellent. I know restraint is somewhat difficult, but it would certainly be wisest in the long run. Of course you needn't hesitate to advertise your services or Lenten series or whatever. Just so there's no tone of gloating how you came by St. Swithums."

"There'll be no difficulty from us, sir," Karl answered. "Dr. Dennis and I and all of us understand the problem. In fact, I shall even try to set the proper tone among the parishioners, though of course it may not be easy to hold down their enthusiasm."

"Quite. We will appreciate whatever you can do."

Karl examined the ancient font with new eyes. No longer was it a mere antiquity but a functional part of the church.

He wondered how many infants would meet the waters of life there. Might it not be wise, for the sake of tradition, to follow the Anglican mode of pouring from a ewer. At one time the symbol of flowing water was as Lutheran as it was Anglican.

What pleased him most, as he reconnoitered the building, was the attitude of the bishop. It would be a pleasure to be on good terms with one's neighbors instead of merely tolerating them. Somehow, in his prayers that night, he might even come to see how a pagan spiritualist like the old squire, along with his right of advowson, in spite of it all, had served as a tool of God.

For the first time Karl noted the heavy scent of pine and fir. In the north transept, piled thickly against the wall, rose a mound of evergreens and laurel. Once the Sunday services were over, the young folk would come in and go to work, decking the arches and the windows for the birthday of the Christ Child.

He had forgotten in all the excitement, quite how close Christmas lay. Only six days away. As a Christmas present, St. Swithums appeared as precious as gold and frankincense and myrrh. Too bad he couldn't mention it in his Christmas sermon.

The men kept their voices low, as if not to disturb the vicar at the organ. They could see him faintly, peering at his music and hunched over the keyboard, with a coat and shawl that half hid his graying hair and steel-rimmed spectacles.

The chancellor watched closely, with a touch of tenderness. Dr. Dennis, noticing, whispered, "Have you told the vicar yet?"

"No, not yet. As I say, he's retiring the octave of Candlemas. Except for not having to preach, there won't be much difference. Hamilton's letting him stay on in the rectory in any case. A kind of stipend for his work in plainsong."

At that moment Geoff Thorkill leaned over the balcony,

without leaving the organ, and waved cheerily toward Karl. He refrained from making a sound, as if he knew it was not proper to shout helloes across the house of God.

In a moment the ancient walls echoed with sound, and the swell of the organ rose to an exquisite crescendo. The tune was scarcely discernible, though the counterpoint was clearly a fantasia in the style of Bach. Perhaps a prelude or fugue or, for that matter, variations on the variations of the Mendelssohn symphony.

From the tenth bar there was no longer any doubt. It was Luther's "A Mighty Fortress Is Our God." Even in the ornate pattern of the fugue it marched along with stateliness and power. A little out of date in terms of the church year, but nonetheless a gesture of kindliness and exuberance.

"We'll love to have old Geoff about," Karl said softly as the party made its way out the aisle. "He thinks you're Lutheran music lovers from Germany and wants to make you feel at home. With Bach and Luther."

Devil Take
the Hindmost

The night held a kind of magic all its own, even had it not been the night our Savior was born. Karl hummed softly as he drove into the lane. "Away in a Manger." It was the carol his first-formers had sung at the Christmas pageant, with faces and voices so shining one could almost imagine them the heavenly hosts of Bethlehem's fields.

This was the kind of Christmas Eve one found in Trollope and Barsetshire, with a touch of snow to pillow the dying landscape, and the sound of carols to waken the darkness. He parked the little Morris at the broad turn in the drive, a good 50 yards from the abbey gate. As he switched off the headlights, the clinging snow glistened under the stars.

The sky had cleared about the time his program at the Community Hall was ending, and in the darkness of December each little star competed for the eye of its Maker. He could spot the brilliant outline of Orion — Betelgeuse, Bellatrix, Rigel, and Saipha — and wondered just where they had lain in the sky that night of Bethlehem when God's star signaled the birth of His Son.

The snow scarcely covered the blades of grass, and already the asphalt had melted the wet flakes. Obstinately the snow clung to the boughs of the laurel and the twigs of the holly, making a kind of fairyland to delight the children and leprechauns.

In the dark night Karl's footsteps made black tracks in the grass. Ahead the gatehouse flickered with lights. From each window glimmered the reds and oranges that spoke of candles and firesides.

With his ungloved hand he touched the cold brass of the knocker — the Angel Gabriel he was coming to know on intimate terms. On so cold a night maybe the old archangel would have trouble getting a good pucker on his trumpet. Brass echoed solidly on brass in a way one could feel as well as hear. In the light of the tiny bulb he could read the brass plate, "Abbey Gatehouse," and in smaller letters, "The Bishop's Residence."

Inside he heard a scurry of feet and the yipe of Alfred the Great dashing down the hall. "Hello, Karl. Merry Christmas." In the half light Josie appeared as entrancing as a Beatrice in Paradiso. "How'd the programme go?"

"Fine. We'd a hundred and seventy-five jammed into the hall and another fifty in the game room. The fire marshal wouldn't've been at all happy, I'm afraid."

"Everyone know his piece?" She led the way down the carpeted hall.

"The little tykes stole the show. First-formers. Real muggers. Playing up to the crowd. Put them on the BBC and they'd take over the Home Service in nothing flat. You should have been there. And 'Away in a Manager,' with no lights except the candles and the Christmas trees. It'd have stolen your heart."

"I'm sorry I didn't, now. Bruce called an hour ago. They've had a good two inches at Peterborough, and the RAC advised them to stay off the roads. Sometimes there's a good deal of drifting in the Wash."

"Won't they get down at all?"

"There's still an off chance even tonight. By tomorrow of course it'll be easy."

"It's a rotten shame. Now we'll have to do all the decorating without the nephews and nieces."

"*Have* to! *Get* to, don't you mean?" There was a sly laugh in her upturned face.

"You're dressed more for an afternoon tea than a session with holly and stepladders." In the light of the fire he examined her closely. In a stranger she might have resented it, but

Karl she knew too well. The bright blue dress sported trimmings of white and a single strand of pearls, setting off the slate blue of the eyes and the chestnut of the hair. Her cheeks glowed with the firelight.

"Father and Granny are in the larder chopping up the holly and fir."

"The King's in the counting house, Counting out his money, The Queen's in the parlor, Eating bread and honey."

"Silly." She poked her finger mischievously at his chin. "Let's go join them."

She was more mature than he remembered, yet playful enough to keep him on his toes. It was one more quality he chalked up to her credit.

The serving kitchen smelled of the out-of-doors. As usual, old Tom Swopes had trimmed the shrubbery just before the holidays, and in his zeal to provide the bishop with greens, occasionally did too drastic a job. The floor rose high with greenery — bay, juniper, pine, laurel, ivy, three or four varieties of holly.

With a pair of pruning shears His Grace whittled at the greens and wove the pieces into an unending garland. Granny sat at the counter with a muslin cloth and shined what seemed a whole bushel of apples. Most were bright red, Cox's Pippins probably, though Karl also spotted a few score of Golden Delicious. On the stem of each she tied a black thread.

In his black waistcoat and gaiters Alred Ellingston-Harte rose from his knees. "Welcome, Karl. A blessed Christmas."

"Thank you, sir. And to you as well."

Granny skipped from the stool, quickly for a woman of 77, and reached her hands up to the newcomer's shoulders. She bussed him gently on the cheek in the French fashion, making him bend a bit forward so she could reach. The second cheek she snapped with her finger. "That's special for Christmas. A love tap. If we can't have Bruce and Genevieve, we'll take you instead."

"Did they say they couldn't make it tonight, Father?"

"It wasn't very definite, Josie. I didn't encourage him if the roads were slick. You know how it is on Christmas Eve anyway, with all the hot toddy and buttered rum. We'd rather see them tomorrow, safe and sound, than not see them at all."

"I should say." It was Granny. "Besides, we've got Karl to do the climbing. Sometimes I dream I'm a great landholder in Tanganyika, with a whole passel of laborers at my beck and call." Her puckish tone filled the room with warmth. "You youngsters want to start hanging, or shall we all work here?"

The clock in the cathedral boomed out the time, with eight strokes of Big Tom counting out the hour. It filled the Gate House with a mass of sound.

"He has a friendly voice, Big Tom. But how do you manage to sleep?" Strange, Karl had never before really noticed how loud it was. Perhaps the quiet air and the pillow of the snow exaggerated the noise.

"The dampers go on from nine through six to muffle him. Otherwise every mother in town'd be on the phone. Waking up the babies."

"Funny I never noticed. And here I've been priding myself I knew all about Bishop's Monksham."

"Alfred, you stop that!" The Corgi had seized a string of evergreens in his teeth and was dragging it down the hall. "I know it's time we get it up, but how about leaving the job to us?" Sarah seemed the true master of Alfred the Great. Immediately he dropped his mouthful and poked a sheepish face into the doorway. "Now behave!" She waggled a wrinkled finger.

The bishop stretched his long, lean arms. "It always sounds a good deal louder in the winter. In summer the leaves catch the sound and deaden it, but on a clear night in winter people say you can sometimes hear Big Tom as far away as Gravesmere if the wind is right."

"I'm glad you don't muffle it completely. Sometimes I lie awake at night and listen at the Cross and Mitre. It's a great comfort. Like the cock atop the spire. A quiet witness that God's in his heaven and all's right with the world — you know, like Browning. Or maybe even Shakespeare."

"Go on," urged Josie like an elf. "Recite. Shakespeare's socially acceptable."

Karl grinned and stood atop a low stool. His voice lowered to a range he thought appropriate to Lawrence Olivier or Michael Redgrave.

"Some say that ever gainst that season comes
Wherein our Saviour's birth is celebrated
The bird of dawning singeth all night long."

"Bravo, bravissimo!" Grandma Sarah clapped politely. "Too bad he isn't C. of E. Just the right resonance for Fulham Palace."

The bishop half smiled as if he couldn't help being amused but wished she'd let it ride at that.

"As long as we're in a poetic mood, why not put the Yule log on the fire? Tom's had it in the weather for a month, so it'll burn slowly. You remember, Karl. The dying old apple by the compost heap. That's our Yule log. Roots and all." She placed a yellow apple on her gray head for no apparent reason. "How is it the old Norse rhyme has it? 'Come bring with a noise, My merrie, merrie boyes, The Christmas log to the firing.' "

She flipped the porch light on and swung wide the door. The gnarled trunk and the swollen whorl of roots lay hard against the stone wall. While Sarah held the door and Josie brushed off the snow, the two men grasped the trunk of the apple. At the root end, Karl had the heaviest load, a hundred pounds perhaps, but the roots made good handles.

Ceremoniously they swung the log through the larder down the hall to the living room. It oozed drops of water onto the waxed red bricks before the hearth. "First a charcoal from last year's fire," Granny argued. She placed a chunk of half-burned ember into the glowing coals. "Now." The men strained, their arms extended toward the warmth of the fireplace. With the roots braced against one side, the trunk reached 5 feet to touch the bricks at the far end.

"Old Tom knows his business," said the bishop. "I had my doubts, but he said he'd bet a half crown it'd fit with an inch to spare. That's just about it, an inch."

Josie piled smaller branches round the massive log. Already the furrows of the bark smoked with the sweet scent of apple wood. Trickles of flame played at the bark.

"Has to burn all night, not to break the spell, Alred. Think it's wet enough?"

"Nothing to worry about, Granny. It'll still be going strong when the children arrive. Bet you my plum pudding."

"That's not fair. You never eat plum pudding anyway. Just pull it apart to find the silver threepenny bit."

"We're not being very formal, Father," said Josie. "If Karl wants to see a real English Christmas, we ought to give him the whole rigmarole."

"Not enough time, my dear. That's what Bruce is good at. Besides, I still must polish my sermon. And there're all the decorations. Still, we could get out the mead and perry and have an Olde English toast or two."

Granny flicked her graying locks imperiously. "It's just that you're consistently opposed to paganism, Alred. Yule logs, demons of the mistletoe, spirits of the oak and apple. Just because you're a bishop, we can still be Anglo-Saxons, can't we?"

The bishop brushed bits of bark from his hands and gaiters. "Of course, Mother. You know I'm just jesting. Besides, if we're all at midnight service, we'll be exorcised anyway." It was difficult to tell who was pulling whose leg.

"The shepherds must have been superstitious too," said

Josie. "Look at the speed they made when they came with haste to find the Babe in the manger."

On a tray of Indian brass with delicate red inlays Bishop Ellingston-Harte arranged tiny porcelain cups holding no more than a thimbleful. He reached for a pint flask of blown glass standing on the buffet. Into each cup he poured a golden brown liquid not unlike rum.

"This is mead, Karl. An old custom in the family. What the Saxons used to drink when they came home from hunting or courting."

"From honey, isn't it?"

"Right. Fermented honey with a bit of sugar added. Tastes like rum but a bit stronger and lighter. Hard to find these days unless you go to Dorset. Bring your own bottle, and the orchard folk'll be glad to fill it up. A lost art, mead."

"Not much loss if you ask me, Son. Sickly sweet and twice as potent as it ought to be." In spite of her words, Sarah was quick to take a cup.

"Waes hael," said the bishop, once to each of his three companions. It was clearly *waes hael,* in two distinct words, and not *wassail.* Karl recalled last week's column in the *Church Times.*

"Drinc hael," he answered. The mead tasted of old honey, strong and potent, as bitter as the mountain gentian of the Alps.

"You need good health after swallowing that," said Josephine, whose lips puckered prettily. "The perry, quick, to wash it down."

"Now that the lords of the *witanagemot* have had their mead," said Sarah, "the rest of us can fill up on perry." From the sideboard she extracted four crystal goblets, and from an earthenware jug filled each. The sparkling liquid had a touch of amber, like rain from a leaf-strewn roof.

"Ah. That's more like it."

To Karl the flavor was almost like cider, with the aroma

of pears rather than apples. A bit hard if one drank too heartily.

"And now," said Sarah, "It's off to the wars. The whole house is still to be decorated. The tree, that can wait for the youngsters. But everything else is up to us. You know how the carol goes. It's not 'God *Rest* Ye, Merry Gentlemen.' There's no resting to it. It's 'God Rest Ye *Merry,* Gentlemen.' And even Tom Swopes knows the only way God can keep a man merry is to keep him busy."

Karl couldn't repress a smile. By normal standards Sarah belonged in a sedate rocking chair by the fire with her dog and her knitting. But there was no doubt who actually ran the house, and very little doubt that both Alred and Josie liked it exactly the way it was.

The bishop glanced longingly at the fire, as if he were meditating on his sermon. "Glad the dean's on tonight and I in the morning." He watched the flames lick higher on the trunk and listened to the sizzle of the water as it oozed from the roots. "O God, who hast made this holy night to shine with the brightness of the true light — " His voice trailed away, though any one of the three knew exactly his mood as he chanted from the old Christmas collect of Cranmer.

They all faced the fire in silence, dreaming not so much of sugarplum fairies as of shepherds on the fields of Bethlehem. Even Alfred the Great sensed the mood of meditation and pricked up his ears as the sound of conversation and merriment died away.

Karl could not but admire this sparse man of the cloth with the hard muscles of an athlete. The bishop was still quite a man, even as he had once been quite a scholar and rower. When one knew him well, those crossed oars above the fireplace were a symbol not only of the athlete but of singlemindedness and devotion, which had given him at so young an age the see of Bishop's Monksham.

With luck and with the right friends he could still go far. Who knows, one day he might succeed to the diocese of London or even to York or Canterbury. Reflecting, Karl had to consider everything. Alred could still rise high, provided all the chips fell into place. But what if he were taken to task for giving up an ancient church to the Lutherans or if his daughter were to marry one?

"It's a shame, really." Josie was at the record player, putting on a London recording of Bach's Christmas Oratorio. "If we enjoy the fire, the house will stay bare. But if we decorate, the fire will go to waste."

Alfred yawned, scratched behind his ear, moved sedately through the hall, and barked once. Sarah rose to let him out into the night air. "Don't be long, Alfred. It's cold and wet out there, and we don't want you to have no room at the inn on Christmas Eve."

Josephine was also on her feet, yawning and stretching.

"Up with the Rosemary and so
Up with the bayes and the mistletoe
Up with the holly and ivy and all
Wherewith we dress the Christmas Hall."

"Very pretty, my little one. The trouble is, that's not the way Herrick wrote it. It isn't *up,* It's *down.*"

"I know, Daddy. But I didn't think anyone'd catch me out. Besides, everyone else's reciting Christmas poetry, and that's the only one I knew."

Karl laid a coil of greens in the hall. He had first planned to lay it before the fire but repented, remembering the luxury of the Persian rug. Get some rosin on that, and you'd really had it, even if the Corgi did chew his bones there when no one was looking.

He and Josie stretched it above the mantle in three great loops, dangling from the oars. "How's that? About right?" Before anyone had a chance to answer, Josie snipped off the end of the garland with the gardening shears and hung a similar strand over the doorway.

Meanwhile Sarah sought out the pile of holly and stuck a branch behind each picture. Those old etchings of Roman towns — Eburacum, Verulamium, Lindum — were the bishop's joy, living proof of England's maturity.

Alred retired to the counter in the kitchen, where he wove clusters of pine and fir into man-size wreaths. One he tried in the parlor window and, pleased, wired in a red candle, a white ribbon, and sprigs of mistletoe.

He dove into the work with the zeal of a shoemaker earning piecework, though if one watched closely one could see he was also thinking through the morrow's sermon. The dog in fact had to sniff four times at the pantry door before a friendly hand admitted him back to the warmth of the fireside.

In the far corner of the living room Karl worked at the tree. On Sarah's suggestion he trimmed away the lower circle of limbs to make it fit the room, then shaved the trunk to the size of the holder. The lights and the ornaments and the tinsel could wait for the holiday, when Greta and Peter would swarm all over it, but at least the tree would be in its stand, ready for the finishing touches.

Josie was arranging a basket of bay and spruce for the hall, with reeds and cattails from the Aublin. Three red apples for the handle gave it a touch of color. She had quite a taste for the unusual, that Josie.

In the whirl of activity the time passed quickly. Twice Josie added new records to the player, Bach after Bach after Bach. A good many of them were motets or preludes on Christmas carols. Though he prided himself on his knowledge of music, Karl was a stranger to most of them.

In terms of music it was a bit U. Outside one could hear the youngsters caroling the usual favorites: "Silent Night," "Hark! the Herald Angels Sing," "O Come, All Ye Faithful,"

"O Little Town of Bethlehem," "As Shepherds Watched Their Flocks by Night," "The Twelve Days of Christmas."

Wary of the bishop's house, they hesitated to beg for handouts. All the same, perhaps a bit respectful of his position, they paused long enough at the gate to let him know he had not been overlooked. Once, he walked out with a handful of shillings, without even his coat, for which Sarah took him gently to task.

As the evening lengthened and the clock chimed half past ten, the bishop excused himself for a final polish on the morning's sermon. As if on cue, also Sarah excused herself and padded up the stairway. "If I should doze off, Josie, you'll wake me a good half hour before we have to go? Mind, not later than eleven-thirty."

"Yes, Granny. Never fear. You have a bit of a nap so the youngsters won't seem so noisy tomorrow."

Josie filled the glasses once more with perry. In the dancing light of the fireplace the goblets gleamed golden.

"Good, this perry. Many people drink it?"

"Not as many as you'd think. It's a cheap substitute for champagne. No tax. But it's nowhere near cider. That's what the old derelicts at the hospital get drunk on when they can't afford mild and bitters. Cider."

In a pie plate the girl laid out a handful of chestnuts and shoved them into the hot ashes of the fire. A flume of sparks climbed up the flue.

"Finished your sermon for tomorrow?"

"Four days ago. Christmas spirit, that's what does it."

"I'm still sorry you can't be here for dinner."

"So am I. It's not that I don't enjoy the Dennises. I do. But they asked three months ago, and I couldn't very well refuse. There's the hour's drive too. That'll be no fun if there's still snow."

"The snow'll be gone, don't you think? And if the Dennises get you for Christmas, it's the Ellingston-Hartes on Boxing Day. Why don't you come early, say ten-ish, and help stuff the goose or at least keep the youngsters out of Granny's hair?"

He leaned back against the leather back rest. It smelled of fallen leaves and tannin and wood smoke. With his eyes on the Yule log, where sap still dripped and steamed, he leaned down as if to untie his shoe, thought better of it, changed his mind again, and then untied both.

"Oh, no, Karl. Not while the Yule log's burning." The firelight outlined her upturned nose and glimmered orange in her eyes.

"What's the matter? Can't I even loosen my shoes?"

She laughed. "Not on Christmas Eve. Anyone walk in the room where the Yule log burns, barefoot, it brings bad luck the rest of the year."

"That's just the Puritan in you. The old *huswif* trying to make things proper. Telling the kids to keep their shoes on." He took off his shoes and stood them neatly beside the chair.

"Who's Puritan, did you say?"

"You. You, Josie. And you, the English."

"Me? It wasn't we that made Christmas Puritan. Look at those Pilgrim fathers in Massachusetts. Sure, Parliament passed some laws against Christmas. No feasting, no singing on the streets, no gift giving. But it only lasted a year or two. You in Massachusetts kept it going a hundred years, and you're still afraid to sing a carol out of doors for fear of waking somebody's baby."

Karl was not exactly *au courant* in Colonial history, especially when it related to Christmas. "Now don't tell me the Puritans couldn't take their shoes off before their own hearths!"

In the fireplace a chestnut crackled. Alfred the Great, who lay dozing on the rug, stirred to his feet and moved a yard away.

Josie's voice sounded almost teasing. "Well, you can't ask

a girl to burn *her* fingers digging *your* chestnuts out of the fire."

For all the banter it was a serious conversation. Relaxed, with a goblet of perry on the table beside him, Karl imagined himself in a duel of words, with his opponent thrusting and parrying as skillfully as he. It was fun, and yet he had to be on guard.

He pulled the pan of nuts off the coals and let them cool on the bricks of the hearth. "Smell them? Can't tell which smells better, the nuts or the pine. A good Christmas, Josie, a good Christmas."

Through the plaster above, Karl could hear the soft foot-falls of the bishop. He was pacing back and forth across his study. "Does he always work so hard on his sermons?"

"No, not always. Mostly, of course, he's on the road. Con-secrations and confirmations and ordinations. And he can preach almost the same sermon at Upper Tenby as at Lower Netherton. Nobody knows the difference. In fact nobody'd know the difference if he preached the same sermon twice at Upper Tenby, provided there was a year in between. Christ-mas, that's different. Eight, ten hours, a whole new sermon — nothing's too good for Christmas."

"I hadn't really stopped to think of it, to tell the truth. Still, it's pretty obvious even to a pup who's preached only three or four Christmas sermons in his whole life. Even I don't usually work at a sermon four days ahead of time, now I think of it. Except at Christmas."

"It's odd sometimes, how people react similarly. Without realizing it."

"It is. Something about Christmas is different. It's — how would you put it? — eternal. Fundamental. Not just tinsel and holly. Reminds me of that passage from the Venerable Bede. You know, the one about the sparrow. Flies into the great hall through an open window, and after a few minutes, out again. Like God coming into our lives and then leaving again.

Or for that matter, like us ourselves, born one year and dying the next."

"It does give you pause, Christmas. All morning I've been thinking of my job at the hospital. Junior almoner. Out to change the world. To give sound counsel to an Irish washerwoman who's pregnant by a Gold Coast wiper. Or make some motherless urchin see he's wrong to lift candy from the confectioner's."

"It's catching, Christmas. Makes you see yourself in a new light. As if you really want to be a shepherd from Bethlehem, now that the heavenly hosts have sung their alleluias."

"Do you really think it's Christmas that does it? Or age and experience? Two years ago I'd have sworn a good social worker could remake the world, conquering at one fell swoop sickness and poverty and ignorance. Now I'm not so sure. I'd be willing to settle for a life like Granny's, in a country vicarage, losing her husband to a heart attack, raising her children and her son's children. Once it's lived, a life like that, there's something concrete to show."

"Change and decay in all around I see. Is that it?"

"No, that's too gloomy. Change maybe, but not decay. The new dream is healthier than the old. More realistic."

"Come to think about it, you couldn't be righter. Four years ago you should have seen *me.* An American engineer at Stony Hinge. First lieutenant. Christmas in merry old England, and all that sort of thing. With a solid Christian background, I won't say I slid as far under the table as the rest of them, who were hardly sober enough to know it was Christmas. John Jameson, that did it. Then, the Christ Child in the manger didn't mean half so much as tonight."

"What is it you really want, Karl? To prove your faith? Are you really happy in a parish? Are you really happy in England?"

"I'm glad you asked. I guess it's been obvious. Do I look unsure, unsettled?"

"No, not to an outsider. Just to one who is really beginning to know you. I don't think it's just the tension between a Lutheran and an Anglican." He was not at all sure whether she was referring to herself or to her father. "It's that there's some kind of inner wall. You can do a perfect job — preaching, calling, visiting — and yet appear not quite as happy as when you're out on the cricket pitch, flailing away with a crowd of schoolboys. As if you haven't really found yourself."

"Maybe I haven't."

He could see a look of intentness and concern on her face, but there was admiration there as well. "Even if you haven't," she said, "you're twice as interesting as most people who have. A kind of Diogenes if you like, too far ahead of your contemporaries. Out with a lantern, looking for an honest man, when no one else even knows how to light the lantern."

"What is it they say about flattery?" He dawdled the pan of chestnuts in his fingers and offered her a choice. She accepted two, but with a peculiar look on her face. It was almost as if she sensed the inner depth of the conversation, and he sensed that she sensed it. "But I guess we've had enough philosophy for one night."

"To thine own self be true, and it must follow as the night the day. . ."

"It's not that I'm not being true to myself, Josie. Maybe I just want to live in the world of Jack the Giant Killer. Confirming a dozen souls a year and visiting a hundred sickbeds seems too puny. To God it isn't, I know; but to Karl Mueller, I'm not so sure. It's exactly what thousands of others are doing, and often better than I."

"Still, it needs doing. Is it England that bothers you?"

"No, I don't think so. It wouldn't be much different in Boston or Indianapolis or Des Moines. Maybe it's that I dream of being a St. Augustine, coming to England with forty helpers, or a Boniface, who can bring the faith to a whole continent."

"Don't you think there were a hundred Augustines for every one who succeeded? And what about Augustine's monks? Do we know their names or what they did or even where they're buried?"

"Still, there're plenty of worlds to conquer. Look at Schweitzer and Bonhoeffer and Laubach. Maybe it's my own faith. Maybe I just can't see why it's necessary to convert a Christian who's fifty percent faithful into one who's seventy percent faithful."

"What is it that bothered Goethe, *Sturm und Drang?* You'll get there; give it time. Already you've got a century's start on your contemporaries. England did that, and the Army engineers."

"I hope so, I hope so. But it takes so long to learn, so long to find oneself."

"Long, Karl? You've been at Bishop's Monksham scarcely nine months. Look what you've learned. About the world and yourself and your faith. All since April. The best year in your life, if you're honest."

"You're right, Josie. It's just impatience, I guess. The mills of God grind slowly, and I try to make them grind at the speed of Karl Mueller."

"I'm afraid the Ellingston-Hartes haven't helped, Karl. It's been a bit difficult for both of us, and father as well. We three are mature enough to understand. But it's hard to maintain a position and not lose face with the bootblack and the chimneysweep. In a way I'm glad I've lived in London. Has it helped at all — or just made matters worse?"

"That depends what you mean, Josie. For the church or for *us?*"

The flames in the fireplace flickered low, gnawing steadily into the wet wood of the Yule log. He tried to study the rapt expression in the slate-blue eyes and wondered whether the upswept nose was at normal tension. She stared intently into the flames, her features as motionless as the dozing dog on the hearth. She did not answer.

"I know this won't make it easier, Josie." In the half darkness of the room you could hear the soft crackling of the fire. "I think we've both known it for months. Sooner or later it's bound to come out. It's not very easy to say, when you're not used to it. I've wanted to say it a dozen times, ever since the harvest festival. But the time was never quite right. I'm not sure it is now. But anyway, would you" — his voice broke a bit — "would you marry me?"

Epilog:
The Time
of Testing

In the soft sunset of April the evening tide surged
up the valley of the Thames. From the boat deck of
the *Jacaranda Queen,* hand in hand with Josie, Karl could
see the oil-slicked waters tug gently at the mooring lines.

The narrow entrance of the Victoria Docks made them almost landlocked in a forest of cranes and warehouses and
sidings. Only the passing collier on the river, its window boxes
full of tulips and its hull loaded with Newcastle coal, reminded one of the sea.

Now that the tide had begun to move, it swelled and
surged like a great wave, carrying the debris of a busy water-
front. On the horizon one could make out the white dome of
St. Paul's silhouetted against the fading sun.

Karl and Josie had the boat deck to themselves. The other
score of passengers were on the promenade below, but for
the most part without friends and relatives to see them off.

Except for the adventurous, the *Jacaranda Queen* was
hardly to be recommended. She was a ship the Union Castle
folk seldom advertised, a kind of workhorse of the South
African run, with stops wherever there was cargo: Dakar,
Monrovia, Accra, Lagos, Lambarene, Capetown, Port Elizabeth, Durban, Mombasa.

For Karl and Josie she was still part of the honeymoon.
Those same billows of cloud dotting the sky were what they
had seen for two weeks in Penzance and the Scillies, a kind
of framework in which they were discovering the world anew,
with each other. Port Elizabeth, in Africa, would have far
more to offer than Mount St. Michael, but for a pair of newly-

weds, *where* they lived was not really so important as *with whom* they lived.

The gulls swooped low over the decks and fluttered about the rigging as if they were eager to pilot the freighter out to sea. A tug puffed gently in the slip like an obedient dog waiting for orders. Karl felt Josie's fingers, warm and moist in his palm, her slim, young body relaxed but spirited.

He remembered those sunsets over the Atlantic, from their guest house in the Scillies, and the sun that sprang up rosy-fingered from the morning sea. He recalled the fond outlines of Mount St. Michael in the bay, a kind of stalwart giant fending off the attacker, whether spiritual or temporal. He remembered Josie's excitement as his spouse, and the new world they had entered together.

The breeze off the Channel swayed her skirt and played with the jaunty ribbon in her hair. She wore a bright, yellow daffodil at her shoulder, the same kind of daffodil he remembered just a year before, when she and Sarah had first taken him to the sale of work and bazaar at St. Swithums. What a long time ago, in terms of all that had happened, but what a short time in days of the calendar!

Twenty feet below, standing on the dock, was the going-away party. Karl was somewhat embarrassed, to tell the truth, however pleased he may have been at the warmth of the friendships. There were too many, and it was too formal — Josie's family, the Lutheran clergy, a dozen of her friends from the hospital, even Alfred the Great.

Even if they were shipwrecked for a year on the Cape of Good Hope, they would never be able to eat the baskets of fruit or smell all the flowers. Josie in fact had been close to tears when the last guest had disappeared down the gangplank — not so much at the parting, to tell the truth, as to realizing how close her friends had been.

There on the cobblestones of the dock, Sarah Ellingston-Harte sported the same kind of daffodil as her granddaughter. It was almost an insignia, not of a garden club but of the family. The gray silk dress and the navy coat made Sarah look like a woman of the world, a headmistress or a doctor or an actress, and far younger than her seventy and seven.

Karl remembered her as a pillar of strength and a pillow of comfort. Somehow she seemed to raise not only her orphaned grandchildren but almost anyone else who needed help, whether it was a one-legged old soldier by the name of Tom Swopes or a foreign-born preacher by the name of Karl Mueller. Bless the old lady anyway! Would that her kind lived long upon the earth!

The bishop must have marked the occasion on his calendar as a red-letter day — as important as Christmas or Easter or Pentecost. Mind you, he even wore his gaiters. Under ordinary circumstances, bishop's stocks and gaiters seldom hit the dockside, especially in so remote a bywater as the Victoria Docks; but with the Lutherans surrounding him he appeared almost like a hen shepherding his chicks.

Dr. Dennis wore his clericals more like a West Ender than a City man, and Ted Gruber and Gene Bratlich were also in their dog collars. The rest of the Lutheran contingent, in business suits, merely hinted at being the clergy without really proclaiming it.

In a way Karl hated to leave them. The bishop, Paul, Audrey, Doug, Sarah. He would be back probably, and certainly at least to visit. He had contracted, with a great deal of enthusiasm and support from Josie, to serve for two years in the Lutheran seminary at Port Elizabeth.

Africa was primitive, he knew, there in the midst of Zulu territory. But he had had challenging reports from one of the missionaries. He didn't really hope to train the Zulus to recite their paradigms from the Greek with the accents of first-century Athenian, but perhaps with luck he could at least drive home the importance of the Scriptures and how a smattering of the Koine could show how God used language, like other human tools, to spread the Gospel.

A Dane who had served there earlier, on the little faculty of half a dozen, had suddenly fallen ill, and at the same time a Zulu pastor had won 18 months of study at a seminary in the States. Would Karl consider serving as a two-year replacement, considering he had done rather well in his seminary Greek? Doubtless his experience at army engineering might also serve well in the mission field.

Most of all, he hoped two years in Africa would give him a truer picture of what he really wanted from his ministry. Was he really cut out to be a second Schweitzer and blaze new paths through the bush? Or would the land of the Zulus merely confirm what he had already discovered in England and America — that the saving of souls was as much sweat and disappointment as it was handsprings and hallelujahs? For that, only time and the good Lord could provide the answers.

For Josie, who had once had a holiday in France but had otherwise never set foot outside England, the venture seemed one great honeymoon. For her as well as for her husband it was a quest for the Holy Grail — promising no sure success but obviously worth the search. A time to get to know each other, a time to let their marriage grow roots, a time to give up the distractions of civilization.

For Karl the hardest decision was giving up St. Swithums. From the beginning of Lent he had discovered a new zest in preaching, holding forth from the ancient pulpit with the fervor of a St. Paul. His decision had not been easy. Even if he should ever come back to England, St. Swithums would doubtless belong to a successor.

It was not that Karl considered himself indispensable. Half a dozen others could do the job equally well. All the same, leaving St. Swithums would be almost as hard as giving up Josie, though of course he was sensible enough not to say so where she might hear.

Leaving Bishop's Monksham caused a certain amount of consternation among the bigwigs in Cleveland. He'd had a letter from David Altschuler urging him to stay and convert all England, now that his start had been so auspicious. But he felt a little like Christian in *The Pilgrim's Progress*. He had to keep moving if he were to finish the course.

In terms of the Ellingston-Hartes, he also felt it wisest to leave Bishop's Monksham. Anyone who really knew him, anyone who understood the Lutheran cause, would not be a nit-picker when it came to criticism. But there were still scores of those who did not understand, the Tom Swopes sort, whose tongues could exaggerate. The memories of Carole Dunning were not yet buried but would surely lie quieter with someone besides Karl in the pulpit of St. Swithums.

The collier was now well up the Thames, and the tide lifted the *Jacaranda Queen* from her moorings. At the bow the tug made fast. She blew steam through the stack at forced draft. The bosun's voice chanted out, "Cast off!" and the lines slipped into the roily water. The ship edged from the dock.

Josie's hand tightened in Karl's, and she waved with the other to her father and grandmother. Alfred the Great dashed to the edge of the slip, yiping in the high-pitched voice of a Corgi. Karl felt the muscles in Josie's arm tighten, not in fear of the unknown but in sheer excitement. Like a Biblical Ruth, she was giving up father and country to cleave only to her husband.

On the pier Alred of Bishop's Monksham raised his arm in farewell, the palm outward, almost motionless. His purple stock, his clerical collar, his black gaiters made the picture unforgettable.

They sensed it together and squeezed their fingers until the blood pounded. There could be no doubt. It was as if he were giving a parting benediction. That the Lord would bless them and keep them, that He would make His face shine upon them, that He would lift up His countenance upon them and give them peace.